SOME T

He used ... g
from the ca... n
she returned.

"I caught you."

"Like you don't eat cake the same way," he countered, offering Amy Jane a lick.

She surprised herself by spontaneously licking the chocolate from his finger.

"You missed a spot," Max said, wiping the frosting onto her neck and then slowly licking the speck of chocolate with his warm tongue.

"Don't do that," Amy Jane groaned, while her hormones clamored for more, more.

"Why not?" he asked, not stopping.

"Because you're a client. I don't get involved with my clients. It isn't ethical."

"Then I'm not a client any longer. I'm firing you." He scooped another finger of icing from the cake and offered it to her.

She gave in, licking it slowly, deliberately. She looked up to find him grinning at her.

"What?" she asked.

"I'm trying to figure out if it's me or the chocolate you like."

"I do like chocolate," she teased.

"Give me a try, plain," he suggested. He pulled her close and lowered his lips to hers. . . .

PRAISE FOR ANNA EBERHARDT'S
WHISPERED HEAT

"Sensual . . . sexy . . . a treat to read."
New York Times bestselling author Sandra Brown

ANNA EBERHARDT

SWEET AMY JANE

PINNACLE BOOKS
WINDSOR PUBLISHING CORP.

PINNACLE BOOKS are published by

Windsor Publishing Corp.
850 Third Avenue
New York, NY 10022

First Pinnacle Printing: September, 1994

Printed in the United States of America

In memory of my friend

KATHLEEN PATRICIA BRUMITT
"The fairest of them all"

ACKNOWLEDGEMENTS:

My agent, Denise Marcil
and my editor, Denise Little
for taking chances and believing

Ken Wilson, Announcer for the St. Louis Blues
John Frederick, Hank Frederick, Private Investigators
William George, Firearms Examiner, St. Louis
Metropolitan Police Department
Donna Julian, Wedding Consultant
Bruce Broder, Entrepreneur

Kathy's Group:
Linda Bickel, Nancy Dumeyer, Marlene Wilson, and
Allyson Kaiser

My writer friends:
Mary Lynn Baxter, Debbie Macomber, Carla Neggers,
Bonnie Jeanne Perry, Suzanne Forster, Olivia Rup-
precht, JoAnn Ross, and Wendy Haley

A special thank-you to Sandra Brown for showing me
the way.

One

Amy Jane Chadwick sat at her desk with her chin resting in her hand, and her elbow propped on the morning newspaper she'd opened to the daily horoscopes. The astral predictions ought to be called horrorscopes, considering hers for the day. It read:

> Planetary aspects focus on your
> latent libidinous side. You'll
> want the man you shouldn't have.

Flicking open her first Pepsi of the day, she enjoyed hearing the rush of carbonated fizz. The sound was as satisfying to her as the feel of a warm afghan on a chilly night. Taking a gulp of soda, she reread her horoscope to make sure she'd read the right one. It had sounded more typical of one for Scorpio.

No, she'd read the one for Virgo, all right.

It was not the horoscope she'd hoped for. Her priority at the moment was more finance than romance. Money was scarcer than men. It was only good men who were scarce. And good men,

well, she hadn't ever shown much interest in
them.

Even her horoscope knew that much.

Smoothing the newspaper, she refolded it
carefully so she could sneak it back downstairs
to the library without her baby sister Claire being any the wiser. Claire would have a fit if she
found anything at all out of place. The morning
newspaper was complimentary for guests of the
Chadwick Bed and Breakfast.

Only last Thursday it had been her bad luck
to upend a Pepsi on the newspaper. She'd had
to get dressed and run out to replace the newspaper before Claire discovered it was missing.
While she very much loved her baby sister, she
hated how Claire made her feel irresponsible.

She put the newspaper to one side of her
desk, frowning at the papers littering the smooth
pecan surface of the piece of Queen Anne furniture she'd bought with her first paycheck. It
wasn't that she had no taste; it was that she had
no patience. Like Carrie Fisher, she thought instant gratification took too damn long.

Claire claimed all the while they were growing
up that there had to have been some mistake on
Amy Jane's birth certificate, as she wasn't your
textbook neat and tidy Virgo.

Amy Jane was inclined to agree. That, or she
must have a lot of schizoid Gemini in her chart.
There was never any telling what she'd do next—
except be neat, tidy and responsible.

Luckily, neat, tidy and responsible weren't the

necessary qualifications to be a private eye. And lucky, too, that she had just enough Virgo in her to pay attention to details even when they bored her.

Claire, on the other hand, was the queen of detail.

It was a quality that had made the Chadwick Bed and Breakfast she'd started two years ago such a successful venture, while Amy Jane's detective agency limped along. Someday she'd have her own office, but for now she had to make do with a room in the bed and breakfast. And someday she'd have a calendar filled with client appointments.

Not like today, when she had nothing scheduled.

Someday. She glanced at the date on the neatly reassembled newspaper. The Friday, April 14th date served to remind her that, unlike Claire, she wasn't in her early twenties anymore. By one's late twenties one should have one's life on course.

It annoyed her to no end that she didn't have her act together. It annoyed her even more that her baby sister did.

But then Claire had had her act together since she was two years old and had started trying to mold her big sister into an acceptable tea-party guest. Claire's teddy bears were much better guests. At least they didn't object to being dressed up for a tea party.

She knew that Claire still to this day hadn't given up hope on her.

Like a new bride, Claire harbored the illusion that she could make someone change.

Amy Jane picked up the newspaper and headed downstairs shaking her head. That was like believing in your horoscope.

It had been a long day.

Since she didn't have any clients, Amy Jane had allowed Claire to rope her into helping out with the bed and breakfast. It was only fair that she do what she could to earn her keep.

Sitting back at her desk, Amy Jane tossed a crumpled paper into a wire mesh trash can full of similar discards, earlier attempts at making ends meet on paper. She wondered if Philip Marlow had ever stooped to making beds and arranging flowers to pay the bills.

Somehow she didn't think so.

The framed photo of her and Claire on her desk made her smile; they didn't even look alike.

Claire was tall, slender and meticulously dressed. Not a strand of her long, flaxen, pencil-straight hair was out of place. Her features were Dresden-doll elegant and her clothes classically feminine. Amy was four inches shorter than Claire, and though slim-hipped, she was curvy. Her clothing was . . . original, though not designer original—Amy Jane was original. Her hair was long like Claire's, but it was light brown and naturally wavy. And her features, while asymmetrically pleasing, were bolder; her eyes big, her lips full.

Suffice it to say, Claire had kept the family pearls while Amy Jane wore her father's leather-strapped watch.

Leaving off musing, she shoved the paperwork on her desk aside, crossed her ankles comfortably on the space she'd cleared, popped a cold can of Pepsi, and considered her predicament.

What money she earned working as a private eye came mostly from insurance companies, investigating suspected cases of insurance fraud. It was pretty tame—boring stuff consisting of sitting in cramped stakeouts watching to see if people who said they couldn't walk, could.

What it did was furnish a modicum of income. What it didn't do was provide the interesting, exciting kind of case she wanted to work on.

The kind of case the detective novels she'd grown up reading had promised.

But then, neither had her horoscope come through with the wrong man it had threatened.

You just couldn't believe everything you read.

Getting up, she went to the rain-spattered window to look out over the Chadwick estate grounds. The family home had come to her and Claire upon their parents' death. It had been two years since they'd been killed in an accident. Her fun-loving parents had lived beyond their means. Money to maintain the estate hadn't come with the inheritance; hence the bed and breakfast.

Neither she nor Claire could imagine selling the estate where fond memories of their parents lingered. It was their link to the past.

In the darkness she could just make out the shape of the tennis court, swimming pool and gardens. A gently rolling hillside led to the horizon. As she stood before the window lost in thought, a grumble of thunder was followed by a flash of lightning that cast an eerie glow to the room.

She almost didn't hear the knock at the door when it came so close after the thunder.

Her sister insisted she keep the door to her room closed at all times, since she couldn't be bothered with keeping the room neat, tidy and without posters on the walls. At the moment, a picture of Andre Agassi decorated the wall behind her desk.

She had a weakness for good-looking rebels.

Yet one more failing for Claire to shake her head about. What dear Claire needed was a husband to distract her, Amy Jane thought, not for the first time, as she went to answer the knock.

And maybe a set of twins, she thought, enjoying the perverse wish for her baby sister. Then we'd see about every hair being in place, every newspaper neatly folded.

Opening the door of her bedroom, she decided it was lucky her weakness for good-looking rebels was one she didn't indulge.

The clientele at the bed and breakfast was definitely looking up. Either that, or Claire had gone and hired a butler without telling her. No, a butler wouldn't be scowling. Or he might be a local hunk celebrity. One who stood before her looking at her like she was an apparition . . . one of the rare times she'd been caught speechless. She stood watching a fat raindroplet slip from his chiseled jaw to splash on his tuxedo.

Of course, she knew rebels didn't usually wear tuxedos; what tipped her off was the pierced ear *sans* an earring, and the top-gun squint of his dark green eyes. If she hadn't recognized him as a local celebrity, she would have pegged him for a military man because of his very short haircut.

She'd never thought she'd say it, but short hair could be incredibly sexy. On the right guy.

He was the right guy.

Actually, he was the male equivalent of the blonde (except his hair was dark) with red lips, long stockinged legs and a problem, in a Raymond Chandler novel.

So her horoscope was late, but it had very certainly delivered what it threatened. Yikes!

"Excuse me, ma'am. I believe I've got the wrong room." He began backing out into the hallway.

That was clearly a subjective deduction, Amy Jane thought, trying not to pout. After all if he needed a place to sleep on such a night, who was she to turn him away? It had been a while since she'd done a good deed anyway.

Lightning flashed.

Okay, a long while.

For the first time she saw the appeal of boarding strangers. Though she was sure Claire would faint dead away at her take on hospitality.

"What room were you looking for?" she called, coming to her senses as the poor guy began sloshing down the hall.

He stopped and turned back to face her. "Actually, I was looking for a person."

"A person?" She should have known. He was one of *those* newlyweds. Had probably gone out for protection out of habit and then forgotten which room his wife was in.

Trouble was he didn't look like the sort of man who would forget where he'd misplaced his woman. And Amy Jane would have read about it in the newspapers if a local celebrity like this man had gotten married.

Unless they'd put it on the sports page. She was going to have to check out the sports page more often if there were more like him. Sports announcers weren't routinely gorgeous. This one was, though. Or maybe the light in the hall was bad.

"Yeah," the guy answered. Looking down at a piece of paper in his hand he read, "His name is A. J. Chadwick. Look, maybe I have the wrong address. This is some sort of bed and breakfast, isn't it? At least that's what I thought the sign outside said when I drove up. It was raining so hard though that it was difficult to read. But then when I came inside to make a phone call to see if I had the wrong address, the pretty lady with flour smudged on her nose said I could find A.J. upstairs here at the room at the end of the hall. Maybe I . . . is there another hall?"

He looked confused.

And wet.

"I think I can help you," Amy Jane said. "Come on in my room, and I'll get you a towel."

He stood where he was assessing her. "Then you know A.J.?" he asked, hesitant.

"On some days better than others," she answered.

He didn't move.

She stuck out her hand. "I'm A. J. Chadwick," she explained.

He didn't look less confused. She wondered if he'd had a head injury in his brief hockey career before he'd turned sports announcer. She'd remembered he'd had some kind of injury that had ended his career early, leaving all his teeth intact and his gorgeous puss gorgeous.

"Amy Jane Chadwick . . ." she explained further.

"Oh." He looked trapped. And uncomfortable. And wet.

"Wait here," she instructed. A minute later she returned to hand him a fluffy towel.

He took it. After he made a cursory attempt

to dry off, he handed back her towel, thanking her, then tried to make good his getaway.

"Listen, A.J., er, Amy Jane," he began, tugging on his ear lobe. "I'm sure there's some mistake. You see I'm looking for the A. J. Chadwick who's a private detective."

"Good, you found her."

"Her. You're a girl."

"A woman," she corrected.

"Yeah, but—"

"Why don't you come on in my office," she said, since the word "room" obviously spooked him. He must have been victim to a lot of palimony suits or something. "I'm relatively certain I'll be able to help you. Who referred you to me anyway?" she asked, taking a seat after adding the damp towel to the pile of clothes she cleared from a chair for him to sit on.

"There's this bartender at a sports bar where the hockey team hangs out when they're in town. His name is James."

"Oh, Uncle James," she said, nodding, everything becoming clear. "He gets a kick out of doing that. Thinks calling me A.J. will get me more business. Maybe he's right. Some men don't have the balls to use a woman detective, believe it or not."

He had the grace to swallow. Dryly. Recovering, he began introducing himself. "My name is—"

"Max Armstrong. I know."

"Oh."

"It must be a pain being a celebrity, huh?" she said, fiddling with a paper clip.

"At times," he agreed, leaning forward and resting his forearms on his thighs.

She chuckled. "You mean times like this when you can't blow me off with some excuse instead of admitting the real truth of the matter."

"The truth?"

She looked him straight in the eye unflinching in her directness. "That you're one of those men . . ." she said, challenging him to deny it.

He rested his head on his fingertips. It was plain he was tired and wet and not up to the fight she was full of. He looked up at her from beneath dark spiky lashes. "You're pretty tough. Where'd you learn to be so tough? I don't remember playing hockey against you the year I played."

"Touché, Mr. Armstrong."

"Max. Call me Max."

"Max. I learned to be tough playing good cop, bad cop."

"You were a cop?"

"Not for long. It didn't suit me."

"Being the good cop, or being the bad cop?" he asked sardonically.

"I've got this thing about life being fair. I can't get used to the idea that it just isn't. Anyway I caught on pretty quickly that what I really liked was solving mysteries."

"So you became a private eye," he said, doubt tinging his words.

"Yeah, I've got a license around here somewhere," she said, searching through the stacks of papers on her desk, ". . . if you care to see one."

He shook his head no. "Your card will do just fine," he assured her, reaching for one from the brass holder on her desk.

She waited while he studied it, picturing it in her mind's eye. It had taken her quite a while to get it just the way she wanted it.

Mysteries Solved   Scores Evened

AMY JANE CHADWICK - PI

P. O. Box 56
St. Louis, Mo. 63146   314-426-2700

"So you don't go by A. J. Chadwick then?" he said, slipping her business card inside his tuxedo pocket as he stood up.

"No, only Uncle James calls me that. He is the most perverse man. Did you know he had heart bypass surgery a few years back and then just last month he went bungee jumping?"

"You go with him?" Max asked, not batting an eye as he headed toward the door.

"He didn't ask me because he knew I wouldn't let him go if I knew about his plan. Wait a minute, where are you going?"

"I ah—"

There was a discreet knock at the door interrupting them, and they both turned to it.

"Amy Jane? Amy Jane, I made a pot of tea.

I thought you and . . . you and your gentleman caller might like some. Can I come in?"

"My sister, Claire," Amy Jane explained. "I was wondering how long it would take her."

"The woman with flour on her nose, I presume?" Max said.

"The same. Be nice."

Max shot her a glance as Amy Jane called out for Claire to come in.

The smudge of flour was gone from Claire's nose, though Amy Jane was certain that on Claire it had looked enchanting. And very feminine.

No matter what Claire did she managed to look feminine, even when she was digging in her prize rose garden. At the moment she was in Laura Ashley from stem to stern and carried a silver service that would have made Martha Stewart weak in the knees. "When I finished the butter rolls and set them aside to rise for tomorrow night's dinner, I decided to make some tea. It occurred to me the two of you might like some," Claire said. "It's such a terrible night out."

"Why don't you put the tray down here on my desk?" Amy Jane said. "You'll join us, of course."

After setting the tray down, Claire looked from Max to Amy Jane for introduction.

"Oh, rats, I'm forgetting my Emily Vanderbilt or whoever," Amy Jane said, upon catching Claire's look.

Turning to Max she explained. "Claire isn't

into sports so, you see, you're a complete stranger to her. Let me introduce you two."

"This is Max Armstrong," she said, turning back to Claire. "He's the announcer for the Lions hockey team. Max, this is my sister, Claire."

"It's my pleasure to meet you, Mr. Armstrong," Claire said, smiling warmly and extending her well-manicured hand to him.

"Max," he said, rising politely to kiss her offered hand.

"And you know Amy Jane from . . ." Claire took after Uncle James.

Amy Jane wished Claire would stay out of her nonexistent lovelife as she caught the spark of amusement in Max's eyes. She wondered if it was Claire, her or both of them who amused him. Whatever, she wasn't amused.

"He's here about a case, Claire," she rushed to clarify before her sister's meddling progressed to full blown. "Max doesn't know me from Adam."

"Oh, he's a client, then."

"I'm not actually a—"

Amy Jane's warning look cut him off. "Well, we haven't discussed my case yet," he said, sitting back down and looking over at Amy Jane in puzzlement.

Claire poured tea for them into dainty porcelain cups and saucers that weren't much different from the set the two of them had played with as children. It would never occur to Claire that a man might prefer his tea in a good sturdy mug, Amy Jane thought with a smile.

Max raised an eyebrow, but accepted the delicate cup and saucer, trying valiantly to balance it on his knee.

Watching, Amy Jane wondered just how much it would cost to clean a tuxedo.

Claire offered a plate of biscuits, then walked over to stand by the window looking out at the rainy night as she sipped her tea.

Tasting his tea, Max voiced his approval, then asked, "So is this some sort of bed and breakfast detective agency you two ladies run here? Are you both private eyes?"

Okay, so he wasn't a dumb blond, Amy Jane thought.

Claire choked on her tea. Regaining her composure she said, "Hardly. The detective stuff is Amy Jane's idea." Unspoken was the word *harebrained*. "She helps me out with the bed and breakfast as well. Speaking of that, Amy Jane, don't forget I need you to do the marketing for me tomorrow."

"Sorry, I can't now. I have a case," Amy Jane said, dodging that bullet. She hated shopping for groceries. Hated shopping period. She'd never understand why her baby sister found shopping of any kind orgasmic.

A smile ghosted Max's full lips, telegraphing the fact that he'd picked up on the reason for her insistence that he was her client even though he hadn't disclosed a word of his problem to her.

He shook his head, shaming her.

Amy Jane refused to look guilty.

Thunder rumbled far off in the distance. The rain had slowed to a light shower, no longer pinging against the window in wind-driven torrents.

"I'd planned on making up sachets from dried rose petals, but I guess I can do the marketing instead," Claire said.

Max's brow furrowed.

Amy Jane jumped in to explain. "Claire makes her own potpourri from rose petals she gathers from the garden. She dries them to mix with other dried flowers and spices, then sells the special Chadwick scent to our guests." Claire might look like a genteel 1890s woman with her polite, refined manner, but she had a knack for running a business.

"It's like putting a pinch of cloves in my peach pie," Claire said with a smile. "Taking the time to make things unique is something our guests appreciate."

"And more important, are willing to pay handsomely for," Amy Jane interjected.

"Do you like peach pie, Max?" Claire asked.

Ascertaining that he did, she excused herself, leaving the two of them alone to talk about the case.

Her leaving reduced the atmosphere to intimacy. Amy Jane felt suddenly shy, and neither of them seemed to know what to say or where to look. They were, after all, strangers.

It was Amy Jane who finally was emboldened to break the silence.

"Do you always dress so formally when you're hiring a detective?" she asked, noting his tuxedo.

He wore it well enough to be a model. Well enough to evidence that he was a man who liked clothes and was particular about what he wore. It wasn't a rented tuxedo, but one tailored to fit.

But he wore his intelligence openly enough that Amy Jane could tell he wasn't a dandy or a fop, as they used to call such men.

"I have an awards banquet to attend tonight," he explained. "I'm one of the speakers." He glanced at his watch. "I've got to run. It's already past seven."

"But we haven't discussed your case yet," Amy Jane objected as he rose to go. "Can't you be a little late? Don't those things go on and on?"

He paused briefly, considering the idea. She could see he was torn. But for whatever reason, he decided against it, heading for the door.

"I've got your card," he said. "Let me think about it, and I'll call you."

And then he left.

If Claire hadn't met him, Amy Jane might have thought he was a phantom in the rainy night. Someone she'd dreamed up like the blondes in trouble who always appeared in detective novels when the private eye was two months behind in his rent.

He'd said he'd call.

She knew he wouldn't.

If she wanted his case she was going to have to pursue Max Armstrong and convince him she was the only private investigator to do the job—whatever the job was.

He clearly hadn't intended to hire a female private investigator. Uncle James, the dear, had set him up. Max was just being polite in saying he'd call.

He was a man with beautiful manners.

Beautiful manners, drop-dead gorgeous, and a lot going on behind those murky green eyes.

But more importantly, he was a prospective client. One she was determined not to let get away despite his reservations about her being a female investigator. For once, she had to thank Uncle James for meddling.

She glanced at the picture of her father and Uncle James as young men. They were twins. And they'd had a pet name for her: Sweet Amy Jane.

They'd called her that since the age of two because she wasn't. Claire had come along seven years later to be the sweet one.

Leaning back in her chair she wondered what Max Armstrong's problem was.

He didn't look like the sort of man who needed help in solving his problems. For all his lovely manners, there was a hockey player when you scratched the surface.

Trying to imagine what sort of problem would compel Max to search out professional help, she let her mind wander.

Did he have a problem with gambling? Was someone pressing him hard to pay up? She didn't think so. He hadn't said anything about needing a bodyguard. And that wasn't something she did anyway.

Maybe it was blackmail. No, if it were, he wouldn't admit the reason to a stranger. That was why blackmail worked. Unless you didn't have the money, and Max Armstrong had buckets of it according to his contract.

Palimony. She remembered her fleeting thought about that earlier. Maybe that was it.

No, she would have picked up on that if there was that sort of rumor about him. It wasn't easy to keep a palimony rumor out of print when you were a celebrity. It was just the sort of juicy stuff newspapers loved to print.

Oh hell, who knew? It could be anything. Anything at all. Whatever it was, her gut instinct told her it was embarrassing. It had almost seemed to her that his reluctance to talk to a female private eye had less to do with sexism than it had to do with embarrassment.

Intrigued, she continued to wonder what it could be, as she went downstairs to talk to Claire. Claire was pretty good at reading people. It was part of what made her such a good hostess for the Chadwick Bed and Breakfast.

She found Claire in the library curled up on the chintz sofa with a romance novel. Claire looked up when she plopped down on the sofa across from her.

"So what did you think?" Amy Jane asked.

"He's a hunk. Are you going to date him?" she asked, putting down her book.

"I can't date him, Claire. He's a client. It isn't ethical to date a client."

Two

"What are you doing here, Claire?" James Chadwick asked, surprised to see his younger niece enter the sports bar. Claire was out of place in the rowdy, burger and big-screen TV joint where he tended bar. She had high tea at the Ritz written all over her elegant blond body.

"Uncle James, you've got to do something about Amy Jane!" she cried, approaching the bar, where she stood instead of trying to maneuver onto the barstool in her pencil-slim skirt.

"Why? What's your older sister done now?" he asked, indulging her, as the St. Louis Lions hockey team poured into the sports bar.

"She's caught up in this Nancy Drew fantasy of hers. It was embarrassing enough when she started doing insurance fraud investigating, but now she's had private-eye business cards printed."

"I need two pitchers of beer, and a glass of St. James white," the petite blond waitress in a black miniskirt called from the nearby table of hockey players.

Claire placed her leather clutch on the bar,

searching through it, while Uncle James filled the order.

"Claire, this is Miranda Sherman," Uncle James said, introducing the waitress, while setting two pitchers of beer on the bar for her.

"You're robbing the cradle there, James, don't ya think?" Miranda said, offering her hand.

"She's my niece," he explained.

"Oh, sorry. Me and my big mouth," Miranda said with a shrug, letting go of Claire's hand. "Don't forget the glass of wine for Max, James."

"Max?" Claire repeated.

"Yeah, the announcer for the Lions," Miranda said, pointing him out. "Is he to die for or what? Looks, culture and money, what more could a girl ask for?"

"Here's your wine, now scram. Claire has a problem for me to solve."

"I keep tellin' you, James, you're supposed to listen to problems, not solve them," Miranda said, picking up the order, and heading for the hot, sweaty, and thirsty hockey players.

"Look at these," Claire said, handing Uncle James a stack of business cards. "I found them on the registry desk, where Amy Jane had put them for the clients of our bed and breakfast to take."

"It's not funny," Claire exclaimed, teary-eyed, when Uncle James burst out laughing after reading Amy Jane's card.

"You have to admit the card sounds just like her."

"That's the problem. I've spent all this time creating an image for the Chadwick Bed and Breakfast. What are our clients going to think? You've got to make her stop."

Uncle James laughed deep and rich. "Now tell me, Claire, has anyone ever been able to make Sweet Amy Jane stop?"

"No, but—"

Seeing Claire was genuinely upset, he gave in. "I'll talk to her, but I can't promise anything."

Amy Jane lay abed, contemplating the beam of warm sunlight playing across the white eyelet cover. It was good to see a cheery bright day after a succession of gray showery days.

She was propped against a mound of white pillows cushioning the white enamel and brass bedstead. The pillows were monogrammed with satiny white C's—Claire's handiwork.

Every touch of elegance could be traced to her baby sister's rarefied taste. To Amy Jane, a pillow's only requirement was comfort.

Her sleepy yawn evidenced her restless night. When she looked around her cluttered room with its bare wood floor, white wooden Adirondack chair and bleached mantel she saw a charming cottage-by-the-sea look. She found her room deeply satisfying.

However, when Claire looked around the room she saw only the piles of clothes discarded carelessly on the floor, scattered magazines and newspapers, and her cluttered desk.

She saw mess.

Claire was forever giving her baskets and brightly papered hatboxes to control the clutter, baskets and hatboxes Amy Jane had stacked in her closet until Claire had given up.

Amy Jane smiled as she considered her room. She'd made a character flaw into an art form.

Not that the room wasn't clean. It was. She was as meticulous about that as she was about her person. It was the picking up that Amy Jane just couldn't seem to master.

She sighed, thinking back to the cause of her restless night's sleep. Beneath the smooth, cool sheet her naked body felt warm and edgy. For a moment or two she wondered if she'd dreamed up Max Armstrong's visit.

While he'd taken one of her business cards from her desk, he'd left nothing behind to indicate he'd ever really been in her room at all. It could have been something she'd eaten or a weird dream.

Heaven knew she was bored enough. Investigating the insurance-fraud cases was tedious work, leaving her mind plenty of time to conjure up more exciting scenarios. But Max Armstrong? Surely not.

She saw it then.

The sunlight had splashed on a black cuff link lying on the bare wood floor by the chair where

Max Armstrong had sat refusing to tell her why he'd been in need of a private investigator.

It was the equivalent of Cinderella's glass slipper.

She continued staring at it, assessing.

Coming up empty, she stretched lazily, then threw back the cover. Getting out of bed, she padded barefoot across the floor, unconscious of and at home with her nudity as she retrieved the cuff link to study it more closely.

Perhaps it would lend her some clue to Max.

Picking it up, she turned it over and over in her hand. It was simple and elegant in design. Claire would approve of it.

She tossed the cuff link in the air and caught it one-handed, as she thought.

Cuff link. Max link?

She could make use of finding it. Was that what Max had intended, maybe subconsciously?

It was difficult to control her gut instinct, and force herself to think things through logically.

Especially when her gut instinct was usually a dependable shortcut to the answer she wanted.

Should she ignore her impulse to insist Max Armstrong hire her, just toss the cuff link in with her collection of her father's cuff links she kept in a blue glass bowl on her desk? She had taken up wearing them since they'd come back in fashion with the dandy look for women.

Maybe she was just grasping at straws because she'd lost out last week on a case she'd really wanted. In her mind she deserved the stolen-jewels case, but the insurance company had given it to a prominent investigative firm instead.

A Cheshire-cat smile crossed her face. She could feel its ear-tilting width. So what, if that was the reason. Her gut instinct told her this was a case she needed, so she'd pursue her impulse. Especially since no logical reason for her not to presented itself. This case could replace the high profile one. After all, Max Armstrong was a local celebrity; if she solved the case, she couldn't help but benefit from it.

Max's missing cuff link gave her the perfect excuse to quest him out.

And she knew just where she'd start.

Uncle James.

She could seek him out at the sports bar and give him the cuff link to return to Max. Of course, she'd package the cuff link so Uncle James wouldn't have an eyebrow to raise. And while she was at it she would pump Uncle James for information.

Maybe he knew what Max wasn't telling.

She checked her calendar. It was a light day. All she had to do was pick up a check at the insurance company and see if they had any new cases for her.

Grabbing a robe and toothbrush, she ascertained the bed-and-breakfast guests were all cleared out, then she luxuriated in a long, hot shower.

Back in her room, Amy Jane splashed on a scent that smelled like lilies after the rain, pulled on a pair of 501 jeans, a white shirt and an antique vest. Digging into her blue glass bowl on her desk, she picked out a pair of silver cuff links and fastened the French cuffs of her shirt.

Her towel-dried hair was already starting to fluff in a cloud around her face. Pulling open a nightstand drawer she picked out one of the bright bandannas to tie her hair back.

After slipping on a pair of sandals, she headed barefaced in search of Claire and a warm butter roll, if she were in luck. Halfway down the hall she remembered and went back to close the door to her messy room.

At the bottom of the stairs she paused. The tantalizing scent of fresh-baked rolls still clung in the air, but the doors to the library beckoned.

Calling up her seldom-used willpower, she forced herself to disregard its siren call. I will not read my horoscope, she vowed. After wrestling her inclination to the ground and foregoing her customary daily check of what the stars had in store for her, she felt a rush of accomplishment.

Sometimes it was better not to know. Look what had happened when she'd read yesterday's horoscope. "The man she shouldn't have" had shown up, sure enough. Late, but then weren't men always late?

To make matters worse, she grumbled mentally, making her way to the kitchen, her libido was yawning and stretching.

And demanding.

And now she had to decipher if her interest in Max Armstrong was professional or prurient.

It could be either. Maybe even both. But if it was professional, then it couldn't be prurient. He'd be a client. Whatever, she could pursue one and ignore the other. Having rationalized permission to see him again, she went off in search of Claire.

On her way, she concocted her plan to reel Max in. She would have Claire invite him to dinner for one of her famous peach pies. He'd agree to Claire's invitation, even if he'd refuse hers.

No one ever said no to charming Claire.

She didn't allow it. The iron butterfly was an apt description of her baby sister. After all, how many tea parties had she attended with teddy bears when they were growing up?

Claire owed her. Big time.

Claire was in the sun-flooded kitchen. The black and white tile floor sparkled and the copper pots, arranged on a suspended rack over the cooking island, glowed. She had just finished arranging a pitcher of roses on a long wooden trestle where the bed-and-breakfast guests ate every morning.

"Any fresh rolls left?" Amy Jane asked, lifting the linen on a basket sitting on the white ceramic-tile counter to take a peek inside.

Claire nodded. "You can warm them in the toaster oven if they've cooled. There's butter, strawberry jam and fresh juice in the fridge."

Amy Jane took a roll to the toaster oven.

"Is there anything you want me to get you while I'm shopping?" Claire asked, looking up from the marketing list she was making out, while Amy Jane rummaged in the glass-front refrigerator for juice. Finding it, she turned to Claire.

Claire was dressed in a long, silky dress patterned in a tiny print and wearing one of her signature straw hats.

"Yeah, as a matter of fact there is," Amy Jane said, pouring a glass of juice while waiting for her butter roll to warm.

"What's that?" Claire asked, her pen poised.

"You can get me Max Armstrong," Amy Jane said.

"Who?"

"Max Armstrong. I want you to charm him into agreeing to come for peach pie tonight."

Claire ripped her marketing list off the pad and considered Amy Jane. "Why do you want me to invite him?"

"If you must know, he's not a client yet."

"And you want me to help you convince him to hire you?"

"No, all I want you to do is be yourself, and put him at ease. I'll do the convincing."

"Are you sure you know what you're doing?"

"No, but invite him anyway."

Claire picked up her purse, tucking her list inside. "Did you read your horoscope this morning?"

"I've given up reading it."

"That's probably a good idea."

Three

Once inside the sports bar Amy Jane blinked, trying to accustom her eyes to the dark interior after the bright sunlight outside. Gradually she began to make out the decor and the deep green and burgundy flecked carpet beneath her feet.

Highly polished wood and brass glowed in the soft lighting. The walls were painted a deep forest green and adorned with autographed pictures and sports memorabilia. Large screen TVs were scattered about at advantageous angles. She was surprised to see a soap opera was on.

"There you are, you old reprobate," she called out, spotting Uncle James behind the bar.

He didn't even look her way as she took a seat at the massive ornate bar. Instead he kept chatting with the young waitress he was filling an order for.

The girl was a petite blonde with sparkly eyes and a cheeky personality. It was clear she got on famously with Uncle James.

Having tried waitressing when she'd quit the force, Amy Jane knew having a great personality and a stomach for hard work were the requirements for pulling in tips. Possessing neither, her waitressing days had been of short duration. She'd quit, right before she'd been fired for making one smart remark too many. It had been her experience that the customer was hardly ever right. Uncle James had said she was just spoiled rotten.

"Let's see, that's a Long Island tea and three beers," the waitress said, checking her order then heading for her table of customers.

Amy Jane waited for Uncle James to finish polishing the spot he was polishing on the bar with his white dishcloth. Finally, unable to stall any longer, he came over to where she sat.

"Hi, Sweet," he said, calling her by the abbreviation her nickname had been shortened to over time. "What are you doing up so early? You working on a case?"

"You could say that," she answered.

Uncle James looked pleased with himself.

"Can I get you something to drink to celebrate?" he asked, sliding her a basket of pretzels.

"Okay, how about a Coke."

A ladies' man all his life, Uncle James had never married. Now, at fifty-one, no woman in her right mind would have him. He was unreformable. He'd never met a bad habit he didn't like. But he was a dear. He'd always been there for her.

Even though she hadn't always been the most lovable of children. Claire was the one who had invited Uncle James's dates to her tea parties when he visited on holidays. Amy was the one who put frogs in their bonnets. Having first tried the frog stunt on Claire, Amy had liked Claire's shrieks of dismay so much she'd graduated to tormenting Uncle James's dates.

Her parents had been horrified, and had on more than one occasion sent her to her room without dinner. Uncle James had sneaked dessert up to her room later. No wonder her parents had always said he was at fault for encouraging her.

She supposed that was what he was still doing—calling her A. J. Chadwick, famous private eye, misleadingly leaving out the word *female*.

"Here's your Coke," he said, setting it down before her on a paper napkin. He took a pretzel to munch on and crossed his long legs as he leaned back against a post, waiting for her to thank him for her new client.

"I know you meant well, Uncle James," she began after taking a sip of her soda. "But I really don't think the client you sent me was any too thrilled to find out that A. J. Chadwick was a girl."

"But he got over it, right?" Uncle James said with a chuckle.

"I'm not sure."

"What do you mean? He's your client, isn't he?"

"Yeah, he just doesn't know it yet."

"What?"

"I'm still working on him, okay? That's why

I came to see you. I was hoping you might be able to give me some clue. I thought, you being a bartender, Max might have talked about his problem."

"Not Max Armstrong."

"So why did you send Max to me? You weren't matchmaking, were you?—sending me a good-looking ex-hockey player for romantic reasons, were you?"

"Of course not. I take your private eyeing seriously. Have you ever known me to patronize you?"

"No."

"All I know is that he was in here after one of the games and he seemed preoccupied about something. I thought I'd throw his business your way, when he asked me if I knew the name of a good private eye. Look, you mean to tell me he hired you, but hasn't told you what the case is?"

"Well . . ."

"*Sweet—*"

"He hasn't exactly hired me, okay?" She took a drink of her Coke.

"Why didn't he hire you?" Uncle James's eyes narrowed. "What did you do?"

"Nothing. I swear," she said, putting up her hand at his doubtful look. "He was late for an awards banquet, and he took my card, saying he'd call me after he thought about it."

"Who's going to call you?" the curvy, blond waitress asked, returning to the bar with another drink order.

"Max Armstrong," Uncle James said.

"Well, that explains why he isn't calling me. I thought sure he'd ask me out after he finally ditched the bitch queen he'd been dating. I've been hitting on him ever since."

Amy Jane remembered seeing a picture of Max and Kerry something. It had been before he'd dumped her in some really horsy way. Was *bitch queen* an accurate description of Max's ex-girlfriend, she wondered, or just a description based on the waitress's jealousy?

Maybe what Max had was a clinging ex-girl-friend problem—that would explain the embarrassing aspect of the case she'd picked up on when he'd declined to give her the case right off.

Although Kerry Something hadn't impressed her as the clinging type, as she recalled. She'd seemed like a Chesterfield kind of girl; high-style short haircut, drove a sports car that needed a trust fund to maintain. Amy would guess she was an interior designer or maybe even a model.

"So you're going out with Max Armstrong, huh? Mind if I hate you?" the waitress asked, interrupting her thoughts.

"Sweet, this is Miranda Sherman. Miranda, my niece, Amy Jane."

"Nice to meet you," Amy Jane said. "And I'm not dating Max Armstrong," she explained. All she needed was for that particular rumor to get back to him. He'd never hire her. Not wanting to respond in any way to Miranda's friendly curiosity. "He's not my type," she lied lamely.

"Glad to hear it," Miranda said, "though if I were you, I'd make an appointment to have my eyes checked . . . or my hormones." Miranda gave James her drink order, then moved off to wait her tables.

"Tell me about Max," Amy Jane said, watching him fill Miranda's order.

"Max has been on the air for about three years. He's popular with the players and fans alike. Well, most of the players. He hacks some of them off occasionally because he isn't afraid to say it when he thinks a player isn't playing up to his ability, or is pulling prima-donna stuff."

Miranda returned to pick up her order, and Uncle James's attention was caught by something on the big-screen TV. Briefly, Amy Jane wondered if he were a closet soap-opera buff. She'd work on weaseling that out of him later. Right now she had business to think about, and a client to snare.

"This is for Max, Uncle James," Amy Jane said, leaving the small box containing the cuff link on the bar.

He waved her off, suggesting she quit annoying Claire.

Back in her Jeep, she began mulling over the sparse information Uncle James had given her. It was a twenty-minute drive to one of the insurance companies she worked for where she needed to pick up a check, and at the same time see if they had any new assignments for her. She always picked up her check as she'd learned about that "the check is in the mail" lie early on.

Waiting at a four-way stop, which St. Louis seemed to have more of than anyplace on earth, she thought about what her uncle had said.

Max had been preoccupied about something. Did that mean worried? she frowned pulling through the intersection. Did men ever worry? Certainly not Uncle James. And not her father either for that matter. Like Uncle James, he'd spent money as if he printed it. Not for nothing had they been identical twins. At least her father had gotten the monogamy thing down. Uncle James hadn't.

Trouble was, she was very much afraid it was Uncle James she took after. How was she, with her low threshold for boredom, ever going to get the monogamy thing down? When she dated a man, she dated him just long enough to get to know him well enough not to like him.

But she was digressing. Back to Max Armstrong.

What was the deal with him?

It could be something job related. She hadn't considered that angle until that moment. Squinting at the bright sunlight—she'd broken her sunglasses by sitting on them yet again—she tried to remember what else she'd heard about him.

He'd taken the announcing job after the knee injury that had ended his hockey-playing career. There had been some kind of brouhaha about his getting the job. She recalled some kind of controversy.

But she couldn't recall what.

Frankly she hadn't paid much attention. There was always some sort of brouhaha going on in sports—men being what they were, testosterone dressed in deceptively evolved packaging.

Not that she was complaining about Max Armstrong's packaging. It was very nice packaging. Very nice packaging indeed.

Too nice.

And tempting.

Very tempting. And she was never one to resist temptation. But she had to. He was her client. Or he would be.

Passing a Taco Bell, she voted with her stomach and overruled her brain, making a U-turn, to the annoyance of a honking red sports car, to gain access to the drive-thru of the Taco Bell. After giving the crackling speaker her order of a taco salad and a glass of ice water, she pulled forward behind the other cars lined up behind the window for their orders and turned on her radio.

It was tuned to a top pop station and Whitney Houston was belting out a song from *Bodyguard*. When the song was over, she picked up her order at the window. Amy Jane decided to eat it in her parked Jeep on the lot. As she dabbed at a spot of sauce she'd dropped on the seat, the music program broke for a sports update.

There was a bit on Bobby McQuaid, hotshot

player for the St. Louis Lions hockey team. He'd
been fined a large amount of money and been
made to forfeit a game for purposeful high
sticking that had broken another player's nose.

Amy Jane could never figure out whether the
NHL was or wasn't in favor of bloodshed,
though of late the trend did seem to be toward
less violence in the games, as opposed to what
was happening in society as a whole.

The announcer read off some other scores
and then signed off.

Amy Jane smiled upon hearing her name—
Chantal Perry. Finally she remembered just
what the controversy had been about when
Max had been hired as co-announcer for the
St. Louis Lions.

At the time, Chantal was being feted as the
first female co-announcer in town. She was to
co-announce the Lions games with veteran announcer Corey Cohen. Max's celebrity had given
him the job over her, acing her out. Displaced,
she'd been relegated to fill-in rather than star.
Corey Cohen's family was locally prominent so
there was no possibility of displacing him.

Could Chantal be Max's problem?

Who knew? Maybe she wasn't even in the right
hockey arena. Maybe he wanted a private investigator for someone other than himself. Maybe
he wasn't involved in a problem at all.

Zoning out, she listened to Michael Bolton
croon a tune from his *Timeless* album while finishing up her taco salad, eating it pastry shell

and all. After disposing of the trash, she headed her Jeep back out into traffic. On the way to the insurance office, she stopped only once more along the way, to pick up a copy of the *Post-Dispatch* at a quick shop.

The next stoplight she came to, she opened the newspaper and turned to the Everyday section where the daily horoscopes were printed.

Claire's comment had been nibbling at the back of her mind since she'd left her. Reading her horoscope, she wished she'd kept her resolution not to.

It read:

> Everyone tries to
> involve you in their
> problem. Help, but
> meditate and hold your
> tongue.

Right, like she could keep her mouth shut when she had an opinion? What was the point of having opinions if you couldn't voice them?

Not that anyone ever listened to her.

Uncle James didn't listen.

No matter how much she preached to him, he continued exploring the boundaries of bad habits.

Claire didn't listen.

No matter how much Amy Jane tried convincing her that she needed to be more adventurous, Claire just kept dating boring Ivy League men.

Hell, who was *she* to talk?

She didn't even listen to her own self.

Instead she kept thinking of Max Armstrong in decidedly non-client ways.

"James, old boy, I have a bone to pick with you," Max said, taking a seat at the bar after announcing the evening's hockey game at the Dome on television.

The Lions hockey team had skated poorly, losing in the fourth quarter in a four-to-three squeaker that could have gone either way. Luck hadn't been with the home team, and Max had been vocal about how poorly the team was playing.

The team members pouring into the sports bar with him were in a dour, surly mood, ready to drown their sorrows in pitchers of beer.

The usual good-natured jostling after a game was subdued as each player dealt with what was turning out to be an extended losing streak for the team.

"You'll have to get in line to chew on me," James said, sliding Max a beer. "I've already gotten a load of grief from my niece about it."

"Your niece? What are you talking about?" Max asked, taking a drink of his cold beer.

"A. J. Chadwick is my niece, Amy Jane. She beat you to the punch, came in here on a tear this afternoon and read me the riot act for suckering you in with that A.J. business I gave you."

"She did?"

"She did." James took a drink order from Miranda and began filling it while Max absorbed the information that Amy Jane was James's niece.

So Chadwick was James's last name. He couldn't recall that he'd ever heard it. He would have remembered if he had heard the name, as being good with names was part of his job description. A smile crossed his face as he pictured Amy Jane confronting her uncle. He would have bought tickets to see that.

"So how come you didn't give my niece the case?" James asked, turning back to Max when Miranda's drink tray was filled with a completed order.

"I thought about it, almost did give her the case, as a matter of fact."

"But you didn't." James refilled the pretzel bowl and waited.

"It's just that I'm not really sure I have a case, is all. Maybe I'm overreacting."

"Overreacting to what?"

What was he thinking, talking to a bartender about his problem? Sure they were supposed to be as closed mouthed as confessional priests, but who knew? James Chadwick was a bit of a character, after all.

"I'd rather not say until I decide what I'm going to do. I may do nothing." His gut reaction to Amy Jane had been to date her, not employ her.

"Did you see the game?" Max asked then, changing the subject to deflect a tenacious James.

"I endured it, is more like it," James answered, ringing up a sale. Turning back he said, "I don't know what it is about the Blackhawks this year, but they seem to have the team's number. The Lions are playing like a bunch of . . ." he backed off when he saw a player approaching, a player known for his bad temper.

"I wish I'd been in there playing tonight; I wouldn't have let them cream us like they did," Bobby McQuaid said, coming up to the bar and ordering a pitcher of beer for a table of teammates.

"It's your own fault you weren't in there playing the game tonight," Max said.

"My fault!"

"Yeah, your fault."

"Aw, Armstrong, you're as blind as the referees," the good-looking forward grumbled. "I suppose you agree with my being fined and my having to forfeit tonight's game as punishment."

"You had it coming, McQuaid. You know as well as I do that you were playing dirty. You're a talented player; you don't have to play dirty."

"What do you know?" Bobby said, referring to the fact that Max no longer played the game—that he'd in fact only lasted one year in the National Hockey League playing as a professional before an injury had sidelined him. "Maybe if you'd kicked more ass on the ice . . . you wouldn't have taken that bad fall that ended your career."

"Max knows enough," James interjected. "He

scored more goals his first year than you did these past two."

Uncomfortable with being the topic of conversation, Max drained his beer and set the empty mug on the bar with a thud. "I don't know about you guys, but I'm ready to call it a night. I think I'll take myself home and crawl into bed with a good book."

"What's that, Armstrong? Did I hear you say you're going home to crawl into bed with a good woman? What happened? Did Kerry Ashton put you off bad women forever?" Richie Allen, the big goalie for the team, teased the announcer about his ex-girl.

"The guys sent me to scout up what happened to our pitcher of beer," he said, jerking his thumb in the direction of the table of thirsty hockey players.

"Here's your pitcher, now go," Miranda said, handing him one.

"I could read you a book," she said, turning back to Max, flirting openly.

"Could we get some burgers over here, gorgeous?" Richie called out, and James sent her over to the table with a nod, squelching Miranda's play for Max.

"My niece isn't going to be dismissed that easily, I'm afraid," James said to Max.

"You got a niece?" Bobby said, picking up on their conversation. "How come you never introduced me to your niece, James?"

"Nieces. I have two."

"Really?"

James nodded.

"Which one did you meet, Max?"

"A.J."

"A.J.?"

"Amy Jane."

"What's the other one's name?"

"Claire."

"You think she'd date me?"

"No," James and Max chorused.

"I bet she would," Bobby insisted.

"How much?" James asked.

"Say fifty bucks."

"You're on," James said.

"Why don't you think she'd date me?" Bobby asked, his eyes narrowed with suspicion as he obviously felt the sucker breeze.

"Because she never dates men who don't have names like Terrance or Clayton. She won't get past that diamond stud in your ear, McQuaid," Max guessed.

"But you're dating Amy Jane," Bobby said.

Max shook his head no, and Bobby looked puzzled.

"I said, I met her. I don't date every woman I meet. I'm not a player."

"So then, James, in reality I have a choice. I can date either niece, and I get the fifty bucks," Bobby hedged.

"Sure," James said, way too agreeably.

Max laughed, high and easy.

"What's so funny?" Bobby demanded.

"Let me put it to you this way, McQuaid. You have no chance of dating Claire Chadwick; you aren't Ivy League enough for her. But you have even less chance of dating Amy Jane."

"Why—what's Amy Jane's deal?"

Max turned to James, not wanting to say anything untoward about his niece.

James let him off the hook by answering Bobby's question himself. "That's because, Bobby, dear boy, Amy Jane is better at high sticking figuratively than you are."

"Ouch!" Bobby said. "Then Claire it is," he conceded, to the sound of James's laughter.

On the drive back to his condo in west St. Louis county, Max thought about Amy Jane. He wasn't going to hire her, he'd decided. He was overreacting; he didn't have anything to worry about, not really.

But since he wasn't going to hire Amy Jane, he could ask her out.

Did he have the balls after Kerry Ashton, or had she emasculated him with her cheating ways?

He wondered what Amy Jane would say to his request for a date.

No freaking way, came to mind.

Too bad McQuaid was going to try to date Claire. He'd have loved to have seen Amy Jane out-stick him. The young hot shot needed to be put in his place. Everything had come too easily to him. McQuaid hadn't had to prove himself like Max had.

It hadn't been a piece of cake doing the announcing after his injury. He wasn't really trained in the field and plenty of people were just waiting for him to screw up, none more than Chantal Perry, not that he blamed her; he'd aced her out.

His mind went back to his problem as he let himself into his condo. It was all furnished in pine antiques he'd bought in Canada, creating a warm, uncluttered place.

He was a man who didn't like clutter.

Who didn't like messy.

And emotions were that.

Or so women had told him. Women he couldn't or wouldn't commit to. Was that what his problem was? Was he just an unfeeling bastard?

He didn't think so. He tried to be a good guy.

Maybe he was ready for a permanent relationship. The mood of the times was changing. Anything could happen in a country where the code name of the president of the United States was Elvis.

And it made sense.

Going into his bedroom, he tossed down his keys on the bed and headed for the bathroom. Stopping in the doorway, he looked back over his shoulder.

A bureau drawer was left open.

He was very neat. Today wasn't the day for his housekeeper.

Someone had been in his condo.

He walked over to the drawer and looked inside. What he saw lying there like a snake made him flinch. Steeling himself, he forced himself to pick it up.

It was a note—typed like all the others.

He read it:

> Dearest Max—
>
> I took a pair of your
> silk boxers to sleep in.
> I want to be close to you.
> Promise you'll think of
> my bare skin on your silk while
> you're announcing the game.
>
> I LOVE YOU

Max slammed the drawer closed. After a moment he pulled open the top drawer of the bureau where he'd placed the other letters. There were thirteen of them now; a chilling number.

He'd been wrong.

He wasn't overreacting.

This was getting out of hand, could be dangerous. He dropped the letter in to join the others that had come roughly once a month.

Closing the drawer, he went to his closet.

Reaching into the pocket of his tuxedo, he removed the business card he'd taken from Amy Jane and stared at it.

Was it smart of him to hire a woman he was so attracted to? Wasn't that just asking for more trouble?

The telephone startled him when it rang.

He took the call. When he hung up, he had a smile on his face; he had an invitation for pie.

With Claire and Amy Jane.

Four

Chantal Perry pulled on her jeans from the Gap. Beat, she bent from her waist to let her arms dangle at her sides. Today's aerobic class had been exceptionally grueling. The brunette dynamo instructor was new, and she had worked them like they were chorus dancers for a Broadway play. *The woman thinks she's Debbie Allen, choreographing Oscar night,* Chantal thought, zipping her jeans. How long had it been since she'd nurtured such impossible dreams?

A couple of years, at least. Since she'd lost the co-announcer job to Max Armstrong.

Life had a way of gradually wearing you down, especially when promised rewards failed to materialize after you'd expended great effort. She peered at the small mirror glued inside her locker door. "Everyone's got to grow up, and learn to live in the real world, kid," she mumbled to her reflection, pushing a loose strand of straight, dark hair behind her ear.

In her clear blue eyes shone the determination of a feminist—neither born, nor bred; she was a feminist shaped by the life experience of being a twenty-six-year-old woman.

A movement a few lockers down caught her attention. She recognized Kerry Ashton slathering pink lotion on her lithe body.

Correction—everyone didn't live in the real world. The mundane rules of life didn't apply to the Kerry Ashtons of the world, any more than they did to the Max Armstrongs.

Chantal recalled their very public break-up. The hockey player Max had caught her cheating with had been traded not long after.

Reaching for her ruffled poet's blouse, she considered Kerry, taking in the expanse of toned skin tanned to a biscuity perfection at the electric beach. Kerry's pretty white eyelet demi-bra and flutter bikini matched.

Chantal wondered what it would be like to actually *be* Kerry Ashton . . . to have perfectly matched underwear, hair the multi-hued shades of a fair-haired child, perky breasts, and most importantly—to have slept with Max Armstrong.

Max Armstrong, she thought, watching Kerry pull on a navy and white polka-dot flare tank-dress. Chantal was curious about every little thing about Max Armstrong.

She had a personal philosophy for business and life: when someone changes the game, quit playing by the rules.

She'd been a good team player, going by the book. It hadn't gotten the promised results. Even when she'd excelled. Promises weren't worth the breath it took to make them.

It made her want to cry when she thought of the work, damned hard work, she'd put into paying her dues; working her way up from the most obscure assignments, doing the grunt work, putting in the grueling hours out of town, and with teeth gritted enduring the lack of respect a female announcer encountered in the male-dominated world of sports.

In the end it turned out all you had to have was *balls*. Balls enough to waltz in and take a job you weren't qualified for, away from someone who was, just because you were a man, and a celebrity. And you could.

Max Armstrong had blindsided her, but he'd taught her a lesson. She wasn't going to take anything for granted ever again. One way or another, she was going to get what she was due even if she had to simply take it.

Checking the locker mirror briefly, she ran a comb through her hair, and slicked on some mauve lip gloss. Since she was scheduled to do a radio spot in an hour, about the Lions' chances of making the playoffs, she didn't have to glam up.

She picked up her stylish shoulder satchel, wincing when Kerry slammed her locker door shut with a metallic thud. Kerry Ashton didn't appear to be in the best of moods, Chantal thought, following her out to the parking lot where her rust bucket and Kerry's Jag were parked.

Kerry's bad mood was further evidenced by her stalk to her sports car; the spoiled brat's snit had most likely been precipitated by something as trivial as a chipped fingernail, which would require a trip to her manicurist to repair. Chantal should have such problems, instead of a Visa charge balance that rivaled the national debt in size and impossibility to ever repay.

Watching Kerry slide into her Jag and drive away, Chantal was not surprised to see the Jag bore a vanity license plate. Peevishly, she thought that if you looked up the word vanity in Webster's, Kerry Ashton's airbrushed photograph would be there on the page.

The vanity plate on the sleek white sports car was apt for a Chesterfield princess like Kerry Ashton. It read . . . *2 CUTE.* Chantal wouldn't have been surprised if it had read, OH BABY.

"Oh baby!" was Max Armstrong's personal tag; his own equivalent of Harry Carey's trademark utterance of "Holy Cow!" Just as Harry went ballistic at Wrigley Field, shouting "Holy Cow, it's outa here, folks!" whenever a baseball player hit one out of the ballpark, so did Max Armstrong get practically orgasmic yelling, "Oh baby, oh baby, oh baby!" when a player put a puck in the net to score a goal.

Women absolutely loved it.

It sexualized the game.

How in the hell was she supposed to compete with that?

When Max had arrived at the Chadwick Bed and Breakfast he'd found Uncle James rounding out the foursome for Claire's peach pie.

The pie was still warm from the oven, when Claire served it on china dessert plates, using the good silver.

As Uncle James fired questions at him about the hockey team, Max felt Claire's gaze on him. She watched each forkful of dessert make its way to his lips. He guessed she was waiting for his reaction to her peach pie.

"You make a mean peach pie, Claire," he said at last, ending his conversation with Uncle James. Sometimes he thought sports was the only subject in the world, as it was all anyone talked to him about.

Lifting his last bite to his lips, Max winked as he savored the warm, flaky crust against his tongue. The sugary aroma of cinnamon-and-clove spiced peaches heightened the sensory pleasure.

"Thank you, Max," she replied, a rosy blush cresting her fair cheeks.

"I hope you don't mind us asking you to come so late in the evening for pie and coffee. Claire was concerned that if you came earlier, the guests might pester you for your autograph," Amy Jane said.

"I wouldn't have minded, really," he assured them. "For some reason I've been relaxed since I drove through the iron gates. I'm not even a guest, and I feel at home."

It was true, he thought, glancing around the rectangular-shaped dining room wrapped in a pastel floral print wallpaper. The cheerful paper and white painted woodwork set off the dark antique sideboard and matching furniture pieces. Lace curtains at the bay window framed a moonlit night.

"Oh, all the credit for the success of the bed and breakfast goes to Claire," Amy Jane was quick to point out. "She's the one responsible for the ambiance of the place. I'm nothing more than her scullery maid—that is, when I'm not working on a case."

"Really, Amy Jane," Claire said, shaking her head, causing several fair strands to escape her secured topknot.

"Well, it's true. Don't let Claire's demure demeanor fool you, Max. She runs the place like a drill sergeant. It takes an iron will to make things run smoothly, and believe me, Claire has one; isn't that so, Uncle James?"

Max was amused by the two sisters; amused that the younger one, Claire, appeared to be a flake and wasn't, and that the older one, Amy Jane, was the wildly enchanting flake—and clueless about it.

Max found his gaze lingering on Amy Jane's lips when she lifted a bite of pie to them, but it had nothing to do with his wanting to know if she liked the pie.

"Oh come, Sweet," Uncle James said with a laugh. "You talk as if your baby sister has a cat-o'-nine-tails hanging in the pantry."

"Uncle James!" Claire said with a gasp.

"Say, Max, now that we've finished with dessert, why don't I give you the ten-cent tour of the grounds?" Amy Jane interceded.

"Sure," he agreed, wondering as he finished the last of his coffee just what Amy Jane had in mind. Normally he was in his element with anyone, but the Chadwick sisters had him feeling just a bit off balance. It was easy to see they'd been raised with a light hand. Their willfulness was appealing and disconcerting at the same time.

"What about me?" Uncle James was clearly reluctant to have his hockey conversationalist taken from him.

Amy Jane tossed him a towel. "Your turn to play scullery maid."

"You were always a brat, Sweet," Uncle James muttered good naturedly, grabbing the towel with one hand.

Claire shot him a look. "And who encouraged her?"

"Now don't you go turning on me, too, Claire."

"Then pick up the dishes and give me a hand in the kitchen."

The scent of earth drifted on the cool evening breeze as Max and Amy Jane stepped through the French doors to the flagstone patio. On the terrace below, moonlight shimmered off the inky dark water of the swimming pool. The pool was set like an exquisite gem in the manicured grounds, which were surrounded by a stone fence.

Max whistled appreciatively. "Pretty impressive."

"Yeah, I guess it is. I grew up playing hide-and-seek here so it's just home to me."

Max laughed.

"What?" she asked, as they walked down the steps side by side to the pool.

"I was just imagining you playing hide-and-seek, that's all. Let me guess, you cheated . . . right?"

She flicked her hair back over her shoulder and looked straight at him. "I always play to win."

Max didn't react. Instead he knelt on the grass terrace and trailed his hand in the water to see if the pool was heated.

"Truthful and evasive at once," he said standing. He spritzed her with a flick of his wet fingers, surprising a squeal out of her. "You're a pretty smart cookie, aren't you, A. J. Chadwick?"

"Smart cookie?" She gave him a double take. "What, do you watch a lot of old movies?"

"No, I just know a smart cookie when I see one." She probably knew skinny-dipping had momentarily flirted across his mind when he'd realized the pool was heated. Luckily, a moment later he'd come to his senses. He wasn't a romantic, he reminded himself; he was a cynic.

Thanks to finding Kerry Ashton in bed with . . . well, the romantic in him had folded.

Amy Jane led the way to the lily pond beyond the stable which had been turned into a pool house. "You trying to tell me you didn't play to win when you were on the team, Max?"

"Sure, I played to win. But teams have to follow rules to be effective."

"Ah, but I work alone."

"Bet it's 'cause you don't play well with others." Max looked down at the colorful koi swimming toward him in the pond.

"With some better than others," she assured him on a throaty, sexy laugh.

Had her tone been suggestive? Or was he only looking for some affirmation of the attraction he felt? He was certain of one thing; Amy Jane Chadwick was a mouthful and a handful.

"About your case . . ." Amy Jane said.

"So this wasn't just about peach pie and hospitality, was it?"

"You never thought it was. You knew, you had to know, how much I want this case of yours. You'd be a high-profile client."

"Amy Jane, you don't know what kind of case it is."

"And I'm not going to unless you tell me."

The sound of fish splashing in the lily pond broke the silence of the moonlit night.

"You are going to tell me, aren't you, Max?"

"I'm still not sure I'm . . . that there is a case exactly."

They strolled back up to the tennis courts.

"Here's an idea. Why don't you tell me what your problem is and I'll give you my professional opinion on whether or not it's serious enough to warrant hiring an investigator."

When they reached the clay courts located off to one side of the swimming pool, Max picked up a fuzzy yellow tennis ball from a wire basket and bounced it absently on the court. "I'm surprised you didn't offer to play me a match for the case."

"Would it have worked?"

He gave her a noncommittal shrug.

She considered the idea. "I don't like the odds," she admitted.

"You never know . . . I could have gotten to be a couch potato since my playing days."

She just looked at him. "If you're a couch potato, then I'm Princess Di."

He made a mock bow. "Your Majesty—don't you sort of like the ring of it?"

"No."

He tossed the tennis ball he'd been bouncing onto the court. "I take it you aren't going to let me off the hook by my besting you at tennis . . ."

"Bingo."

"Anyone ever tell you you're stubborn, Amy Jane?"

She nodded. "I'm told it's both my best and worst quality."

"Tell you what, I'm going to take you up on your offer. I'll tell you what my problem is so you can give me your professional opinion. But I'm not making any promises here, okay?"

"But you're not saying no—right?"

"I'm not committing either way," he answered, leaning back against the chain-link fence walled around the tennis court.

Amy Jane nodded her understanding.

He rubbed his cupped hands over his short hair, trying to think how to say it. "I feel pretty foolish about the whole damn thing," he said finally.

"Why?"

"Because it's about a woman."

"Palimony?"

"No. No. It's nothing like that. I'm the ah, wronged party, come to that." Oh, hell, he felt really dumb. Why had he ever thought—trouble was, he hadn't thought this out, not really.

He slid down the fence until he was hunkered with his forearms braced on his knees.

Amy Jane lowered her body, comfortable sitting cross-legged in her jeans on the ground beside him.

"If this is Kerry Ashton and alienation of affection we're talking about, I should tell you that you need a lawyer, not a private eye. And that you're probably in the wrong century for that sort of suit."

"You know, if I'd wanted abuse, I could have gone to see Corey Cohen," Max said, thinking of his co-announcer for the Lions hockey team, who was clueless that his family's prominence in the St. Louis community tethered his job.

Corey thought his talent was responsible for his position, not realizing the ménage à trois composed of the married couple of talent and hard work and the lover, luck was what triumphed in the world of Sports, Arts and Entertainment.

Corey's youthful ego ruled him. He never missed an opportunity to point out a perk he received that Max didn't. It took all of Max's effort to hold his tongue. But he did, telling himself Corey was too easy a target. An adult, Max realized that compromise was the cornerstone of being civilized.

"Okay, I'll be quiet," Amy Jane promised from beside him. "Go ahead . . ."

He glanced over to see she was tugging at the blades of grass around her sneakers. She wasn't watching him while she waited to hear what he had to say. Her head was bent forward, her hair curtaining her face, as she performed her aimless task.

Good. It would be easier to tell her if she wasn't watching him. He felt dumb enough as it was.

"There's a strange woman in my underwear drawer," he blurted out.

Her head popped up and she looked at him.

"I mean . . ." he began, ". . . she's not in my . . . not now, but she . . . she was."

Amy Jane started to laugh, but she stopped,

seeing the look on his face was frustrated, but serious.

"Maybe I should start at the beginning," he said, figuring he'd gone this far, he might as well continue. Besides he had to tell *somebody*. "At first I didn't think anything of it; the initial letter, I mean. The letter was fairly innocuous, and weird fan mail is more usual than not when you're a celebrity."

Amy Jane tilted her head. "Do you get a lot?"

Had she really just asked what he thought she had?

"Fan mail. Do you get a lot of fan mail?" she asked as if he were dense.

"Oh. No, not really." Shrugging, he added, "It straggles into the station, and they pass it on to me when they think of it."

Cramped, he stood to stretch his long legs.

She followed suit. "The ground was getting kinda cold," she said, dusting off the trim seat of her jeans. Her action thrust her chest forward, Amy Jane unconsciously silhouetting what Max couldn't help but notice was a generous C to D cup. He wasn't seeing anything really, but his imagination was making his palms itch.

Why the hell was he rambling on about what was probably nothing, when what he really wanted was to ask out this sexy, enigmatic woman? What, he wondered, would she say, if he did?

Would she be surprised?

Annoyed?

Pleased?

God, you'd think he was fifteen years old instead of thirty.

"Yeah, this is probably spring's early teaser," he said, making a lame response to her mention of the cool ground. The day had been unusually warm for early March. Dusk hadn't brought a lowered temperature. It was still a warm night.

As they headed back up the flagstone path to the patio, Max watched a gentle breeze tease her long tresses.

He found himself leaning closer. She smelled like lilies—though she was anything but as fragile and weak as the flower.

What would she do, he wondered, if he pulled her into his arms, and stole a moonlit kiss? Stole it with a sound romantic thoroughness.

Would she be surprised?

Annoyed?

Pleased?

"So, did you encourage this woman?" Amy Jane punctured his night fancies, picking up the thread of conversation from which they'd strayed.

"What?" he asked, taking umbrage at the implication inherent in her question. Did she really think he was the sort of lowlife who'd feed off something like that?

"Well . . . *did* you answer the letter?"

"No. I don't answer fan mail—as a point of policy."

"You don't?" Amy Jane said, a note of genuine surprise in her voice.

"While I'm a celebrity of sorts, I'm no longer a hockey player. I don't give out my autograph, unless I'm pressed to do so. I just do my job."

"Maybe this particular fan really wants your autograph. It's a reasonable assumption that by not answering this woman's letter, you might have angered her."

Max rubbed his hands together slowly, giving her point some consideration. "I hadn't thought about it, but I imagine it's possible. You never know what motivates someone."

"How about Corey Cohen?"

"Corey! You can't mean you think it could be him sending the letters?" He dismissed the idea out of hand. "Corey Cohen doesn't have the imagination to pull off such a stunt. And I don't even want to think about him rifling my underwear drawer . . ."

"That wasn't what I meant. I was asking if Corey gets fan mail, too."

"Anything's possible," Max answered drolly.

Amy Jane grinned. "Well, let's assume he does. Do you think he answers it?"

"Yeah, probably. He would, sure. Why?"

"Well, I hate to shoot down your balloon, but it could be that Corey's also gotten a letter from the same fan. It might just be that you aren't the only one."

Max let the idea from left field sink in. Now he felt really foolish. Here he was, obsessing about his fan, when Corey in the same position would probably hoard the letters like some grandmother clipping newsprint, just waiting for the opportune moment to gloat. Funny, he'd feel as if their shared fan was actually cheating on him. If they did indeed have a shared fan. Was that perverse of him, or what?

Maybe he'd pay closer attention to what Corey said on the air, and off.

"I don't suppose you brought the letters with you tonight?" Amy Jane asked hopefully.

Max laughed. "Not hardly. I'm not Corey Cohen."

"You know . . ." she said, trailing her finger over the beveled glass top of the patio table, "if I could see those letters, it would help me to give you a better-informed opinion on whether you have a case or merely a major fan."

"You mean now? *Tonight?*"

"Is that a problem?"

"No problem," he answered, considering her request. "Okay, why don't we say good-bye to your sister and uncle. Then we can go back to my place."

"You're going?" Claire asked, coming out to the patio with Uncle James behind her.

"Yes," Max answered. "A good guest doesn't overstay his welcome, eh, James?"

"I was only waiting for my doggy bag," Uncle James hinted broadly.

"But you don't have a dog," Amy Jane said.

"I do," Max said. "And he especially likes peach pie."

Claire shook her head at the two men, but

was obviously pleased. "You two are hopeless,
but I'll wrap you both up a pie anyway," she
said, heading back inside.

"And I'll just get my keys," Amy Jane said,
following her.

Inside the house, Amy Jane fetched her purse.
Returning to the kitchen, she dumped the contents on the tile counter.

Claire rolled her eyes as she watched her search
through the pile of loose change, lip gloss, crumpled receipts and assorted pens and pencils.

"Aha, found 'em," Amy Jane held up her set
of keys triumphantly.

"So, you did learn what the case was about,
then?" Claire looked up from wrapping pieces
of pie in cellophane, and putting them in white
sacks.

"Sure did." Amy Jane put the upended contents back in her purse.

"Well . . ."

"What?"

"What's the case about?" Claire asked, following Amy Jane to the French doors leading to
the patio.

Amy Jane looked back over her shoulder.
"Claire, you know I can't tell you that. It's privileged between the client and me."

Claire shrugged, "It was worth a try."

Five

Corey Cohen went through his mail, using his peripheral vision to dodge the people in his on-coming path to the equipment room at the Dome. The charity match the Lions had played against local celebrities was over. The players had lingered to sign autographs and were now starting to mill about after their showers.

There was nothing exciting in his mail; a utility bill, a bar-mitzvah invitation, a sale no-tice from European Autos and a request that he judge in the Miss American Teen Pageant to select the finalist.

He made a mental note to have his secretary make the proper response to the invitation, and pay his utility bill. He figured he'd take care of looking at the fancy cars and pretty women.

His peripheral vision failed him and he plowed full on into Chantal Perry, who'd stopped to get something from her satchel.

Unable to break the momentum of their colli-sion, Corey took them both down. As he sprawled across her, his mail scattered every which way, and the contents of her satchel spilled out onto the floor.

Slender and agile, Corey did manage to land his body atop Chantal's without doing her any damage.

He braced himself above her on his hands, assuming the gentleman's position. There was, however, nothing gentlemanly about his pelvis touching hers, even though it was accidental. Looking into Chantal's startled blue eyes, he knew it was a position he would relive over and over in his mind. And that there would be nothing gentlemanly about the thoughts he'd allow himself later.

But that was his own secret. No one knew about the crush he had on Chantal Perry. If only super jock, Max Armstrong, hadn't come along to spoil everything. When he took the job of being co-announcer, it had nipped any chance of something developing between the two of them. Now if he wanted to spend time with Chantal, he had to announce his desires. He had to risk.

He told himself it didn't matter, that there was no chance for him with Chantal Perry. Even if a beautiful woman like Chantal knew he was alive, his mother would have a stroke if he brought Chantal home to dinner.

"I'm sorry . . . are you . . . okay?" Corey asked, finally gaining his voice, and moving to assist Chantal up.

"I'm fine, I think. What happened?" she asked, taking his offered hand.

"I don't know exactly. I was looking at my mail." He glanced around at it scattered on the floor. "I guess I wasn't paying attention to where I was walking. I'm really sorry."

"No need to apologize." Chantal held up her hand to stop him. "I'm not hurt, really. And I suppose it's partly my fault. I shouldn't have stopped to look through my bag in the middle of traffic."

At the mention of her satchel, they both looked down to see her lipstick, some papers, and a black lace bra lying near her satchel where they'd fallen.

"Here, let me help you with your things, at least." Corey bent to gather them up.

"No! No, that's all right." Chantal quickly scooped everything into her hand.

"Ah, I think that's mine," Corey said, when she began tucking what she'd scooped up into her satchel.

"What?" Color stained Chantal's cheeks as she looked down at the black lace bra in her hand.

"The invitation." Corey reached to pull it from beneath the bra. "My nephew's bar mitzvah."

"Oh." She quickly shoved the rest of her things into her satchel.

"Look could I buy you a soda or something?" he asked. "I feel bad that I ah . . . bowled you over . . . ah," oh great, had he really said that? Where was his glib tongue when he needed it?

She looked down at her watch. "I've got to be somewhere and I'm late, but thanks."

Corey watched her hurry away. He supposed it was possible she really did have an appointment. His ego validated the positive spin he put on the rejection. As he bent to pick up his mail, his original errand was completely forgotten. Instead his mind lingered on the scrap of black lace that had fallen from Chantal's dropped satchel.

Had it meant that she didn't wear a bra occasionally . . . frequently . . . ?

Damn Max Armstrong. Why couldn't he still be playing hockey instead of playing on *his* turf?

"Hey, Corey—"

He turned to see Lance Thomure, the Lions' defenseman and Richie Allen, the Lions' goalie, approaching from the equipment room. Oh, no, had the two of them seen what had happened? If they'd seen his collision with Chantal Perry, they'd never stop ribbing him.

"Just wanted to ask what you thought of my penalty killing in the last couple of games," Thomure asked, when they joined him.

Corey relaxed, the tension easing from his muscles he'd clenched for the verbal hit. They hadn't seen. "You've been converting the power plays pretty well, I have to admit," he answered, looking at Thomure. "Seems like you've managed to find the 'on' switch."

"How about you, Corster?" Allen asked, elbowing Thomure.

"Did you manage to find the 'on' switch yourself?"

"What?" Corey asked, puzzled.

"You know, a few minutes ago when you and Chantal were wrestling on the floor? Didn't know wrestling was your sport . . ." Both athletes broke up with laughter as they high-five'd each other, then sauntered away from pranking him.

Corey shook his head, rolling his eyes at their good-natured—though juvenile—behavior. He took a deep, calming breath. He wouldn't allow the pair to get to him. Some days he thought maybe his mother was right; he should have gone into medicine—should have listened to her, and become a doctor like every other male in his family.

Oh well, a bloodsport like hockey held the same kind of excitement. Someone was always being checked head first into the boards, or being taken out with a mid-ice check to the side of the knee.

He hadn't been a player, like Max. He hadn't even intended announcing the sport. It was something he'd just sort of fallen into. To him, any sport was exciting. At least it was, if he was the one announcing it, he thought, giving himself a mental stroke.

He knew he was likely to see blood in the weeks ahead as the Lions played the Blackhawks.

Their intense rivalry was more like war than sport, and the games between them were never pretty.

After the series with the Blackhawks, the playoffs loomed. The division games were typically rough and tough with on-ice battles and histrionics. It was an exciting time.

He hoped everyone was going to be healthy for the playoffs. Everyone, the announcers as well as the players, benefitted financially if the Lions took it all the way to bringing the Stanley Cup home to St. Louis. They hadn't had such a good shot at it since the early seventies when the town had had a real power franchise.

Besides, the more broadcast coverage, the better the chances were that he'd be thrown together with Chantal Perry. Yeah, he liked that idea a lot.

Thrown together . . .

The image of her beneath him, flushed and breathless, flashed in his mind.

He wondered if that same image would also surface in her mind. Would she recall him above her today? Would the image tease her . . . haunt her . . . as it did him?

And if it did, would she be thinking the same sort of provocative thoughts he was thinking?

He shook his head, clearing it of erotic images. The business at hand, he reminded himself. He'd been searching out the Lions' coach, Tom Quinn, to check out a rumor.

He'd take any avenue to get the edge on Max

Armstrong and leverage him out. Yeah, Max was a thorn in his side.

Amy Jane pulled her Jeep up to the curb, parking behind Max's luxury car. After exiting their respective vehicles, they walked together to the entry of his condo.

"You didn't need to drive. I would have taken you back," he said, repeating his earlier offer.

"No, the trip is too far. Your condo is at least a forty-minute drive from our place. I don't know why anyone would want to live in Chesterfield. It's far from everywhere."

Not commenting on the regionalism of the locals, Max unlocked the door and she followed him inside. "Figures," she said, upon looking around.

"What?" he asked, puzzled.

"That you'd be a neat freak."

"There's nothing wrong with being organized. It enables me to find things. It doesn't mean I'm a neat freak."

"Really? I'll bet you have the letters all in one place, maybe even tied with a ribbon."

"Come on back to my bedroom and I'll show you," he said, catching her hand.

She trailed along behind him, feeling very much a fly to his spider.

He pulled open the top drawer of his bureau. Withdrawing the letters, he handed them to her.

"Together as you suspected, but no ribbon.
Sorry to disappoint you."

Amy Jane took the letters he offered, scanning
the one on top. "Seems tame enough." Amy
Jane let it slip to land on the bed, while she
moved on to the next letter in the pile.

"They get gradually more demanding," he assured her.

"I've got a bulletin for you, Max. Most women
do." Amy Jane glanced up at him.

He arched an eyebrow, but said nothing. She
returned to scanning the letters, which were actually nothing more than brief notes. They all
began with "Dearest Max." A compliment
and/or request followed. They were all signed
off with "I Love You."

And they were all typed.

Someone else was a smart cookie.

Finishing the pile of letters, Amy Jane let the
last one slip to the bed. "Did you tell anyone
about these letters, brag to anyone?"

"You're confusing me with Corey Cohen
again . . ."

Max bent to restack the letters in a neat pile.
"I didn't mention the letters to anyone. I didn't
think it amounted to anything more than a
harmless fantasy—"

"Until she showed up in your underwear
drawer . . ."

"Right." As he replaced the letters in the top
drawer of the bureau, he asked way too solici-

tously, "Would you like to see my underwear drawer?"

"Where is it?" she asked, reading the surprise on his face at her query.

"Third drawer down." Max stepped away from the bureau after closing the top drawer.

She went to the bureau, pulled open the drawer, and glanced inside. Reaching into it, she made a thorough search, leaving the contents in total disarray. Her quick visual survey confirmed what her fingertips had discerned; nothing more in the drawer than a few foil packets and silk boxers. "You ever hear of cotton underwear?" Amy Jane looked back up at him, the sensual feel of silk imprinted on her fingertips.

"You ever hear of the word neat?" Max moved beside her to straighten the mess she'd made of his bureau drawer.

"Yeah, it's a four letter word," she replied, quickly moving away from the intoxicating scent of his dangerously sexy aftershave.

"You know, you've probably built up the fantasy in your fan's mind even further . . ." she said from behind him.

"What are you talking about? I told you I've never responded in any way to the letters."

"You kept the letters all in a nice little stack, saving them—maybe even rereading them to her mind. It's more than likely she came across them when she was searching for a memento."

"Oh."

"How do you suppose she got in?" Amy Jane

asked, beginning her survey of the condo's lay-
out with Max on her heels. She gave a cursory
check to all the windows and doors, even climbing on a kitchen chair to check a skylight that
opened.

Max grinned. "I don't think we're looking for
a cat burglar."

Annoyed that he wasn't really taking her or
the matter seriously, she shot back, "Oh, I don't
know. It appears she got pretty close to the family jewels."

"Oh, a wiseacre . . ."

"You'll watch anything in black and white,
won't you—including the Stooges. So tell me
Sherlock, if there aren't any windows or doors
broken, then how did your fan get in? Unless
maybe it was an old girlfriend with a key she
conveniently forgot to return." Amy Jane
groaned. "I don't even want to think about the
size of that list I'd have to check out."

"She didn't have to break in," Max said quietly.

"Why not? Don't tell me—" she said, seeing
the sheepish look dawn on his face.

He nodded. " 'Fraid so. I'm not careful about
locking up." He shrugged. "I come from a small
town and just never got in the habit, I guess."

"Your door was locked tonight."

He laughed ruefully. "I may learn slowly, but
I do learn."

"I'd keep locking my door if I were you," Amy
Jane advised. "You've got some valuable pine
pieces from the looks of it. Your insurance com-

pany isn't going to be any too thrilled with you if someone can just waltz right in and rob you."

"You don't think—"

"No, I don't. I think this fan is much more interested in you than in your valuables. But you *are* an excellent target for anyone who would want to rob you. When you're announcing a game live on television, you're like a mourner at a funeral—completely vulnerable. All a burglar has to do is find out when you are announcing, turn on the television while you're telecasting, and he's home free."

"I'd never considered that." Max checked the contents of the refrigerator.

"That's because you're not the wife of a newscaster, and in an even more vulnerable position. It's the sort of set up a rapist looks for. Just ask the police. Speaking of them, did you report the break-in to them?"

"Yeah, that's the headline I want to wake up to . . . FAN IN ARMSTRONG'S DRAWERS."

Amy Jane shook her head no to the wine cooler he offered. "I think you should see what you can find out about this fan."

"You're saying you think I have a case?" Max took a long drink of his wine cooler.

"I'm saying I think it bears investigating. This woman could be dangerous. At the very least, she's breaking the law. For certain if she broke into your condo for the sole purpose of stealing a pair of your underwear, she isn't coloring with the same set of crayons as the rest of us."

Max considered her point, then shrugged. "I don't know. Maybe she's not using good judgment, is all. Didn't you ever get a crush on someone and act a little foolish?"

Amy Jane cocked her head to one side, and gave him a look.

"What?" he asked, setting down his wine cooler on the counter.

"You like it, don't you?"

"I what?" he asked, incredulous.

"You like it. You like women having mad, passionate crushes on you. You get off on it."

"You're crazy!"

"Am I?"

"I think it would be a good idea for you to leave," he said, leading the way to the front door. "Like I said if I wanted insults, I'd call Corey Cohen. Please leave."

"Does this mean I don't get the case?"

"What do you think?"

Amy Jane smiled when she heard the lock click.

He did enjoy it.

Who wouldn't? she thought, heading for her Jeep.

Unfortunately, she wasn't the sort of woman men had mad, passionate crushes on. It had something to do with her attitude.

Where her Uncle James had never met a bad habit he didn't like, she'd never met a stodgy convention she didn't want to overturn.

Especially difficult to resist was the one about

women having the proper respect for male anger. You'd think by now she'd have learned it wasn't cool to laugh at men when they were angry.

Oh, well, Max would come around when he cooled off.

Amy Jane parked her car a block away from Max's condo.

She walked back to it to follow up on a hunch she had. Women had better hunches than men. She was fairly certain that was fact rather than sexist thinking. At least, her hunches usually played out.

Max may not have hired her tonight, but she was confident he would. She was only getting a jump start on working the case.

Taking her sweet time, she circled his condo, checking out what could be seen from the outside when the lights were on. The view inside from outside the kitchen window was minimal. There were mini-blinds in the dining room and living room and they were closed, closing off any view at all.

Making her way to the side of the house where Max's bedroom was located, she hit pay dirt.

The light was on in his bedroom.

His bedroom had a small wooden deck off it, with sliding glass doors leading to it; hence he had drapes instead of mini-blinds. The drapery didn't close perfectly. A narrow slit at the closing gave her a look at a portion of his bedroom.

She jumped at the sound of a sudden loud clang, then realized it was the water pipes. Max was probably taking a shower. She could see light at the entry to the bath adjoining his bedroom.

That gave her a few minutes to be bold in her survey without worry of detection. She could make out the four-poster soft pine bed and the wicker chest beside it from where she stood.

A telephone and clock radio were on the chest. She smiled when she spotted the wine cooler sitting on top of the bureau, imagining she'd driven Max to drink.

She coaxed her mind back to the job at hand. Had Max's fan stood out here in this very spot watching? Was she that bold? It was possible; she'd been bold enough to enter his condo and go through his things.

The fan clearly wanted a relationship with Max.

Was it because she'd already had one? One that she missed? Was Kerry Ashton behind the letters?

Somehow Amy Jane couldn't picture the classy Miss Ashton standing outside his condo watching, yet she did live in Chesterfield. Maybe even within walking distance. Not that anyone walked in Chesterfield. And Amy Jane could easily imagine Kerry wearing silk.

And, of course, there was Chantal Perry, the

announcer Max had aced out of a promised spot on the Lions co-anchor team. Where did she live? Amy Jane made a mental note to check on it. She didn't think Chantal wanted anything of Max's but his job. Still, you never could tell.

The light in the bathroom went out.

Max entered her line of view in the bedroom. *Naked.*

Yes, this *was* the kind of case she needed to relieve the boredom of insurance investigating.

Already the stakeouts were getting lots more interesting.

Seconds later, the light in the bedroom went out. As Amy Jane turned to go, she stepped on something, and bent to investigate it.

It was a small gold hoop earring.

Pierced.

Six

The following evening found Amy Jane at work on an ongoing insurance fraud case. She positioned herself on the end of the wooden bleachers, enabling her to hold her arm out at a forty-five-degree angle without disturbing anyone else watching the amateur softball game. The crowd of interested friends and family allowed her to go unnoticed.

Televised Cardinal spring training had the weekend jocks out on the first warm evenings.

Amy Jane's hand steadied the video camera. The guy she had under surveillance was next up to bat. At the moment he was taking practice swings, trying out different weight bats. He looked far from disabled, as he'd claimed. He and his slick attorney had collected a bundle from the insurance company retaining her. The insurance company felt the man's claim was bogus, no matter what the jury had voted. They had hired her to prove he did not have a serious back injury that permanently disabled him.

The guy had been smart enough to hire a

slick attorney, but not smart enough to give up being a weekend jock.

She already had him on tape, the very tape she now had in her video camera. A few evenings ago he'd tagged up to run for a buddy who'd slid into second base, injuring his knee so he couldn't continue running. He'd only played for him for the last inning of the game, but she had him on tape hauling ass only to be thrown out at the plate in a double play.

Tonight she'd played one of her hunches that once he'd had a taste of playing again, he wouldn't be able to resist the lure of the game.

It wasn't as if she wasn't sympathetic to that lure herself. After all she'd been something of a jock herself as a kid. And softball had been her game.

She'd played in summer leagues, and sneaked her transistor radio into school to hear the broadcasts of the World Series games. In fact, she could still remember the day when it had dawned on her that she couldn't grow up to be a professional baseball player. Sometimes being a woman really pissed her off.

Max Armstrong flashed into her mind. She'd really pissed him off. And she'd seen him naked.

Well, it wasn't the being a woman she minded. She quite liked that. It was the restrictions placed on you when you were a woman that frustrated her. Whoever had invented those stupid rules of gender privileges ought to have to *be* a woman in a girdle and three-inch high heels, getting a permanent while downsizing their dreams for life. One week—no, one day of that, and the rules would be forever changed.

She returned her attention to the business at hand, pushing what was wrong with the world, and what was right with it . . . a naked Mr. Armstrong . . . to the back of her mind. The things she did for money.

Her hunch had played out just as she'd expected; once a jock, always a jock—if you could move at all. This guy could move just fine. If he had a bad back, then she was Babe Ruth. Not with a .211 batting average, she wasn't. No, what this guy was, was a big, healthy guy without a conscience about being on the dole.

There was a pink cast to the evening sky, signaling that tomorrow would be another gorgeous day, as she pressed the record button on the video camera and the little red light went on.

No one was paying any attention to her, assuming she had a boyfriend playing in the game. Looking through the lens, she saw him swing and miss at an inside ball, high.

He let the next ball pass.

And the next.

On the two-one count he swung and juiced the ball, getting it up in the wind. She taped the guy circling first, then second, and tagging up at third where he was held by the strong arm of the left fielder.

Using the zoom lens, she got a clear picture

of him so there could be no dispute about who he was.

And then she shut off her video camera.

She wished she could shut off her thoughts of Max Armstrong as easily.

She had to deal with him. But he would have to wait until tomorrow. Somehow she'd have to make amends for baiting him. But what? And then she remembered that old adage about the way to a man's heart being through his stomach. Maybe breakfast in bed would do the trick, she thought with a considering grin. And she had a clue—the gold earring.

As she walked toward her Jeep, she made a mental note to have Claire take care of the breakfast in bed.

Max flailed his arm out, reaching for the incessantly ringing instrument.

"Hello . . ." he mumbled into the phone, fighting his way up from a deep sleep.

No answer, but the ringing continued.

"Hell-low . . ." he repeated, the greeting tinged with sarcasm.

It took a few minutes, but it finally registered that he was getting a dial tone, while the ringing continued. It took a few seconds after that for him to realize it was the doorbell ringing and not the phone.

He wasn't expecting anyone.

What the hell time was it anyway?

He threw back the covers with an oath. This was probably a player's joke, he thought, stumbling half asleep to the door wearing only the silk boxers he'd slept in.

"Yeah, what do you want?" he growled, yanking open the door.

It wasn't one of the players.

Nor was it the pizza delivery guy with a dozen anchovy pizzas the players had pranked.

It was Little Red Riding Hood with a basket tucked beneath her arm. "Amy Jane said to tell you she's sorry and *bon appetít.*"

"Oh, hi," he said, feeling like the Big Bad Wolf standing before her in his silk boxers. "Would you like to come inside?"

Claire Chadwick looked a bit uncertain.

"Come on, I promise not to eat you," he said with what he hoped was a more sheepish than wolfish grin.

He stood to one side to allow her to enter the foyer, and she acquiesced.

"Ah, if you'll excuse me for just a moment, I'll get ah, decent, and be right back with you."

She nodded, and he hurried back to his bedroom to change. Pulling on a pair of jeans, he glanced over at the clock on his nightstand. Its digital numbers read 9:30. That meant it couldn't possibly have been one of the players on his doorstep.

They had a home game tonight, which meant the morning skate was at 10:30. He would have realized that—if he'd been fully awake when the doorbell had started up.

Grabbing a T-shirt, he headed back to the foyer and his guest.

A noise in the kitchen sidetracked him. It was Claire popping something into the microwave; something that smelled scrumptious enough to set his stomach growling.

"Here you are," he said, joining her, as he pulled the T-shirt in his hands over his head.

"I hope you don't mind," Claire said, looking up from the rasher of sugared bacon she was putting on a plate. "Amy Jane insisted I make up this breakfast for you, and deliver it along with her apology." Wiping her hands on the dishcloth that had covered the basket, she handed the handwritten note from Amy Jane to him.

Max scanned Amy Jane's apology.

The timer went off on the microwave, and Claire withdrew a plate of eggs scrambled with cream cheese.

"Do you forgive her?" Claire asked, when he'd finished reading the note.

"On one condition."

"What's that?"

"If you agree to join me for breakfast."

"Really?"

"I insist."

"Well, okay, if you really want me to."

Max watched Claire fuss with putting the finishing touches to the breakfast Amy Jane had had her arrange for him.

She was a blonde confection in pink, from her pastel city shorts and matching linen jacket to her manicured nails and shiny lips. Baby sister was nothing like big sister. For all he tried, he couldn't for the life of him even begin to imagine Amy Jane putting this much effort into making breakfast for him. If Amy Jane had had to do it, he would have been lucky to have gotten a cup of coffee that wasn't instant . . . a cup of coffee period.

"You know, you're going to make some man a great wife," Max mused out loud.

Claire blushed as she unpacked the remainder of the morning meal; croissants, jam, sliced fruit and a thermos of hot Irish blend coffee.

"So, Max," Claire said, sitting down across from him after pouring him a steaming cup of coffee, "do you like being a hockey announcer?"

Amy Jane had really pulled out all the stops to get his business, Max deducted. She'd even prepped Claire to flatter him, with that note of awe in her whispery little-girl voice. He wondered if Claire had any inkling of its innocent seduction. Probably not. It was no doubt just his being in the business that made voices so interesting to him.

"I love it," Max said, taking full advantage of the female charm Claire unconsciously exuded. It was a welcome change from Amy Jane's bruising of his ego the day before yesterday. It was a wonder the woman had any clients at all.

* * *

Amy Jane's neck ached. She'd been camped out in her Jeep since dawn. Though the van parked in front of her pretty much shielded her from view, she was still careful to keep out of sight. Gingerly, she stretched her cramped legs, and then her arms. Her wrist was tingling from falling asleep.

She supposed last night's softball game had taken it out of Lazybones, or more likely the beers he'd had with his buddies afterward. He was just now coming out of his house to find he had a flat tire on his car to fix.

He wasn't real thrilled to make the discovery. As she kept watch, he swore and kicked the tire as if to punish it. Instead of punishing it, he punished his toe. Swearing again, he hopped up and down on one foot.

Darn, she should have gotten that on tape. And she would have, normally. This morning she was distracted by thoughts of Max Armstrong. She wondered how Claire was faring with the breakfast truce she'd had her take Max. Not that she was worried; Claire and her cooking were a fairly safe bet.

Reaching for the video camera, she dismissed all thoughts of Claire and Max from her mind, watching the guy go to open his truck to retrieve the jack and spare tire.

"Yes!"

She had to control her enthusiasm. It wouldn't

do to get careless now, and let this guy catch her. He wouldn't be too pleased to know he was being recorded doing the strenuous physical activity of jacking up the car, loosening the lug nuts, and then changing the flat tire. Not when he was supposed to be permanently incapacitated with a serious back injury.

As she pressed the record button, she knew he would be even less pleased to know she was the cause of his flat tire.

It had only taken a little puncture on her way home last night . . .

Poor Max Armstrong didn't stand a snowball's chance in hell against her determination.

She smiled.

"Do we have to go, Mom? It's so-ooo boring. Can't we just go shopping instead?" the teenage girl pouted, while her minister father jotted down Claire's directions to the Arch. "We didn't come all the way from Vermont to go shopping," the pretty mother chided her.

Amy Jane smiled, watching the teenage girl's cute little brother make a face. "Shopping, yuk! I want to ride way up high in the Arch."

"And so you shall," his father said, smiling down at the boy. He gathered up the directions he'd jotted down, and Claire waved the four of them off.

"So, how'd it go this morning?" Amy Jane

asked, when Claire turned her attention from the bed and breakfast's guests to her.

Amy Jane had only just arrived back home from dropping off the tape she'd made for the insurance company. "I hope it went as well as my morning," she added, thinking of the bill she'd presented the insurance company along with the tape of the evidence they needed to void the pay out awarded the claimant by a jury.

The bill was going to make the bean-counters choke; but they would pay it because the evidence she'd collected would save them such a considerable sum.

"I woke him up," Claire said, twisting the opal stud in her ear.

Amy Jane laughed with delight. "So tell me, how is he early in the morning—what time did you go?"

"Not that early. I deliberately waited until nine o'clock to go to his condo, so I didn't actually get there until about nine-thirty."

"And he was still sleeping when you got there? What a life. And here I've been up hard at work since dawn. Try to tell me it's not a man's world out there."

She opened the fridge, lounging in front of it like a teenager.

"So was he grumpy?" she asked, looking to find something in the fridge to tide her over until dinner. In the excitement of getting the goods on tape, she'd forgotten to eat. It was lucky she hadn't been so excited she'd forgotten to press the record button on the video camera.

What a disaster that would have been. Since she'd first started out, she hadn't done anything that boneheaded.

She smiled, recalling Uncle James's guffaws, when she'd put an early tape in to play for him, and there hadn't been anything on the tape—only fuzzy static. She hadn't been near as amused, but she had learned her lesson. And she had gotten Uncle James back for laughing. The details escaped her now, but she seemed to recall mustache wax being involved.

"Grumpy?" Claire considered, tilting her head to one side. "Only at first, when he opened the door thinking it was one of the players pulling some stunt on him. When he saw it was me, he seemed relieved."

"I guess that basket of goodies you had packed didn't hurt either. Did he like the food?" Amy Jane slapped her forehead. "What am I saying? Of course, he liked your food. You're a freaking gourmet cook. It's one of the reasons this place is such a huge success."

"He did say he liked it," Claire said, taking a box of salt from the cabinet. "He ate every crumb, at any rate."

"What'd he do . . . make you serve him breakfast in bed? Trust a man to milk it for all it's worth."

"No. No, he got dressed, and we ate in the kitchen." She stood on tiptoe, stretching to reach a box of pepper. "He insisted I join him," she said, locating the pepper, and taking it down.

"Oh, great, I hope his table manners didn't appall you. Never can tell with an ex-hockey player," she teased, with a quick wink.

Claire looked perplexed. "He has beautiful table manners. Really, Amy Jane, you'd think he crawled out from under a rock, the way you talk."

"All men crawl out from under rocks, baby sister," Amy Jane said, settling for an orange, before finally closing the fridge. She began peeling the fruit while watching Claire fill the individual crystal sets of salt and pepper shakers she placed at each table setting for the guests. It was one of her special little touches. "So we've got a good start, he dressed for breakfast, and he didn't put his elbows on the table. What about the good part?"

"The what?"

"Did he accept my apology after you bribed him with your great cooking?" Amy Jane said, as though Claire were dense.

"Oh. Well, he said he'd consider it if—" Claire twisted the sterling tops back on the miniature shakers she'd just filled.

"If . . . ?" Amy Jane bit into the orange, wiping at the juice sluicing down her chin. "If . . . what if?"

"He said to tell you he'd talk to you about accepting your apology tonight."

"Tonight?" Amy Jane said, swallowing.

"Yeah, after the hockey game."

"But I'm not going to the hockey game to-night—wait, maybe I am . . . we are."

"Oh, no, *we* aren't." Claire gathered up the shakers turning her back on Amy Jane and her proposal.

"Oh, come on, Claire," Amy Jane said, following Claire into the dining room, where Claire set the shakers down on the breakfront, at the ready for setting the table.

"I'm not going. I don't like sports, remember," Claire said, heading back to the kitchen.

"Cl-a-aire, come on, go with me. It'll be fun," Amy Jane promised, close on her heels like a pesky dog, begging for a treat from an indulgent owner. "We never do anything, just the two of us."

"But a hockey game . . . Amy Jane? Couldn't we just do a movie or something. There's that fantasy playing at Ronnie's Multi-plex about Redford having to pay a woman a million dollars to sleep with him."

"Must have been a man who wrote that movie," Amy Jane said with a shake of her head.

Claire threw her a soft dishcloth to wipe her sticky hands and mouth. "Really, Amy Jane, you eat like a two-year-old."

"I know," Amy Jane said, unrepentant. "It makes food taste better." She moistened the monogrammed towel, then dabbed the stickiness her snack had left on her lips and fingers.

"Really, Amy Jane."

"Oh, come on, Claire. You work too hard. You've got to lighten up. Loosen up. Stop spending so much time with those minor-league types."

"Ivy League—" Claire corrected, before she could catch herself.

"Same difference," Amy Jane said, shrugging. "Come on, say you'll come to the game with me. It'll be a hoot. We'll pig out on junk food, eat with our fingers," she wiggled her eyebrows with exaggerated sexiness, "maybe even be so bold as to flirt with some guys . . . what'dya say, huh, Claire? Do it, please."

"Okay."

"Okay? No argument?"

Claire grinned, then lifted her hands, palms up in a surrender gesture. "I finished my book."

Amy Jane shot her a considering look.

"Okay, you're right . . . we haven't spent much time together lately. And I do work too hard."

"Good, I'm going up to start getting ready," Amy Jane announced, pleased Claire was joining her for a fun girls' night out.

"Don't use all the hot water," Claire said after her as Amy Jane left the room. "Leave enough for my bath."

Her bath. Claire's baths were long, leisurely soaks that lasted until the candles burned out. They'd be lucky to get to the Dome by the third period.

Seven

The sports bar was filling up with fans who'd left the Dome early to beat the traffic jam, Amy Jane saw, as she and Claire were swept inside with a group of eight celebrating a member's birthday, loudly. The birthday song they were crooning was hilariously off key.

The crowd inside the sports bar was fairly young. Here and there couples sat alone at tables, but there were a lot of groups of friends out for a good time. Dating didn't seem to be as popular among those in their early twenties as it once was. Nowadays twenty-somethings seemed to prefer to live at home and travel in packs. She didn't know if it was fear of AIDS, the poor economy, or some other sociological trend.

She thought it was a good one. It took a lot of pressure off everyone, and eliminated those terrible blind dates. This way you could be around someone without even the commitment of a date.

And you could bail, before anything even got

started, and without either party feeling guilty or embarrassed.

The only thing worse than being dumped was doing the dumping. She always liked to let the guy think it was his idea.

Sometimes she wondered if she had a soft head as well as a soft heart.

As they walked to the bar, two seats opened up.

"What are the two of you up to tonight?" Uncle James asked, trying to look innocent of having shooed away two customers in favor of his nieces. "Did the two of you go see the Redford movie, what's the title, *Indecent Behavior,* isn't it?"

"Proposal," Claire corrected. "No, someone wouldn't go," she said, nodding to Amy Jane, as the two of them sat down at the bar.

"Really? How come?" he asked, putting out paper napkins for their drinks. "I thought every woman breathing was in love with Redford."

"I suggested the hockey game. I thought it would be fun," Amy Jane explained. "But someone takes three hours to take a simple bath," she added, nodding to Claire.

In the background she could hear Max announcing the final minutes of the Lions game. The home team was ahead by four goals.

"The center forward for the Blackhawks cannons a shot, but it bounces off Allen, who makes a great save, folks."

His next words had all heads in the bar turned to the big TV screens. Most of the fans' interest had wandered because the Lions were so far out in front late in the game. Only a little bloodlust could lure them back.

"Uh-oh, folks . . . looks like McQuaid's in big trouble at the far end of the ice . . ." Max's words had provided the bloodlust.

Everyone watched a goon defenseman for the Blackhawks whip up on McQuaid—his action piled the entire Lions team out onto the ice to McQuaid's defense.

"It's the ref's fault," Corey Cohen was explaining into the mike. "He didn't call the lumber facial McQuaid gave the cementhead."

Finally the fight was stopped, and penalties were issued to both sides. McQuaid limped off the ice.

"Oh, the poor guy," Claire said, watching.

"Aw, McQuaid's a hothead," Uncle James said. "He deserved the hockey stick."

A few minutes later the game was over and the Lions had won, no surprise.

The surprise was in one of the two messages handed to Max as he left the announcing booth.

Recognizing the first envelope, Max put off opening it.

He was reading Amy Jane's message to meet her at the sports bar after the game when he passed McQuaid and Allen on their way to the parking lot.

"You going to celebrate the win with the team

at the sports bar?" McQuaid yelled out. "Did we kick Blackhawk butt, or what?"

"Yeah," Max answered absently, with a wave. His mind was on Amy Jane. She was one determined woman.

"See you then," Allen called. "If Kerry Ashton doesn't see you first."

"Grow up," Max mumbled at the goalie's reference to his ex-girlfriend's dumping an entire bucket of ice water over his head in public.

Max ripped open the other envelope. He scanned the message inside quickly. Then he stood stock still, rereading it word for word.

Maybe it was going to be Amy Jane's lucky night.

It certainly wasn't his.

He reread the message a third time.

Dearest Max—

Why haven't you secretly
acknowledged me on the air?
I've been waiting. I don't like
to wait, Max. Don't keep me
waiting, I warn you.

I LOVE YOU

"You're looking like the Lions lost the game tonight instead of winning it," Uncle James shouted above the din of the crowded sports bar, sliding Max a cold beer.

Max's reply was cut off by Bobby McQuaid's arrival at the bar. "So, James, are these two lovely ladies sitting here the nieces you've been bragging about?"

Uncle James nodded.

"Aren't you going to introduce me?"

"Bobby McQuaid," Uncle James said reluctantly, filling a drink order.

"Center for the Lions," Bobby quickly added.

"Nice to meet you, Mr. McQuaid," Claire responded, offering her hand properly.

"Call me Bobby," he said with a wink.

Amy Jane didn't offer her hand. She just nodded, then turned her attention to Max. "I hear you wanted to see me, is that right?"

"Yeah, let's get us a booth where we can talk in private," he suggested, steering her away from the bar.

He chose an empty booth that had a bad view of the big-screen television. "I've got something to show you," he said, after they were seated.

"Then we're even. I've got something to show you as well."

"What?" he asked, a curious glint in his eyes.

"You go first," she insisted, chewing on the straw from her Pepsi.

Max pulled an envelope from his dark green blazer. The blazer had the Lions emblem on the pocket, and was his on-air apparel, the color matching his eyes perfectly.

He took a sip of his beer while Amy Jane

slipped the message from inside the envelope and read it.

Amy Jane looked up at him quizzically. "I don't get it. This is the message I sent you telling you I'd meet you here."

"Oops, wrong message." Max searched his pockets to find the other message, then handed it to her.

She scanned the second message, and looked up at him.

"What do you think?" he asked.

"You need me."

"You don't think it's harmless?"

"I don't know. It could be. But I do think you should find out for certain. She's upped the stakes by issuing you a warning."

Max didn't reply.

"Why don't you think about it while I go to the ladies' room," Amy Jane suggested, making an excuse to casually check the attention he got when he was sitting all alone.

She stopped at the bar to order another Pepsi and beer be sent to their table. Uncle James was up to his armpits in alligators with the thirsty crowd, and Claire and Bobby McQuaid were deep in conversation, so she moved on to the ladies' room.

When Amy Jane returned to the booth, Miranda was batting her eyes at Max and taking his money for the beer and Pepsi. Amy Jane got the distinct impression Miranda wanted more than a good tip and that she wasn't real pleased at her for interrupting the flirtation.

"Let me know if I can get you anything at all," Miranda said, before moving off. She'd been looking at Max.

All the trip to the ladies' room had gleaned Amy Jane was who had been drilling holes in the back of her neck with a fixed stare while she'd been sitting in the booth with Max. It was Kerry Ashton, who was in a booth with Richie Allen, the popular Lions goalie. Evidently Kerry still carried a torch and was jealous of any woman spending time with Max.

"So, have you decided?" she asked Max.

"I don't know. If I hire you, I wouldn't want the team to know I have a woman stalking me. They'd ride me unmercifully."

"You want to know the main reason you should hire me?" Amy Jane said, pulling out her best sales pitch. "You're being stalked by a woman. Who better to catch a woman than another woman. I know how she thinks."

"Okay," Max agreed, resigned.

"You won't be sorry," Amy Jane promised.

"How do you know?"

How was she going to answer that? She didn't know. Not for sure. But suddenly she did know how to answer him. He was a man. Flatter him, play to his ego. She smiled and then said, "Because, Max, I'm as good at my job as you are at yours."

He didn't comment. Just considered her with

that sexy squint of his. He let her parry pass, moving on. "You were going to show me something . . ."

"Right." Amy Jane showed him the small gold hoop pierced earring. "Do you know who this belongs to?"

He picked it up.

"Well, do you?" she persisted. When he didn't say anything, she began laying down the rules of her investigation. "You can't have any secrets from me, withhold any information. Does it belong to someone you know?"

He nodded.

"One of your girlfriends?"

"I don't have any girlfriends."

"I told you that you couldn't have secrets if I'm to get to the bottom of who is stalking you. Now, do you want to know or not?"

"I want to know," he assured her. "Where did you find this?"

"First, who does it belong to? If you don't have a girlfriend as you claim, then maybe an old girlfriend—?" Maybe Kerry Ashton. The woman's stare was giving her a headache.

"No."

"But you said it belongs to someone you know."

"It belongs to me."

"You?"

"I lost it some time ago. Where did you find it?"

"On the deck outside your condo."

He thought a moment, then slipped the earring in his pocket. "I didn't show you the deck." It was a question, and an accusation.

"I know. I found it all by myself. I'm a private investigator—it's my job to be good at finding things."

"But I only just now hired you. What were you—"

"I knew you'd hire me."

"You're pretty obsessive when you put your mind to something, aren't you? Let me ask you something. You aren't the one sending me the notes, are you?"

Amy Jane laughed. "I can assure you I have much better things to do with my time than stalk you."

"But you were lurking around outside my bedroom . . ."

"I was working, not lurking."

"Right."

"You forgot to tell me how much you're going to cost me," he added.

"You can afford me."

"Anybody ever tell you you aren't very accommodating?"

"All the time."

"Doesn't it bother you?"

"Nope. It's my opinion that women are way too accommodating by far," she answered, swirling her straw around in her glass of soda.

"You have a lot of opinions, don't you?"

"Is there something wrong with that?" she challenged him.

"No. Do you carry a gun?"

"You mean to get people to listen to my opinions? It's illegal for anyone other than a police officer to carry a gun in this state."

"Do you own a gun then?"

"Sure. I used to be a police officer. I still own the weapon."

"Really? Did you ever shoot anyone with it?"

"No. I find it very effective just to point it. People tend to pay attention when you have a gun aimed at a vital part of their anatomy. On the rare occasion I've had to use it as a tongue depressor on a hard case."

Max laughed. "Remind me not to piss you off."

The crowd started booing and Amy Jane looked up to see the sports had come on the news. It was an item about ice skating. Hockey players didn't consider ice skating a sport. What they considered it—well, that wasn't said in polite company.

"Neanderthals," Amy Jane muttered.

"You like ice skating?" Max asked.

"It's the only sport I follow since I found out I couldn't grow up to be a baseball player."

"Someone told you no?" Max said with a hearty laugh.

"Shut up."

* * *

Max slipped the latest note into the stack with the others and closed the drawer. He'd been surprised Amy Jane hadn't wanted to keep it. Instead she'd suggested he keep them all together for the moment. He shrugged, and hoped she knew what she was doing.

He still couldn't believe he'd hired her.

As he went to take his shower he noticed the drapes, or rather the small gap where they didn't quite fit. Amy Jane had been standing out on the deck. Just what had she been able to see, he wondered. He opened the sliding glass doors, then closed them behind him without disturbing the drapes.

He stood outside looking into his bedroom through the gap in the drapes; he shook his head when he discerned her view. She'd been able to see his bed. More importantly, she'd seen the doorway to his bathroom where he'd showered after he'd thought she'd left.

And she had the gall to suggest he was keeping something secret from her. The view she'd had hadn't allowed that.

A half hour later he was showered and propped against a stack of pillows in his silk boxers. He was lying in bed in the dark thinking about Amy Jane.

About her watching him emerge from his shower naked. He rose from the bed and stalked to the sliding glass doors, whipping back the drapery.

Nothing but his reflection and the dark night greeted him.

"So how'd it go?" Claire asked Amy Jane as they bounced along home in Amy Jane's Jeep.

"I got the case," Amy Jane answered on a note of satisfaction.

"I suppose I should be pleased?"

"You're not?"

"You know how I feel about this Nancy Drew stuff. Why can't you do something normal? First a cop and now this. What is it about danger that attracts you?"

"Danger doesn't attract me. Power does. The power to change things. To make things right."

"Right according to Amy Jane Chadwick, you mean."

"You sound just like him," Amy Jane said on a snort of derision.

"I suppose we have Uncle James to thank for this. I don't know why he insists on encouraging you."

"It's because he leads such a boring life."

It was Claire's turn for a snort of derision as Amy Jane pulled the Jeep into the driveway of the Chadwick Bed and Breakfast.

"Do you have anything scheduled for tomorrow morning?" Claire asked as they went inside. "I could use some help polishing the silver. We've got six college roommates booked this weekend for a twenty-fifth reunion. Unlike you, these ladies will be the type to notice a speck of tarnish."

"I guess I could help," Amy Jane said with a marked lack of enthusiasm. "I don't have anything until around noon. I want to question the hockey players after they finish their morning skate. It will give me some time to think up a list of questions."

"About what?"

"Claire, you know—"

"Yeah, yeah. It's a secret. You can't tell me you don't like all the skullduggery. If you ask me, being a private eye is just an excuse for you to play and call it work."

"I said I'd help with the silver. By the way, didn't I see you chatting up a hockey player at the bar?"

"You mean Bobby McQuaid?" Claire said innocently.

"Yes, I mean Bobby McQuaid," Amy Jane answered, her tone telling Claire she wasn't taken in by her guile. "What was that all about?"

"If you must know, he was asking me out for Saturday night."

"And you told him to go suck an egg, in a mannerly way, of course, right?" Amy Jane opened the refrigerator door as soon as they entered the kitchen, scavenging.

"No. As a matter of fact, I didn't. I said . . . I said yes."

"You're kidding." Amy Jane gave wide berth

to the ambrosia and other "guest" food, and came up with a ham and cheese sandwich sans the bread. She closed the refrigerator door with her hip, waiting for Claire to grin and give away the ruse.

But Claire didn't grin.

"You aren't kidding."

Claire tucked a strand of long blond hair behind her ear. "Well you're the one who's always telling me to date outside my . . . my . . ."

"Species?"

"Amy Jane!"

"Well, you'll have to agree a hockey player is about as far as you can get from your usual Ivy League type. Where are you going on this date, or do I even want to hear?"

"The ballet."

Amy Jane groaned. "Let me guess who picked that."

"He said he had never been to the ballet, so I thought—"

"No, the ballet is fine. At least I won't have to worry about my baby sister dating a hockey player. I'll bet you a week of dusting that the ballet will finish off Bobby McQuaid."

"You're on," Claire sniffed.

The Dome was suddenly quiet, the scrape of the skaters' blades slicing the ice, silenced as the team piled off the rink.

Amy Jane stood waiting beside the rink where

the players exited for the dressing rooms. She shook off a shiver. Though she was cold, she was happier sleuthing than she'd been in the warm kitchen polishing the silverware.

McQuaid spoke to her first. "I didn't do it."

"Do what?" Amy Jane asked.

"Whatever. Your sister told me you were a private eye, so I figure one of the Blackhawks must have been, ah, damaged."

"More likely she's here 'cause you're dating her sister," the goalie said, shoving McQuaid with a boisterous laugh.

Amy Jane made a mental note to tell Claire not to discuss the fact that she was working on a case for Max Armstrong. She cast about for a ruse to cover the questions she wanted to ask the players about Max.

"I'm not here about business," she lied.

Lance Thomure, the big defenseman, joined them. He elbowed Richie. "Whatcha got here, an autograph seeker?"

"Actually, I was hoping you guys could give me some information," Amy Jane said.

"Information?" Lance tugged the edge of his mustache. "What kind of information?" The group looked at her suspiciously. She was an outsider asking questions.

"I'm curious about the Lions announcer."

"Which one?"

"Max Armstrong. I'd like to know if he's involved with anyone."

"You mean like a chick?"

"Yeah, like a . . . a woman."

The three players looked at each other before deciding to answer. McQuaid fielded her question.

"I don't think so."

"I'm surprised. He's sort of a celebrity like you guys, isn't he? Surely he has girls hitting on him all the time."

"Kerry Ashton wouldn't appreciate that," Lance volunteered.

Amy Jane played dumb. "Kerry Ashton?"

"He used to date her," Lance explained.

"That was before—"

"She's my girl now," Richie announced, cutting off what Lance had been about to say.

Bobby's head whipped around. "Since when?"

Richie grinned. "Since this Saturday night. I asked her out."

"And she said yes?" Lance and Bobby chorused.

"She did, and I don't want to hear any more about it. Besides, maybe I'll be getting some of the heat from Armstrong now, instead of you, Bobby."

"In your dreams. Armstrong is never going to stop riding my butt."

"How come you want to know about Armstrong, anyway?" Richie turned back to ask Amy Jane.

She fed him the first believable lie that came to mind. "I'm in charge of making up the guest list for a surprise birthday party for him."

"Then I guess we'll all be invited, huh?"

"Well, ah, sure. If you want. What about fans? Does Max have any particular fan that I should invite? Someone who really—"

"A fan . . . Max doesn't play hockey any longer," Bobby said with enough patience it couldn't not annoy her.

"I know that. But he is a celebrity as the Lions announcer. Have you seen anyone hanging around worshipping him?"

"Worshipping who?" Chantal Perry asked, a cameraman in tow as she came over to get some sound bites from the team on their road trip to Minnesota to play the North Stars.

"We were just talking about how Corey worships the ground you walk on and how he longs to sweep you off your feet . . . again," Bobby said, referring to the collision he and Richie had witnessed between Corey and Chantal.

"Knock it off, you guys," she said, fielding their teasing, then proceeded to do her job. "What are the chances of the Lions coming out ahead on the road trip?" she asked, shoving the microphone in Richie's face. "The North Stars are on a winning streak."

"*Were* on a winning streak," Bobby said confidently.

Amy Jane took the opportunity to leave as Chantal began interviewing the players. Amy Jane had noted the players respected Chantal enough to tease her, so she must be good at her job. Even if she was second string.

It was a man's world everywhere, but most especially in the world of sports. Still, Chantal struck her as a very determined woman. A woman who would persist until she got what she wanted. A quality that worked well for both sexes.

And a quality she would have to adopt herself, if she was going to get anywhere with her investigation.

Talking with the players hadn't yielded her any new information.

There didn't appear to be a rabid fan lurking.

And Max's old girlfriend, Kerry Ashton, was old news.

Saturday afternoon found Amy Jane sprawled in a white wooden rocker with her cut-off high tops propped on the gingerbread railing of the spacious Chadwick Bed and Breakfast veranda. She gazed suspiciously at the purple pansies peeking out of the ice cubes cooling the lemonade she sipped while reading her horoscope in the newspaper. She'd depleted her stock of Pepsi, and Claire had gone all out for the college roommates in town for their reunion.

Claire's high anxiety over the guests and her date with Bobby McQuaid for the ballet had nearly driven her nuts. She looked to her horoscope for solace.

Today it didn't fail her.

It read:

> Your workload is heavy, so
> protect yourself with plenty
> of rest.

Smiling, she closed her eyes for a nap; after all, she had the equivalent of a doctor's excuse in her horoscope.

Just as she was drifting off to la-la land, she heard a car speed up the drive, jerk to a halt, and then she heard the thud of a car door. A juvenile revelry.

Either Bobby had sent Claire flowers or the pizza delivery kid had the wrong address. Amy Jane opened her eyes reluctantly to deal with whichever.

It wasn't pizza or flowers being delivered.

It was Max Armstrong. And he wasn't bringing anything with him but a scowl. His dark brows were knit together purposefully as he climbed the veranda steps two at a time.

She closed her eyes, hoping he'd pass right by her. Hoping it was something Claire had done.

No such luck.

"What in blazes do you think you're doing?" he demanded, glowering over her.

"I was trying to take a nap. That is, I was before I was rudely interrupted by your crashing in here like a moose in antler-bashing season."

Max dashed her feet from the railing, obviously annoyed she wasn't showing the proper respect for male anger.

"I'm talking about your questioning the

hockey players," he explained. "Chantal mentioned you were at the rink."

"She did, did she? And what else did she tell you?"

"Nothing. McQuaid asked if you and I wanted to join him and Claire tonight at the ballet since you were my new girl."

"Your what?" she demanded, sitting straight up in her rocking chair.

Max unwrapped a piece of chewing gum and stuck it in his mouth, his tongue folding it in half. He began chewing, making her wait. Punishing her. Finally he explained. "Seems the players think I have a very jealous new girlfriend on my hands, and that's the reason you were at the rink asking all those questions about me."

Amy Jane tapped her foot and began rocking back and forth in the chair nervously. "Don't worry. I'll set them straight on that score."

"Don't," Max said, putting his hand out to still her rocking.

"I'll rock if I want to," she informed him, pushing his hand away in a show of perverseness.

"I meant don't tell them you aren't my girl."

"What?"

"I told the players you were my girl."

"You did what!"

Max shrugged, resting his hip on the railing of the verandah. "It was the only excuse I could come up with for you asking all those questions about me. I'd rather the players think you are my girl than know I hired you to protect me . . . from a woman. Cripes, I'd never live that one down."

Amy Jane was quiet for a moment considering. "You know, if you think about it, it isn't a bad cover until I find out who's stalking you."

"What have you found out so far?"

"Nothing."

"Oh, that's reassuring."

"These things take time."

"How much time?"

"Don't worry, we aren't going to have a long courtship."

"Speaking of which, I'll pick you up around seven-thirty."

"What for?"

"The ballet."

"But I don't want to go to the ballet. I hate the ballet."

"Like I don't."

"You're enjoying this, aren't you?"

"Not really."

"Uh-huh."

"See you at seven-thirty." He reminded her as he headed down the steps to walk back to his car.

Amy Jane frowned after him. So much for her nap.

Claire came outside to ask her opinion on the dress she planned to wear to the ballet.

"Do you have another one like it I can borrow?" Amy Jane asked, approving it and know-

ing she didn't have anything suitable for the ballet in her own closet.

"You want to borrow a dress from me? Why?"

"Max just invited me to go to the ballet with
you and Bobby McQuaid."

"Oh, good, a double date!"

Yeah, goodie.

Eight

"Come on, wake up, sleepyhead."

Amy Jane wrapped her pillow over her head to drown out her sister's cheery admonishment. "Come on downstairs and join me for breakfast. The guests have checked out and it's just the two of us. We can discuss our dates last night."

Amy Jane groaned as she heard Claire close the door and head back downstairs. She knew there was nothing for her to do but go downstairs and eat with Claire. If she didn't, Claire would be back. Still annoyingly cheerful, but persistent until she got her way.

Peeking open one eye, she saw the dress she'd worn tossed over the wooden chair by her bed. She was glad to be out of it. It was way too cute by far.

Just like Max Armstrong.

He ought to steal Kerry Ashton's vanity plate.

Recalling Claire's saying the guests had checked out, she didn't bother getting dressed when she got out of bed. Instead she pulled on her white terry robe, and ran her fingers through her hair to comb it. She purposely didn't look in the mirror before going downstairs.

She didn't need seven years' bad luck.

Claire was fully dressed and eating ambrosia from a pretty glass dish. Beside the dish was a green and yellow program from a class reunion—one of the guests had left it behind.

Amy Jane grabbed a bagel and added cream cheese and a Pepsi from the refrigerator, then joined Claire at the trestle table. Popping the tab on the Pepsi, she stretched her bare feet to rest on a nearby chair.

"Okay, let's get the post mortem over with," she ventured, giving in to the inevitable while slathering the cream cheese on her bagel.

"Amy Jane! I wish you wouldn't use those awful detective words at the table."

"Yeah, and I wish last night had never happened, but it did."

Claire played her fork against a slice of banana floating in ambrosia juice. "Really? I thought I saw Max kissing you good night . . ."

Another thing she wished hadn't happened. Max kissed her good-night for Bobby's benefit, to sell the idea that she was his girl. A fact she'd had to keep reminding herself of, because it would have been as easy as take-out pizza for her to have gotten lost in that kiss.

"How'd it go with you and Bobby?" Amy Jane asked, throwing her off the scent.

"Fine. It went fine."

"He fell asleep during the ballet."

"So did you."

"At least I didn't snore." Amy Jane took a bite of her bagel, looking smug.

"Yes, actually you did."

Amy Jane choked on her bagel and washed it down with Pepsi, anxious to defend herself. "I do not snore."

"Wanna bet?"

"Yeah."

"I wouldn't be so quick to bet if I were you," Claire advised.

"Why not?"

Claire tossed her a dust cloth. "Bobby asked me out again. I believe that was a week's worth of dusting you lost."

Amy Jane picked up the dust cloth and stared at it glumly. It just wasn't turning out to be her week at all. Oh well, Max would be out of town for a few days on a road trip, she thought brightening. That would give her time to work some more on his case without him meddling.

The sooner she solved his case and stopped having to pretend she was his girl, the better.

Max Armstrong sat in his hotel room in Minnesota flipping through a hockey magazine. He was still keyed up from the excellent game the Lions had played to win 4-3. It had been a wideopen, up-and-down game.

There were times like tonight when he got the

itch to move the puck; times when he really missed *playing* hockey.

He hadn't been this restless since . . . well, since he'd kissed Amy Jane Chadwick and gone home alone.

That made him smile. Who'da thought?

He straightened a picture on the wall.

He thought about calling her, then discarded the notion. What would he say? He felt foolish enough as it was, for having hired her.

He was usually decisive, but this whole thing had him off balance.

He flipped on the TV, looking for something mindless like a Stooges show to help him fall asleep. It was lonely being awake at three in the morning when you were at home. It was worse when you were in a strange city.

Less than a mile from the radio station where Chantal Perry did her sports updates she heard the pop and then felt her wheel jerk when her tire blew flat.

She was standing beside it, just barely restraining herself from kicking the car, when another car slowed down and pulled over to offer assistance.

It was Corey Cohen.

Oh, great, like he could change a tire.

"Looks like you got a problem there," he said, coming to stand beside her and stare at the flat.

"Looks like."

"Have you called anyone yet?"

She shook her head. "No, it just happened."

"If you'll give me your keys, I'll open the trunk and get out your jack and spare and change your tire for you."

"No, that's all right. You'll mess up your suit."

"Just give me the keys."

She decided to let him change the tire. Not that she couldn't, but she was in a suit with a short skirt. Besides, she didn't really believe Corey would know how to change a tire. She didn't think his privileged background would have provided that experience.

She was wrong.

He had no trouble at all with the difficult lug nuts, showing a surprising strength for his slight build. He probably actually made use of the classy gym he belonged to, she thought as the traffic whizzed by them.

"Are you coming or going?" Corey asked, replacing the flat tire with her spare.

"Going. I already finished doing the spot."

"Then I'd suggest you stop at a tire store and pick up another spare. The one I put on is in pretty bad shape. It should do you for a little while, though."

She watched him tighten the lug nuts and wondered if her Visa limit would stand the price of a new tire. And wondered what it would be like to be Corey and assume making a purchase over a hundred dollars didn't bear planning.

"Did you watch the game last night?" Corey asked, wiping his hands on a snow-white handkerchief while she cringed, embarrassed.

"Yeah. Great game. I'll replace your handkerchief. Listen, I feel bad about you having to stop and do this for me. I owe you one."

Corey grinned. "You ever been to a bar mitzvah?"

Amy Jane spent most of Tuesday at the computer in her room working up copy for a yellow-pages ad, clearing a lot of piled up paperwork and accessing the transactions at the ATM of a friend's ex-husband who wasn't paying his child support regularly. From monitoring the deposits to his account she gleaned that he had gotten a large bonus or was on a lucky streak with the ponies. A few more strokes on the keyboard turned up the information that he was living with a woman and how much money he owed on his credit cards. The file she built on him would enable her friend to force payment from the deadbeat.

A knock at her door came just as she finished up a bit of illegal hacking.

"Come in," she called out, turning off her computer and rolling her head from side to side to ease the cramp in her neck.

"I figured you'd be hungry, so I brought you up a new recipe I just made," Claire said.

"Ummm . . . it smells heavenly. What is it?"

"A recipe I clipped out of the paper. It's called Crazy Sam Higgins' Chili. It's pretty spicy, so I thought I'd test it on your palate first before I tried it on the guests."

Amy Jane dug into the steaming bowl of chili. "This stuff is delicious. It's got a really . . ." she thought a moment, ". . . zesty Southwest flavor. Since when are you serving guests chili for breakfast?"

Claire shrugged. "The party booked this weekend is from Texas. By the way how's the dusting going? I noticed the library wasn't touched when I put out the newspapers this morning."

"I'll get to it. I've done the whole downstairs with the exception of the library. Libraries are supposed to be dusty. It makes them seem so, so permanent. Besides, when I finish dusting, you'll just find some other chore for me."

"I'm sure I could think of one or two," Claire agreed.

"Never mind. I'm working on a big case, remember?" Amy Jane licked her spoon. "Have we got any soda crackers to go with these, you know, the little bitty round ones?"

"I swear, Amy Jane. You are such a child. No, we don't have any little bitty soda crackers."

Amy Jane frowned. Half the fun of eating chili was those little bitty crackers that got all mushy.

"So what's the deal with you and Max?" Claire asked. "I thought you had a rule about not dating a client."

"I'm not dating a client."

"But—"

"Max is a client, that's true. But we aren't dating."

Claire watched Amy Jane polish off the rest of the bowl of chili. When she was finished, Claire persisted. "Max took you to the ballet, didn't he? You went with Bobby and I. Are you trying to tell me that wasn't a double date?"

"It only looked like one. Which is what Max wanted Bobby to think."

"I don't get it."

"Max doesn't want anyone to know he's hired me, especially not the hockey team."

"Why not?"

"Because the reason he hired me is sensitive, sort of. So we're pretending to be dating as a cover."

"Sensitive . . . ?"

"Don't ask," Amy Jane said, dropping her spoon in the empty bowl with a clatter. "Let's talk about you and Bobby McQuaid instead. I can't believe you agreed to a second date with him after he fell sound asleep during the ballet."

"He told me he was tired because he'd been doing a lot of special appearances for the team."

"Don't tell me you like him . . . ?"

"Well, he's big and strong—"

"And a hothead."

"You were the one, I believe, who's been telling me I need to date more passionate men."

"But—"

"And maybe you can sell that pretense line about Max to others, but I'm not buying. I'm your sister and I know you. You like him."

"Okay, so Max Armstrong is cute as hell and maybe I like him. Are you satisfied? All that means is that there has to be something wrong with him."

"Like what?" Claire asked, picking up the empty bowl from her desk.

"Like maybe he has a wife somewhere. Or a gambling problem. Or he likes to dress up in bustiers and stockings. I don't know. But if I like him, you can count on there being something wrong."

"You're only looking for trouble. Max Armstrong is a celebrity. If there was anything like that wrong with him, the press would have picked up on it and had a field day with it."

"Maybe, maybe not. Anyway, this is just business to him. As soon as I find out . . . well, it's business pure and simple."

"Uh-huh." Claire's voice was lightly mocking, indicating she still wasn't buying Amy Jane's avoidance.

"It's business and nothing more, believe me." Amy Jane continued to insist. "Now go, and let me work in peace, okay?"

Claire moved to the door to return downstairs.

"Oh, Claire—"

"Yes?"

Amy Jane shot her the thumb-up sign. "The chili is killer."

Claire smiled.

Early the following morning there was a pounding at the front door to the bed and breakfast.

Claire opened her eyes, having slept late because the guests from Texas weren't due until Thursday. She got up and threw on a robe, knowing Amy Jane wouldn't hear the door. A tornado could carry the house away and Amy Jane wouldn't wake up to find out about it before ten.

"I'm coming, I'm coming," Claire called out to the persistent knocking. She stopped to pull up her socks. Her feet were always cold, so she slept with her socks on. She peered in a hall mirror on her way to the door and pulled the rubber band from her limp ponytail, shook her hair loose in a straight fall to frame her face.

The door was still rattling when she reached it.

"Okay, oka—" She stopped in mid-word when she found out who was pounding on the door.

Max Armstrong scowled at her. "Where is she?"

"What?"

"Where's your sister?"

"She's still in bed."

Max stepped around Claire, and stalked to the

stairs, taking them two at a time. Frustration eddied around him in waves.

"You can't—" Claire whirled to object, but Max had already disappeared from sight at the top of the stairs. "Incoming . . ." Claire called out to warn Amy Jane with the sinking feeling it was too late.

"Get up," Max called through the closed door of Amy Jane's bedroom. When there was no response to his demand, he began pounding on the door.

Amy Jane's, "Go away," was muffled, as if she'd pulled her pillow over her head to make him disappear.

"Not a chance. I'm coming in. Get decent fast. I want to talk to you." He waited for about thirty seconds after issuing fair warning, then shoved the door to her bedroom open to be met with one of her shoes sailing through the air.

He ducked, but Amy Jane's aim was true and painfully unpleasant.

"Ouch!" he swore, wincing and covering himself. "What'd you do that for?"

"Because I couldn't reach my gun," Amy Jane muttered, sitting up in bed, and tucking her sheet around what appeared to him to be her naked body.

"Lucky for me," he said, wondering just how handy her gun was. He'd have to make sure he kept her in bed—and unarmed.

She tugged at the sheet. "Tell me, do you make a habit of bursting into women's bedrooms uninvited, or is this a sudden perversion you've acquired?"

"Is that any way to talk to a client? No wonder you operate out of a bed and breakfast. You can't have many clients with a mouth like yours." He realized he was digressing and shoved his hands on his hips, getting back to his reason for being in her bedroom so early in the morning. "You've been spying on me. I thought I told you I wanted to keep the investigation thing quiet. So instead what do you do?"

Amy Jane shrugged. The sheet dipped provocatively. "I asked a few questions, that's all."

"That's all!"

"Yeah, that's all."

"Didn't it occur to you that the hockey team would get just a little suspicious, a little curious about why some female private eye was asking them questions about my sex life."

"I did not ask them about your sex life."

"Is that a fact?" He picked up a pile of clothing from the edge of her desk. After glancing around uncertainly for a place to put them, he opted for the floor. "I was told you were asking about my old girlfriends," he said, resting his hip on the cleared spot on her desk.

"I explained that. I told the players I was planning a surprise birthday party for you."

"Remind me to be surprised in ten months."

It didn't help his mood any that Amy Jane didn't look as contrite as he'd have liked. She had a lot to learn when it came to how to deal with male anger, with how to placate a man. And somehow he knew learning it wasn't high on her list of priorities. That supposition only inched up his anger.

"You're pretty steamed, huh?" she said, stating the obvious.

"I'm steamed because you used me."

"What are you talking about?"

"You deliberately talked to the players when I told you not to. And now I find you asked them really personal stuff. I think you did it to gain your own celebrity for your private-eye business. Don't do it again. You're the one who convinced me I have a problem. Prove it, *quietly.*"

"I must be doing something right," she countered. "You haven't gotten any notes lately from your secret admirer, have you?"

"No, I haven't," he admitted.

"So perhaps I've scared her off."

"How could you have scared her off, you haven't done anything but embarrass me."

"Make up your mind," she said, pushing her long hair away from her face. "I thought you just said I was being too visible—that I was stealing your spotlight."

"Just do your job and cut out the funny stuff, okay?"

"Don't tell me how to do my job."

"Somebody needs to if you stay in bed every day until noon."

"I get up early when I have to."

"Whatever, just stay away from the players," Max warned, standing.

"Anything else?"

"Yeah. Put some clothes on," he said, leaving as abruptly as he'd come.

Amy Jane gave him a few minutes, then got up and walked to the window in the bathroom that overlooked the drive. She lounged in the window naked as the day she'd been born, but Max didn't look back up at the house.

He was on his cellular phone as he eased his luxury car down the drive.

Amy Jane smiled as she watched him drive off. Max looked sexy as sin when he was angry. She'd have to see what she could do to facilitate keeping him that way.

Meanwhile she needed to shower and get dressed.

And track down her horoscope for the day.

Fifteen minutes later she was in the kitchen sneaking a bowl of the guest chili and warming it in the microwave oven, planning to wolf it down for breakfast with a Pepsi while she kept one eye peeled for Claire.

"Do I smell . . . ?" Claire called. She appeared just as Amy Jane raised the first spoonful of chili to her mouth, and caught her red-handed.

Claire raised her hands to her hips. "Amy Jane, that's guest food and you know it."

"But it's so good," Amy Jane said with a smile, trying flattery.

"You know the rule about guest food," Claire stated, not budging.

"Okay, okay. You want me to put it back in the pot with the rest of the—"

"No!"

"Good." Amy Jane sat back down and lifted another spoonful to her lips, then popped open her first Pepsi of the day.

Claire shook her head, and threw up her hands in defeat. "You're a hopeless case, Amy Jane. How are you ever going to raise your children with any manners to speak of?"

"In case you haven't noticed, Claire, I don't have any children . . . so there's nothing for you to worry about, is there?"

"I meant when you do have children."

"But I'm not going to have children," Amy Jane said around a swallow of the spicy chili, enjoying tormenting someone after having had Max torment her.

"Of course you are. Why wouldn't you have children?"

"Because I'm never going to swallow . . ." Amy Jane said, her tongue playing with the inside of her cheek.

Claire looked puzzled for a moment, then got the drift of just what Amy Jane was implying and blushed furiously. "Amy Jane!"

"Well, I'm not."

"What did Max want?" Claire asked, changing the subject. "He didn't appear to be in a very good mood. What was wrong with him?"

"Emotional dyslexia."

"What?"

"He's immature."

"Like you're the poster image for emotional maturity . . ."

"Uncle James says—"

"That reminds me. He wanted to see you. Said for you to stop by the bar when you had time."

"I've got time this afternoon. I'll go see him as soon as I finish up my dusting in the library with Colonel Mustard."

"You can't fool me. You're not having domestic guilt. You're just going to the library to read your horoscope in the newspaper," Claire said, taking the bowl and empty Pepsi can.

"I promise I'll dust."

"Uh-huh."

"I will."

"I swear, Amy Jane, I don't know how someone as smart as you are can believe in that horoscope mumble jumble."

"I don't believe in it necessarily. I just like to have some advance warning when things are about to go wrong."

"Then you believe in it."

Amy Jane knew it was pointless to argue with Claire, so she didn't. Instead she went into the library to dust, and search out her horoscope in the morning newspaper.

When she found it, she wished she hadn't. She scanned it once again:

> Warlike Mars in your
> relationship sector
> will stir up conflicts
> in both your personal
> and business life.

That was just great. Hardly the news she
wanted to read after arguing with Max. She
wondered what sign he was. He'd said his
birthday was in ten months. That would make
him either a Capricorn or a . . . no, he was
definitely a Capricorn, she decided. He was
stubborn as a goat.

She let her gaze scan down the column of as-
trological signs until she came to Capricorn,
then read Max's forecast:

> Keep your ego in check
> or you won't be able
> to avoid a major tussle.
> You'll wind up ego dancing
> with opposing partner.

Max obviously hadn't read his horoscope. His
ego had certainly not been in check when he'd
blitzed into her bedroom and started throwing
around accusations and orders.

She picked up the dust rag and began dusting, thinking about how much he'd been bothered by her being naked beneath the sheet she'd
had tucked around her. She'd dusted the mold-
ing and bookshelves, and come up with snappy,

pithy comebacks for all his accusations. She wished she'd thought of them when Max had uttered those words. Then Claire called out that the telephone that had been ringing moments ago was for her.

Amy Jane picked up the extension in the library.

It was Max.

He was not in a good mood. Still.

"You've gone too far this time," he was shouting over the phone.

"I haven't gone anywhere. What are you talking about?"

"I'm . . . I'm . . ." he was so angry he was sputtering like a choked-up lawn mower. "You've been investigating me," he accused, finally getting the words out.

"You mean I've been investigating for you."

"No. I mean you've been investigating me. I got a call from the credit bureau about an unauthorized person checking my credit."

"And you think it was me?"

"Are you trying to tell me you don't know how to run a credit check on someone, finding out personal information?"

"Of course not."

"So of course it was you. Who else would it be? That's why I want you off the case as of right now."

"Are you firing me?"

"Exactly."

"But—"

She found herself trying to rebuttal a dial tone. He'd hung up on her.

"Real bright, Max," she muttered, staring at the receiver in her hand. If he'd listened to her explanation he would have found out that he'd been wrong.

To fire her for starters—because he did need her.

Because he'd also been wrong about her having run an unauthorized credit check on him. He was right in assuming she did know how to do it. But he was off target thinking it had been her.

It hadn't.

If she had run one, she would have been successful. She was a very good computer hacker because she possessed a lot of qualities Max didn't; charm, nerve, curiosity, intuition, patience and composure.

Okay, so maybe he had nerve.

And a little charm.

But he also had someone very interested in him. Someone with more than just the interest of a casual fan.

Max might not know it, but he needed her. Her intuition told her Max's secret admirer was dangerous. And she'd learned, when her intuition talked, to listen.

Unlike Max, who'd never learned to listen at all.

Nine

James Chadwick stood at the bar drying some glasses and watching Miranda Sherman as she set the chairs down from the tables, getting ready for the lunch crowd. He liked her sparkly eyes and cheeky personality. It was a damned shame she had a crush on Max Armstrong.

He'd like to ask her out. Their flirtation was one of those friendly working-together things. He wondered if Miranda would go out with him, if he did ask. It wasn't like he was interested in anything serious. He'd never been the monogamous type; couldn't imagine himself settling down with any one person.

He was a thrill seeker who always needed change and excitement in his life. One change though he hadn't liked. His twin brother and sister-in-law's death had changed him. Made him more melancholy.

They had been the anchor that had allowed him to drift. Their home was his home. Their family, his family. Now Sweet and Claire were all he had left. Claire remained the anchor, but Sweet . . . well, there was no telling with her.

Sweet might just as well have been his own daughter.

Sweet appeared to be handling her parents' death a little better than Claire. Claire, on the other hand, had become more controlling, less flexible. It was as if she thought you could control something as random as death.

Along those lines of being in control, Claire had called him again about talking to Sweet about her private-investigator business she was running out of the bed and breakfast. He'd promised Claire he would talk to Sweet, if she came by the bar. Though for the life of him, he didn't know what he was going to say.

He'd have to think fast, though. He'd just caught a glimpse of Sweet as she entered the bar.

"I hear you wanted to see me," her reflection in the mirror behind the bar said, as she took a seat on a stool at the bar.

"It's always good to see you," he said, stalling before he turned from putting away the bar glasses.

Amy Jane waited, smiling. "Claire put you up to this, didn't she?"

"She wants you to keep your private-eye business low key."

"Doesn't everybody," Amy Jane mumbled, reaching for a bowl of pretzels.

"What are you talking about?"

Amy Jane took a pretzel, and broke it into little bits. "Claire might not have to worry about

my trying to expand my business. I might just
wind up doing only insurance-fraud cases after
all."

"How come?"

"Things haven't exactly been going swim-
mingly to date."

"Is that why you're making pretzel dust all
over my clean bar?" Uncle James asked, wiping
up the mess she'd made. "Tell me what's wrong,
and stay out of the pretzels."

"Max fired me," she answered glumly.

"Fired you? Why?"

"It seems I didn't, ah, keep my investigation
low key enough to suit him."

"Oh. You want a drink?"

Amy Jane laughed.

"What's so funny? I thought you told me Max
fired you."

"He did. I was just laughing at how things
change and yet stay the same. You've gone from
offering me cake to make my hurts feel better,
to offering me a stiff drink."

"So, are you planning to stay fired?" Uncle
James asked, biting into a pretzel.

"What do you mean?"

He shrugged. "I don't know . . . for as long
as I've known you, and that's all your life, you've
never taken no for an answer very well."

"You mean I should just ignore Max firing
me?"

"It's not like you haven't done it before, is it?"

"You know, you're right. If I can get used to

dealing with your antics, Claire's perfectionism, the wackiness of insurance-fraud cases and the even wackier clientele at the bed and breakfast, I should be able to handle Max."

"Go get 'em tiger," Uncle James encouraged as the sports bar began filling up with the lunch rush. Miranda joined them at the bar with a drink order.

"Hi," she said, then her attention was caught by a sports story on the noon news on the big-screen TV.

The sports reporter was interviewing Max about an injury one of the hockey players had sustained in a fender bender.

"What do you think I've got to do to get him to notice me?" Miranda sighed.

"Who?" Amy Jane asked.

"She's got a crush on Max," Uncle James explained. "I don't know why, when she's got me working with her. I guess sometimes you just can't see what's right under your nose."

"James, behave," Miranda scolded, her gaze still on the large screen TV and the interview with Max.

Amy Jane slipped off the barstool unnoticed, and left the sports bar. Desperately wanting Max for a client, she'd decided to take Uncle James's advice; she wouldn't stay fired.

Max needed her. He just didn't know it.

She'd have to prove it to him.

* * *

Amy Jane sat in her Jeep on the parking lot of the Channel Two television station. She'd taken the chance Max would still be there, as he'd been interviewed live instead of on tape. Spotting his luxury car, she slouched down to watch and wait for Max to exit the building.

She'd decided the best way to get Max to re-hire her was to follow him around. That way she could find out if anyone else was following him around while she tailed Max.

She surveyed the parking lot again. All the parked cars appeared empty. As she waited, people came from and went into the small one-story building. She recognized a few of the reporters.

A steady cold rain began to fall.

The windows of her Jeep began to fog up just as Max came out of the television station. Amy Jane stopped fiddling with her radio, watching as Max looked up at the sky and then down at his soft leather loafers, and scowled.

He gingerly made his way to his car, trying to avoid ruining his shoes, got in and drove off the parking lot.

Amy Jane followed, several car lengths behind, with one hand on the wheel as she slouched to avoid being seen. One-person tails were almost impossible in the city, what with traffic lights and congestion causing a snarl-up to foil the best-laid attempt.

Max made it easy. He went to the Dome.

Once he was inside, Amy Jane searched the junk in her back seat to come up with a roll of neon tape. She'd read once that a private eye made tailing a subject easier by spray painting the subject's bumper with neon paint. She couldn't bring herself to do that, opting instead for the neon tape.

With one eye on the entrance to the Dome, she made her way to Max's luxury car. Dropping down on one knee she taped a strip of the neon tape across his right tail light, then hurried back to her Jeep to wait.

Afternoon radio sucked, she decided as she waited. At least, morning stakeouts were bearable because of J. C. Corkran. The local disc jockey kept things stirred up, and while she didn't always agree with him, he was interesting to listen to when he was on. And he had a female partner who held her own.

Finally Max came out of the Dome and returned to his car. He'd snagged an umbrella somewhere and used it. He didn't have to worry about the rain frizzing his hair the way she did. On days like today, she didn't even attempt to control her hair. Instead she wore a black baseball cap to hide her unruly mane. It was embroidered with the words, "Bad Hair Day." She pulled the bill down to hide her face and left several car lengths before following Max from the parking area.

She lost him at a light.

Just as she was about to give up catching up to him again, she saw him nose out of a fast-food lot. She began tailing him again, her eyes on the neon tape as he weaved in and out of traffic a couple of times before she followed him onto the highway.

The rest was an easy tail as he was obviously going to his condo. She could hang back pretty far.

When he left the highway at the exit by Chesterfield mall, she picked up the slack and tailed him to his condo.

When he parked his car she was certain of two things. One, no one was following Max, except her. And two, he'd spotted her.

She slouched even further down in her seat as he approached her, and she closed her eyes to make herself invisible.

It didn't work.

Max jerked open the door of the Jeep. "I thought I fired you," he accused.

"Were you yelling like this when you did it?" she asked, opening her eyes and looking up at him, all innocence, from beneath the bill of her black twill cap.

"Maybe," he conceded. "Why?" he asked, resting his weight on one leg in a macho stance while he scrutinized her with his piercing green eyes.

"You must have been. That's probably why I didn't hear you. I never listen when someone yells." She sat up straight, so he wouldn't think she was being cowed by his anger.

"Really? Well, am I yelling now?" he asked, his voice whisper-soft, but clipped.

She shook her head no.

"Good. You're fired."

"You don't want to do that," she said, still not listening.

"Why not?" he demanded, then before she could reply added, "Anyway I hired you to find someone, not to stalk me."

"I know that. But what better way to find out who's stalking you, than to follow you?"

"Did you find someone?"

"No."

"So then we can safely assume whoever sent me the notes isn't dangerous. It's just an over-zealous fan who let her enthusiasm get the better of her. I haven't gotten any notes in a bit so maybe she's moved on to . . . to who's that romance model you see everywhere . . . Fabian?"

"Fabio. And you're wrong. Just because you haven't received any notes lately doesn't mean you're not in any danger."

"Are you always this obsessive?"

"Are you always this angry?" she countered.

"No. You just seem to know how to push the right buttons to infuriate me."

"Maybe if you weren't so buttoned down . . ."

He let her comment about his neat streak ride. "Okay, let's say I listen to what you have to say."

"That'd be novel—"

"And you listen to me. What makes you think I'm in any danger? And I mean besides some hunch you have."

She gave him the comment about her hunches

and answered his question calmly. "You know how you accused me of running that credit check on you . . . ?"

He nodded.

"It wasn't me. If I'd checked on you, you wouldn't have found out. Someone else was checking up on you. If I were you, I'd be feeling uneasy about that. If I were you, I'd rehire me."

Max braced his hands on the frame of her Jeep and leaned forward. "You would, would you?"

She nodded.

"Okay, but I want you to keep in mind that this isn't something I want people to know about. Do you understand?"

"Yes, I'll be as discreet as possible conducting my investigation. But you've got to agree to let me do my job my way without any interference from you every time you don't like something. In other words, Max, I don't tell you how to announce, and you won't tell me how to detect."

"As long as you're as good at your job as I am at mine," he agreed, having the grace to grin when he said it.

"No wonder you never wear a hat," she retorted, starting up her car. "Your ego wouldn't fit inside one."

She didn't give him time to deny it, as she pulled away from the curb. Nor did she look back. He'd rehired her and she didn't want to muck that up.

Her mind was on his case a few miles down

the road when a sports car sped past her, nearly driving her off the road. Some people. Some people thought they owned the road. Or their daddies did.

Max stood in the shower letting the hot water beat down on him. He'd had an extra-large hot-water heater installed in the condo because he loved taking long, hot showers. They relaxed him.

As the hot water sluiced down his body, matting the dark hair on his chest, he wondered if he was crazy to believe Amy Jane's warning that his fan could be dangerous. Normally very pragmatic, he found himself more than willing to believe anything Amy Jane told him. Found himself wanting any excuse at all to spend time with her.

She was a woman outside his experience.

Amy Jane Chadwick was tough and full of moxie.

Moxie . . . he shook his head, sending a spray of water droplets on the tile. He didn't think he'd ever used that word. He certainly hadn't ever dreamed moxie was something he'd find appealing in a woman.

Claire was more the type of woman he'd been involved with in the past; very feminine and passive, even if in a manipulative sort of way. It was refreshing to find a woman who didn't mind telling him off, didn't mind telling him what

she really thought . . . instead of what she
thought he wanted her to say.

Maybe he was just becoming masochistic.

Or had he spent so much time on his career
that he had become self-absorbed? So self-absorbed he needed someone to tell him he was
in danger. So self-absorbed he needed someone
to wake him up to the fact that he was lonely.

He turned off the water and stepped out of
the shower, reaching for the bath towel. As he
rubbed the plush towel quickly over his body, he
continued thinking of Amy Jane. He'd hired a
woman to protect him . . . that was all he
needed—the players or Corey Cohen finding out
that little tidbit of information. They'd never let
him live it down.

It had been bad enough with Kerry Ashton.

Finding her in bed with one of the players
had been shocking only to him. It seemed he
was the last to know. He'd expected to be more
hurt. He'd merely been embarrassed. Was there
something wrong with him? Why hadn't he ever
been in love enough to care when things went
wrong with a relationship?

Kerry's pleas later that she'd slept with the
player only to make him jealous, to get a commitment from him, had fallen on deaf ears.

He went from the bathroom to his bedroom,
opening the bureau drawer and taking out the
notes. Sitting down on the bed, he reread them.
He supposed Kerry could have sent them.

But he was embarrassed that he didn't know

her well enough to tell after dating her for six months. He'd been attracted to her cute little body, not her mind.

Now it appeared the shoe was on the other foot.

Someone was attracted to him—someone who didn't know him at all.

"Listen to this," Miranda said, reading from the newspaper.

James Chadwick leaned his forearms on the bar and did just that.

"St. Louis has gone hockey crazy. People are scheduling their social commitments around Lions games. Attendance is up with the games averaging over 18,000 wildly cheering fanatic fans a game. The Stanley Cup Playoffs being televised are putting the old image of hockey players to rest. Instead of toothless brawlers, hockey is sporting some popular hunks. Even in the announcing booth," Miranda finished reading with a smile.

"So someone's into Corey Cohen, eh?"

"Are you nuts? They're talking about Max."

"Guess I'd better warn my niece, eh?"

"Guess you'd better."

"Do you think the Lions are going to win the Central Division?"

"Is Hillary a feminist?" Miranda said, rolling her eyes.

"Give me a break. I was just trying to make

conversation, okay?" James pleaded, defending his inane remark.

"Please, that's almost like asking if the Penguins will qualify when they've been in three of the last four—actually they've won three out of the last four cups."

"So, maybe you could go out to dinner with me and explain the finer points of hockey to me," James proposed.

"Don't go trying to smooth talk me, you old rascal. You know way more about hockey than I do."

"Don't be saying the word 'old' to someone having a midlife crisis."

"Midlife?" Miranda said, arching an eyebrow. "Hey, turn up the sound, our soap is on," she announced as the opening credits appeared on screen.

"How did I ever let you get me hooked on this damn thing?" James grumbled, watching.

"If it's good enough for Max Armstrong, it's good enough for you."

"How do you know it's good enough for Max?"

"I read it in an interview in the *Post-Dispatch*. Max got hooked when he was playing hockey. The players all ate at noon, watched the soaps and then went to the game."

"You need to get a life, Miranda."

"Look who's talking."

"Have *you* been bungee jumping?"

"No, I have a brain."

* * *

It was the same hotel room Max had caught
her cheating in.

Kerry writhed beneath the Lions goalie, making all the right moves to drive Richie wild.

"You're so big and strong," she whispered, in-
fusing her voice with girlish awe.

"No, it's just that you're so tiny."

Kerry smiled, knowing Richie was amazed
she'd chosen him from all the other players on
the team. Richie didn't know just how carefully
she had chosen him. She hadn't given up on making Max Armstrong jealous. Not by a long shot.
No one *ever* ended a relationship with her before
she was ready for it to end. She was the one who
broke hearts.

"How does that feel?" Richie asked, his voice
needy.

"It feels so good, Richie."

"But I'm afraid I might hurt you . . ."

"No. I'm ready for you. Can't you feel how
wet I am? Put your hand between my thighs.
I'm not wearing any panties."

Richie groaned as she guided his shy hand
there to prove her words.

"Are you hot for me, baby?" she asked, moving against his hand.

They fell on the bed, Richie eager and not
nearly as experienced as she. It was the way she
liked it.

She liked having Richie's full, undivided attention. "Richie?" she asked, her voice a pout.

"What is it? I didn't hurt you, did I?" he asked, levering his body up from hers, while still kissing her.

"No. I was just thinking. You ought to talk to someone about the way Max picks on you. I don't like it. It's not fair."

"Oh, you're just being too sensitive, Kerry. Max comes down hard on all of us when he thinks we aren't doing our job." Richie's hands were busy shedding his clothes.

"But he—"

Her words were cut off by his insistent penis.

Her mouth did its expert work, her tongue flicking, her teeth trailing. And while she had Richie in a state of thoughtless bliss, she thought a mile a minute.

But not about Richie Allen.

Moments later she was swallowing, and positioned to lead Richie around by the oldest and most reliable method known to woman. She would get her way.

She would.

Claire sat in the living room with a cup of tea, sipping it as she flipped through the thick, glossy pages of a bridal magazine. She had a subscription for each of the monthly bridal publications, reading them with the same addiction as Amy Jane read her detective novels.

Everything was magical in the magazines, from the fanciful floral bouquets, to the fairy-tale wedding cakes, to the frothy white dresses. Her dreams and desires were all based within the glossy pages.

She wanted to be married.

She wanted a husband.

She didn't want to be in charge. But she didn't have a choice. Her parents' death had forced her to become strong. There was no one else to make sure the family estate wasn't lost.

Uncle James was hopeless.

Amy Jane, well, she didn't have the domestic gene.

So it all fell to her.

For now.

She supposed she should take pride in how well the bed and breakfast was doing. And she did. But it was a lot of work. A lot of daily reality.

"You know what I wish?" she asked one of her favorite dolls sitting on the bookshelf. "I wish Mommy and Daddy were still alive. You know, when I turn the corner or enter a room, I still sometimes think I catch a glimpse of them. And then I have to remind myself that they are gone. That things won't ever be as they were. I'll never hear their laughter again. Hear them practicing their lines, rehearsing in the library until all hours of the night. Sometimes I feel so lonely."

She wiped at the moisture gathering in the corner of her eyes, chastising herself for giving in to self-pity. It wasn't so bad really running the bed and breakfast. Plenty of people had it much worse. She was living in a beautiful home with spacious grounds.

And when there weren't guests she could imagine things were still as they once were.

Tossing aside the bridal magazine after ripping out a recipe for almond pound cake, she went to add another log on the fire. It wasn't cold really. She kept a fire burning for atmosphere. Aesthetics mattered to her. Probably too much. Sitting in an ugly room could make her physically ill.

Unlike Amy Jane, whom nothing seemed to make physically ill. Her sister had the constitution of a horse. One would have to when one made a habit of eating things like tacos and Pepsi first thing in the morning. She wondered what it would be like to be Amy Jane and not be trapped by her own standards.

Looking around the room, she imagined Bobby McQuaid sitting in the wing chair by the fire. He didn't look out of place. He added to the room. Yes, the place needed a man.

Almost as much as she did.

Ten

Feeling ridiculous, Max made another entry in the journal Amy Jane insisted he keep on any untoward incidents. She'd insisted he needed to document everything, just in case.

When he'd asked her just in case what, she'd told him he didn't want to know. That he should just leave everything to her. To trust her.

She didn't know how much she was asking.

Nevertheless, he dutifully noted the series of hang-ups on his answering machine. It was creepy to think that someone was constantly checking up on his whereabouts by calling his condo. He preferred to think the hang-ups were merely sales calls. He never would have thought he'd be hoping for computer-generated phone calls, instead of being annoyed by them.

After jotting down the information in the journal, he closed it and put it with the notes in his bureau drawer.

With time to kill, he decided to go to the mall. He needed to replace the pair of expensive loafers he'd ruined in the rain. He wished he could get insurance coverage for his fetish.

As luck would have it, the kid with a crewcut who waited on him was a broadcast journalism major. So, while Max got exactly the pair of shoes he'd ruined replaced, it took him twice the normal time to make the purchase. The kid wanted to pump him for all sorts of hints on how to become as successful in the career as Max had.

Max's answer was always the same. A good speaking voice was, of course, a given. Next came hard work and endurance. The traveling was a grueling part of the job. Luck usually played a walk-on part as well.

A luxurious sweater caught his eye in a window display when he left the shoe store to browse. He passed on it in the end, but did stop to buy a white shirt made of Egyptian cotton.

He moved on then to the food court for tacos and an import beer. As he poured hot sauce on his taco, he watched a little girl of about two use tears to get her way. Feeling someone staring at him, he turned, expecting an autograph seeker, but there was no one at the table behind him and none of the people at the food booths seemed to be paying any attention to him. They were busy jostling for position.

He must really be getting paranoid, he decided.

Finishing the last of his beer, he left the food court and stopped by the bookstore on his way out of the mall. He lingered long enough to pick up a couple of paperback mysteries to keep the boredom of road trips at bay.

The parking lot was crowded. Blue sunny skies had brought casual shoppers out in droves. When he reached his car, he saw something white stuck under the windshield wiper. He quickly glanced at other nearby cars to see if one of the stores was putting out a sale flyer. But no, it was just as he'd feared; his was the only car with something under the windshield wiper.

He knew what it was before he retrieved it.

It was another note. A Dearest Max note.

He was tempted to fling it on the ground and just drive off. But he couldn't. His curiosity and Amy Jane's certain censure made him rip the envelope open with his finger and withdraw the note. It was as he'd expected:

Dearest Max,

Why are you playing
hard to get? There is
no woman in your life.
I'm growing tired of
waiting. If you don't
act soon, I will.

I LOVE YOU

He crumpled the note in his fist.

Damn. He hadn't been imagining things. Someone had been watching him sit down to eat at the food court. And then while he'd been eating and buying his paperbacks, she'd put the note under his windshield wiper.

It gave him the creeps. Creepier still was the knowledge that she knew his car. Might even have tailed him to the mall and put the note under his windshield wiper before she'd gone inside the mall.

He spun on his heel, hoping to catch someone watching him. His quick action was to no avail. All he'd done was startle a bird who'd been lunching on a spilled bag of French fries on the pavement two cars away.

Feeling foolish, he unlocked his car and got in, tossing the crumpled note on the passenger seat. For a moment he considered the idea of not telling Amy Jane about the note. But he realized ignoring the problem wasn't going to make it go away. He'd have to tell her.

As he pulled out of his parking space, he punched her number on the cellular phone.

Someone picked it up on the fifth ring. "Hello . . ."

"Claire?"

"Yes."

"I was looking for Amy Jane. Is she there?"

"Ah, no. I picked up the phone because I'm in her room laying out fresh linen. I think she went to the DMV to check on a license or something. She said she'd be back in time for dinner."

"Tell her I need to talk to her. It's important that she call me tonight."

"Well, why not join us for dinner tonight, then?" Claire suggested.

"What time?"

"Around five."

"Uh, Claire, would there be peach pie involved in this dinner?"

Claire's laugh radiated pleasure. "No. But, there will be dessert. Amy Jane insists."

It was Max's turn to laugh. "Good. I'll be there."

Once again Max found himself feeling relaxed when he pulled up the drive to the story-book estate that was the Chadwick Bed and Breakfast. Having been raised in a small farming community, he hadn't had much exposure to canopied beds, English silver pieces and gourmet foods. But it was something he found pleasing.

Claire made him feel welcome, making polite conversation while they waited for Amy Jane, who was late.

"Did you do a lot of research before you opened the bed and breakfast?" Max asked, watching Claire check the dish she was keeping warm in the oven while they waited.

"Not really. It sort of happened without a plan. But luckily we've had good word of mouth, and the place is thriving."

"I'm not surprised. You're such a wonderful hostess. Still it must be a lot of hard work . . ."

"Oh, it is. It's labor intensive, as Amy Jane

likes to say. Too labor intensive to suit her. But I like keeping a home."

"Who are you talking to?" Amy Jane asked, as she rushed into the kitchen. "Sorry, I'm late."

"I invited Max to dinner," Claire said, nodding to him.

"Oh, I didn't see you." Amy Jane turned to him.

"I wanted to talk to you about a business matter and Claire invited me to stay for dinner."

"Why don't we eat first, so dinner doesn't dry out? Claire tends to get a little cranky when I ruin dinner by being late."

After a bowl of white beans and buttermilk biscuits they polished off a good portion of the still-warm almond pound cake. Claire cleared the dishes then, while Amy Jane and Max adjourned to the library to talk business.

He pulled the crumpled note from his pocket and handed it to Amy Jane. "You said to let you know when I got another one. Apparently you were right. She hasn't lost interest."

"So, guess you're happy, as it leaves your ego still intact," Amy Jane said, flattening out the note on the desk she sat at by the bay window. She switched on the green lamp and studied the note.

"I don't know why you keep insisting that I like this. I don't. It's pretty creepy stuff. I'm beginning to feel really paranoid."

"You're not paranoid if someone is following you," Amy Jane observed. "Where did you find this note? Did it come in the mail, or did someone put it where you would find it?"

He came over to the desk and stood just behind her, inhaling the fresh fragrance of her shampoo, admiring her clever hat. "The latter. I came out of the mall and when I got to my car on the parking lot it was just hair, I mean, there." If you asked him, Amy Jane was having a great hair day. He found himself wanting to touch it. The lack of mousse or spray made it inviting. That and the fruity scent of her shampoo that lingered.

"Where?"

"Beneath the windshield wiper on my car."

"And you didn't notice anyone?"

"No. Well, I thought I felt someone staring at me when I was eating at the food court, but when I looked around, I didn't catch anyone."

"It could have been your stalker. Or it might have only been a fan gawking. That's the trouble with celebrities—you can't be sure."

"Do me a favor. Let's don't use the word stalker, okay? It makes me uncomfortable."

"It should. This person is making threats to act. You have to take it seriously. You can't be sure she won't act to carry out her threat. Even you have to agree this person is obsessed."

"Are you trying to scare me?" Max teased, moving to slouch on the sofa.

"Think," Amy Jane dismissed his touch at lightness. "Is there someone you've encouraged?

Someone who might have gotten the wrong idea?"

"What kind of man do you think I am? I don't do that sort of thing."

"I wasn't implying that you did. But either you've got a fan with a fantasy that's gotten completely out of hand, or you've got a total nut case on your hands. Either is trouble."

"You got any suspects?"

"I'm trying to narrow it down to a couple thousand," she answered glumly.

"What were you doing at the DMV?"

"Running a check on a license. No luck, though. I didn't have enough to find out anything. You know anyone who drives a dark Mercedes sports car?"

"Only everyone in Chesterfield, except, of course, for those who aren't driving light-colored ones. Or Porsches."

"Don't be cute. If I could get a lead on who your stalker is, you could file a complaint with the police. Once you did, then you could get a court order of protection. Police respond more aggressively when there is a court order."

"No police. I'm already going nuts with the creepy feeling someone is watching me. I don't want to make it worse."

"Even without a court order, I could call in a few favors from my buddies at the precinct— have them keep an eye on your condo and the Dome to see if anyone is putting in a regular appearance."

"No police."

"But—"

"I told you from the start that I don't want this to become public information."

"What do you want—?"

He thought about telling her. Wondered what her reaction would be if he told her he wanted to lock the door and make love to her on the desk she sat behind.

Hey, but that was an idea.

"The question is what does my . . . stalker . . . want. She mentions in the note that there is no woman in my life. But what if there were?" He rose from the sofa and walked toward her. "Do you really think she'd be so obsessed with me if I were involved with someone. Someone, like *you*. If she saw us together, she might decide she didn't want me any longer, and move on to someone else. Someone who was more available."

Amy Jane shook her head no. "I don't date clients."

"But—"

"No."

Amy Jane stood at her bedroom window later that night looking out over the grounds wondering why she'd lied to Max. She didn't have any hard-and-fast rule about not dating a client. There hadn't been one she'd wanted to date until Max.

But she'd told him no for one reason only. A reason that had nothing to do with principle.

He was the man she shouldn't have. He was all wrong for her.

So she wanted him.

That was the real reason she'd told him no.

She had a business to build. There was no room in her life for the distraction Max Armstrong would be. A smart woman didn't get on a plane she knew was going to crash, or at the very least lose her luggage.

She moved away from the window wondering when she'd become a coward.

The creepy sensation of being watched followed Max around, as unshakable as a shadow. He wanted to put a stop to it, but how? There was no one to confront. He'd done all he could by hiring Amy Jane.

Now it was a waiting game. They had to wait until the stalker broke the law.

Max couldn't actually say he was afraid. But he was certainly unnerved.

And his job required concentration. He had to pay close attention to announce the game or risk blowing it.

He tried to dismiss the whole thing from his mind that night as he began announcing the Lions game.

"Bobby McQuaid isn't suited up tonight due to an injury he sustained showboating once again. One of these days he's going to surprise us all and live up to his press clippings, if he can control that temper of his."

"Don't you think you're being kinda hard on Bobby?" Corey asked as they led into a Busch commercial.

"No." Max knew it annoyed Bobby and the other players when he rode them hard. But Max's logic was that the players were being paid a lot of money. Enough money so that they should be adult role models rather than childish prima donnas.

The commercial was over and Max went back to announcing the game, with one eye on a blond fan in the stands.

"Kenny LeBac, a second-year pro, passes up the middle. It's in his own end and—"

"LeBac is a fourth-year pro," Corey corrected.

"Isn't that what I just said?" Max stated, still watching the fan who was staring at him. Was it the one? he wondered.

Corey let it ride, and Max continued announcing the game. "They go down to the corner and circle the net. Allen bumps the puck away from the net."

The woman in the stands got up.

"With 1:20 to go . . . the shot is blocked in front of the net by Allen again. The kid is hot tonight, ladies and gentlemen. Uh-oh, Richie just lost it and is fighting with the—"

"The other guy hit him first," Corey defended.

"Hockey isn't about fighting. It's about skating. Richie needs to learn that," Max insisted.

"The Flyers push the puck in front of the net, but LeBac interferes. He shoots the puck out to center ice and his pass comes right back to him. It's a power-play goal. Oh baby! That makes the score two to one in the Lions' favor," Max shouted wondering where the blonde had gone.

"Three to one," Corey corrected.

"What? Oh, right," Max agreed recovering.

Chantal joined them in the booth. "I think you need a vacation, Max. You're blowing calls. I'd be happy to sit in for you," she offered.

"Yeah. Why don't you take a few days off and rest," Corey eagerly agreed.

"I'm fine," Max insisted, feeling anything but.

"He sure was in a hurry to leave," Corey said when Max cleared out of the announcing booth right after the game wrap-up. "Wonder if he had a hot date. He certainly seemed distracted enough tonight."

"He's probably going home to sleep. He looked tired to me. I wish he'd take me up on my offer to sub for him. I could sure use the money. My car is about to fall apart," Chantal said, looking glum.

"Why don't you let me lend you the money," Corey offered. "Interest free."

"Why would you want to do that?"

"It's a loan, nothing more," Corey assured

her. "I happen to think you got a raw deal by the station when they pushed you aside to make room for Max. I'd like to make it up to you."

"Thanks, but no thanks. I take care of myself."

"Well, if you change your mind, my offer stands," Corey assured her, stepping aside to let her go first as they exited the booth.

"What a jerk. I'd like to pound him, wouldn't you?" Bobby snarled to Richie when Miranda mentioned Max's lecturing them on-air again.

Richie nodded.

"Don't you boys go messing up Max's gorgeous puss," Miranda said, pouring them each a beer and leaving the pitcher on the table while she went to wait on another table.

"How's it going with Kerry?" Bobby asked Richie, nudging him as they watched Miranda walk away in a pair of Guess jeans just made for her sassy tush.

"Man, she's wearing me plum out. I barely had the strength to make it through the third period," Richie said, not seeming too unhappy about his complaint.

"Does she ask you to wear your goalie mask in bed?"

"How'd you know?" Richie asked suspiciously. The question of whether Bobby had nailed her was plain on his face.

"She's a sports groupie, man. It figures she'd ask you to wear your mask."

"Oh. How about you and James' niece? How's that going?" Richie asked, taking a swig of beer.

"It's not. I think she's a frigging virgin. And to think I took her to the ballet for nothing. You want to trade women?" he suggested, brightening.

"Not a chance," Richie vowed, scotching Bobby's offer. "Did you collect on your bet from James that she'd go out with you?"

"Come to think of it, no. Guess I'd better do it before I dump her. Let's go over to the bar and collect."

"When you planning to dump her?" Richie asked, trying to pat Miranda's tush as she passed by.

"I don't know. Guess I'll give it a few more tries. She is a looker."

"Besides we go on the road tomorrow, and what she doesn't know won't hurt her," Richie said.

Bobby nodded. They lifted their beer mugs and clunked them. "To road trips," they toasted.

"What are you guys toasting?" Lance Thomure asked, setting down a bowl of pretzels and joining them.

"The playoffs," Richie answered.

"Let's hope we win some games," Lance said.

"That, too," Bobby agreed, exchanging a glance with Richie.

* * *

Amy Jane unpacked the new phone she'd bought. It had a feature that allowed you to press a button and redial the number that had just called you. A handy way to trace a call. When Max returned from his road trip, she'd have him plug in the phone and they'd try it out. With any luck they might be able to trace his hang-up calls to his stalker.

Or maybe . . .

Claire came in from the kitchen where she'd just finished up a sausage and egg casserole she planned to serve their guests for breakfast. It had smelled so good—Amy Jane hoped there were leftovers.

"What's that?" Claire asked, stopping to watch her repack the phone.

"It's for a case," Amy Jane explained.

"Oh." Claire flipped on the television and sank down onto the sofa. "I'm bushed. Want to watch the first game of the playoffs with me?"

"Later. I've got an errand to run first. I should be back in time for the third period." Amy Jane picked up the boxed phone and headed out of the library for her clandestine mission.

Thirty minutes later she was circling Max's condo, casing the area. She was relieved to find no cruising patrol car. The only one out was a man walking his dog and he'd already turned a corner and was out of sight.

Satisfied she wouldn't attract any notice, she parked her Jeep and went to the door of Max's condo, carrying the boxed phone. She set the box down at the entrance and took a quick surreptitious glance around before picking the lock on the front door of Max's condo.

Moments later, she'd slipped inside and expelled the breath she'd been holding. Her body slumped against the wall while she caught her breath. It was quiet and dark. She let her eyes get adjusted, then searched out Max's phone.

It was easy work to replace it with the one she'd bought. It was only a matter of attaching Max's phone jack to the phone she'd bought and plugging it in.

There, she was done. She began gathering up the spare cord and papers that had come with the new phone.

The phone rang then, so startling her that she picked up the receiver.

Damn. Now what? She decided to answer.

"Hello . . ."

"Yes, this is the *Post-Dispatch* calling. Do you receive your daily newspaper at this address?"

Amy Jane had no idea. She glanced around the kitchen and saw in the wastebasket a yellow cellophane wrapper for the paper.

"Ah, yes."

"And have your deliveries been satisfactory?"

"Yes . . ."

"Thank you," the woman said. "This is a service check." A moment later Amy Jane heard the dial tone when the caller hung up.

Was it a service call? Did the phone company do that sort of thing at night? Or was it Max's stalker? If it was, Amy Jane hadn't recognized the voice.

She hit the star button and punched in 69 to test out the feature.

"Hello," the same voice she'd just talked to answered.

Amy Jane hung up.

It worked. Now Max would have to see if he recognized the voice on the other end of the line when he tried tracing his hang-up calls.

If not, the next step would be a visit to Radio Shack to get a device that would actually trace the calls. Just then she remembered to replace Max's message to the new phone, switching his tape.

It was time to go, but she found herself lingering. What would be the harm she asked herself, in having a look around?

She couldn't rationalize that she was doing it for any business reason. No, her interest was personal. What she was doing was tantamount to reading someone's private diary. It was against the rules.

She smiled. And delicious fun.

Max accommodated her by having a flashlight plugged into an outlet above the kitchen counter. Unplugging it, she used the flashlight to begin snooping.

His kitchen was typical of a bachelor. An undomesticated one. The lack of a wide variety of utensils told her that he ate out most of the time. A sensible man.

Still, what there was, was in place.

His bedroom followed suit. All his clothes were pressed and hung neatly. Nothing was half off a hanger. His shoes were shined and lined up perfectly on the floor of the closet.

She lifted one of his blazers to her nose. His aftershave lingered. Picturing him as she'd seen him fresh from his shower, she wondered what he was doing at that moment. She realized immediately that, of course, he was announcing the game.

After hanging the jacket back up, she moved to the bureau. The notes were still in the drawer. She'd traced the paper to a common kind used in every office copier. She hadn't had any luck tracing the typewriter that had been used, either.

Closing the drawer, she flicked on the television at the foot of his bed, and began switching through the channels with his remote, trying to find the game. He had a lot of channels. It was then she recalled the satellite dish he had in his yard that would enable him to pick up even more hockey.

Finally she found the channel carrying the Lions game.

Max looked real uncomfortable.

The clothes he wore told her he'd lost his luggage.

Amy Jane smiled, and laid back across his bed to watch him squirm.

Eleven

"This is St. Louis Lions hockey. With 1:20 to go in the period, a long shot is stopped by Lance Thomure and the Lions stay out ahead two to one."

Max finished announcing the period, fresh and on top of the game. It wasn't like the last game he'd announced in St. Louis when he'd blown some calls. Being on the road had helped to settle him down. And tonight he hadn't seen the blond fan who had unnerved him at the last home game.

The only thing that had unnerved him since he'd been back was finding out Amy Jane had been in his condo to install the phone. It wasn't that he had anything to hide, it was just unsettling knowing.

"The Leafs are hot tonight," Corey said. "Richie Allen has been defending the goal all period and looks like he's fading."

"He needs to stop partying. He's celebrating too early in the playoffs," Max said. "Just because we won two on the road from the Leafs, doesn't mean it's going to be a sweep of the series."

Max's prediction proved right. The Leafs rallied and scored goals late in the third period, spoiling any plans for a Lions victory party.

The mood of the fans at the sports bar was downbeat when Max reached it. And the crowd was thin.

But not thin enough. The blond female fan whose stare had distracted him at the last home game was there waiting for him. Smiling at him.

He thought about leaving, but James called out to him, motioning for him to come to the bar. The woman frowned as Max made his way to the bar, instead of approaching her.

"Amy Jane wants you to call her when you get home," James said, relaying the message and handing Max a cold beer.

"Where is she?"

"On an insurance stakeout, but she said she'd be home later. You having any luck with your problem?"

Max shook his head.

"I'm sure Amy Jane will clear it up sooner or later. She's one stubborn child."

"Woman."

"What?"

"Amy Jane's a woman."

"Depends when you catch her. Sometimes she's still a child."

Max could feel the woman staring at him. But

he ignored it. Instead he engaged James in conversation about his niece.

"So tell me about Amy Jane," he said, swirling the beer in his mug, but not drinking it.

"What do you want to know?" James asked. He deftly handled a drink order Miranda called out.

"Like why she's so stubborn, for instance."

James laughed. "I suppose I come in for my share of the blame for that. Although we're a pretty eccentric lot, the Chadwicks. You may have noticed Claire is just as stubborn, though she uses wile to get her way. Amy Jane doesn't bother with that. I suppose she was her father's favorite. Her mother tried turning her into a lady along with Claire. But Amy Jane just wasn't interested in rules and regulations. Manners and such. She always wanted to get at the truth even when it hurt. For that matter, I think she's accepted her parents' death better than Claire or I."

"How come she hasn't married? Don't tell me she doesn't like men."

"Hardly. She just has about the same luck in picking out the opposite sex as I do. Amy Jane keeps picking men she thinks she can save—men who can't be saved."

Max was quiet a while, digesting the information James had given him about his niece. So the way to get to Amy Jane was to appeal to her need to save him . . .

It occurred to him that he didn't feel anyone

staring at him any longer. Not wanting to chance looking, he appealed to James. "Is there a blond woman sitting across the room behind me?"

"Nope."

Max let out a sigh of relief. Maybe it was just his overactive imagination.

"She's coming over here," James explained.

"What?"

Someone tapped Max on the shoulder. "Excuse me."

Max turned.

It was her.

"Would you mind signing my Lions jacket. I've got all the team members' autographs."

Max took the pen she offered and waited for the woman to take off the jacket. It became obvious that she wanted him to sign the jacket with her in it.

He cleared his throat. "Ah, where did you want me to sign it?"

"Just above my name," she said pointing to a spot on her breast.

Max looked at James. He wasn't offering any help. He just smirked while wiping the bar.

"You'll have to take off your jacket," Max finally said.

"But all the hockey players agreed to sign it while I was wearing it. This is my lucky jacket," the woman pouted.

Max outwaited her pout, and the woman finally caved, taking off her jacket for him to sign it. But she let him know she wasn't happy about him disappointing her. He tried to pacify her by asking her how she wanted him to sign it. He was being polite, of course, but he also had an ulterior motive for asking her name. If he got it, he could have Amy Jane check it out.

The woman considered a moment, then brightened.

"I know, how about if you sign it 'Love, Max Armstrong,' " she suggested.

Max didn't quibble. Instead he pressed ahead in his determined effort to gain her name. "Don't you want me to personalize it with your name, too?"

"Sure, okay. Make it out to Snoozy."

"Snoozy?" Max repeated, disappointed. He could just imagine Amy Jane's response if he asked her to track down that name. "Cute nickname," he said, signing the woman's jacket. "What's your real name?"

"Hey, Armstrong, what's the deal with you being on our butts all the time?" Bobby McQuaid demanded as he and Richie Allen stopped to confront Max on their way out of the bar.

"You guys aren't doing your job. I'm doing mine by saying so. I announce the game I see, not the one your agents see. I wouldn't be on your butts, if you guys were to party less and practice more. You've got to put some effort behind the talent."

"Sounds like sour grapes to me," Bobby said. "Maybe you're just sore because Kerry Ashton is seeing Richie here instead of you. You know what I think, Armstrong? I think you're jealous."

"Grow up, McQuaid."

"Well, I don't see you dating anyone. Maybe you're still carrying a torch for Kerry, even after she dumped you."

"Kerry did not dump me," Max said, wishing he hadn't said it almost instantly.

Bobby elbowed Richie. "I don't know about you, but if I found my woman in bed with another man, I'd consider myself dumped."

Max wanted to paste him, but he held on to his temper by a thin thread of control. He could have pointed out that he'd gone to the ballet with Amy Jane, but he knew it was lame, as he hadn't been seen with her since.

"Aw, come on, Richie," Bobby said, seeing Max wasn't going to be provoked into fighting. "Let's get out of here. We've got women waiting for us."

As the two left, Max closed his eyes and tried to regain his temper. He turned back to finish his business with the blonde, but she'd disappeared.

Damn.

After ascertaining that James didn't know the identity of the blond autograph seeker, Max spent the rest of the evening at the bar discussing the Lions' chances of making it all the way through the playoffs to the Stanley Cup.

At closing time, the coach, Tom Quinn, had left, and the last stragglers were saying their good-byes at the door. When Miranda had finished tallying up the take for the night, she joined Max and James at the bar.

"Which one of you handsome gentlemen wants to walk me to my car?" she asked, nervous over the increasing crime rate the news detailed nightly on television.

"I'll walk you," Max offered.

Ten minutes later when James had locked up, Max and Miranda were still trying to start her car.

James looked under the hood, and pronounced the car dead electrically. "Want me to drive you home?" he offered, closing the hood.

"No, Max can take me. I live closer to him."

"Okay, but give me a call tomorrow if you need a lift anywhere. Unless you don't want to be seen with an older man," he teased.

"Wait a minute, I'm older," Max said.

"Will you two quit? I like older men. They make me feel real protected."

"Just as long as it isn't rich older men you like. I'd be out of that ballgame," James said, glancing at Max's expensive luxury car as James got in his own mid-sized sedan and drove away.

"I think he likes you," Max said, opening the passenger door for Miranda.

Miranda laughed, "James likes women period. He's a consummate flirt."

"Okay, where do you live?" Max asked, when he'd settled into the driver's seat.

"Creve Coeur, on Ballas off Olive," she explained, running her hands over the soft leather seat lovingly.

"Where does James live?" Max asked, heading for the highway.

"I don't know," Miranda admitted.

"Then how did you know I live closer to you?"

"I wanted to ride in your car. Is this a great car or what? It's the kind of car I bet you never want to get out of."

"It's a car," Max said with a shrug. He'd reached a level of success that made material things less coveted. It was hard not to take a lot of things for granted, not because you didn't appreciate what you had, but because you were so busy.

"No, what I left sitting back there on the lot was a car. This . . . this is heaven."

Flattered in spite of himself, and a little touched, Max pulled the car over to the curb a few blocks before the entrance ramp to the highway.

Max switched off the engine and turned to Miranda. "Do you want to drive it?" he asked, dangling the keys before her.

"Are you kidding me?" she asked, awed.

"No. Go ahead. You know the way to your place and I don't. I'll just catch some z's. Besides, while I know how to nurse a beer for an hour, so I can drive safely, you haven't had anything to drink at all. Let's call you my designated driver."

He didn't have to ask her twice.

And catching *z's* was out of the question with her driving. She was a good driver with a deft hand on the wheel, but she had a lead foot.

"Do you always drive like that?" he asked when they pulled off the highway onto Olive Boulevard.

"No, but then it's not often I get a chance to drive a car like this one."

They were at her apartment in five minutes.

"Why don't you come in for coffee?" she invited, after she'd parked the car.

"It's late."

"I insist. Come on, you gave me a ride. Heck, you let me drive. And you didn't even flinch about my speeding. At least let me make you some coffee before you go on home."

"Okay," he agreed reluctantly.

"Good."

Not good, Max decided when he got a look at her apartment. It was practically a hockey shrine. She had hockey sticks, jerseys, caps, you name it. And posters and publicity photos on the walls. There was even one of him.

Miranda put on coffee while he had a look around at all the hockey mementos. Each thing he commented on she could tell him exactly when and how she'd acquired it.

"Here's your coffee," she said, setting it down on the coffee table.

Had her hand lingered a moment too long when she gave him a spoon to stir in his sugar?

What was wrong with him? She was just a kid.

A kid who liked hockey. This stalker business had him all crazy, suspecting everyone.

He took a sip of his coffee. "It's good," he complimented her.

"Would you like something to eat? I could make you a sandwich."

"No, just the coffee to wake me up, and then I'm on my way."

"Why don't you take off your shirt first," she said as he lifted his cup of coffee to drain it.

Max nearly choked on the swallow of coffee he took. "What?" he asked, after he'd finally managed to swallow the warm liquid.

"If you take off your shirt, I could get that ink stain out for you," Miranda explained.

Max looked down at his shirt. Sure enough there was a streak of ink across the front of his shirt. No doubt a souvenir from his blond fan. He wondered briefly if it was a deliberate act, or an accident.

"It's no problem, really," he heard Miranda saying.

"No, it's okay. I have a great cleaners. They get everything out. Even blood."

Miranda looked at him strangely.

"Well, not that they've ever had to . . . ah . . . I'd best be going. Thanks for the coffee," he said, rising to go.

She followed him to the door.

"Max?" she said softly.

"Yes?"

She reached up and brushed his lips with a

kiss. "Thanks for letting me be your designated driver."

"Yeah. I gotta be going," he answered, making good his escape.

Amy Jane felt like a teenager waiting for a boyfriend to call. Only Max hadn't called. It was past midnight, she could see from the clock's lighted dial.

Who was she kidding? She'd been on the other end of an unringing telephone long past her teenage years. Something in her made her pick men who made promises they couldn't or wouldn't keep.

But this was just business, she kept trying to tell herself.

Max Armstrong, just business.

Right. And Swiss chocolate almond was just ice cream.

Well, she had David Letterman. The permanent man in her life who never disappointed her. The old Letterman with his khakis, sneakers and wise-guy smirk was as comfortable to her as a second skin. They shared an irreverence for the postured, pompous authority that deserved to be mocked. He had made being an outsider in. Made being different cool.

The new Letterman had gone from "I won't behave, you can't make me" to "I have made it bigtime, and I can do Yoga relaxation while hosting my show and still make you laugh."

No matter, his best attitude was silliness; his sense of the ridiculous that he'd honed to sheer perfection.

Why, Amy Jane wondered, didn't men know that if you could make a woman laugh—you could get to home plate with her on a walk.

And if you called when you were supposed to, you could probably get her to swallow.

The telephone rang, interrupting her late-night musings. She followed the phone cord until she unearthed the phone beneath a pile of clothes. When she picked up the receiver and heard Max's voice, she deliberately dropped it, knowing the clatter would hurt his ear. When she picked the receiver back up, he was still there.

"Hello, hello . . ."

"I'm here. I dropped the receiver, sorry," she lied with a pleased smile.

"James gave me your message earlier in the evening when I stopped by the sports bar after the game. I just got home. Is it too late to call?" Max asked.

"Yes," she answered, peevish, only barely restraining her urge to demand to know where the hell he'd been. The sports bar closed at eleven.

And then she found herself saying so, inwardly groaning at her stupidity. He'd probably gone to East St. Louis to one of the clubs there that stayed open to all hours of the morning.

His explanation was sorta worse. She was surprised he even voiced it.

"I drove Miranda home. She had car trouble."

"I see." Cute little Miranda Sherman. She saw, all right. More than she wanted to. Well, she didn't have any claim on Max. If he wanted to see teenagers it was none of her business.

"What were you calling about?" Max asked.

"I wanted to check and find out if you'd had any more contact from your stalker. Have there been any more notes or gifts? Any hang-up calls since you've been back?"

"No, it's been pretty quiet. I did get a couple of hang-up calls though."

"Well?" she said, waiting.

"Oh. Yeah, I pressed the star button to redial the number that had called me, but all I got was a ringing telephone."

"Keep trying if you get any more. Maybe next time we'll get lucky."

"How about you? Did you catch any bad guys tonight? James said you were working."

"Nope, I struck out, too."

"Did you listen to the game while you were working? It turned out to be a real squeaker."

Amy Jane wondered whether to acknowledge that she had indeed listened to the game. It would be giving away her interest. "I heard," she finally said, noncommittal.

"What were you working on last night? Something juicy like a cheating spouse? I bet you were out looking in windows, weren't you?"

"I was not!"

"Can I go along next time?"

"I do not go around peeking in people's windows," she claimed, indignant.

Max laughed, obviously delighted at having riled her. "Aw, come on, Amy Jane, why else would someone become a private eye unless they were nosy."

"To help people," she insisted. "Good night, Max. I'm going to sleep and I'd advise you to do the same," she said, hanging up.

A second after she'd hung up on him, she realized he'd been tweaking her about having looked in his bedroom window.

Ticked, she redialed his number.

When he answered, she hung up, clueless about what to say.

He made her crazy.

A few seconds later her phone rang.

She reached to pick it up, then realized just in time he'd pressed that damn redial button. She let the phone ring and ring.

And she smiled. Maybe Max wouldn't sleep so easily after all. It served him right.

The problem was, she didn't fall asleep so easily either.

What, if anything, had been the import of his taking Miranda Sherman home? Miranda was very open about her interest in Max. Had her car trouble been Miranda's play for Max? And if so, had Max . . . ?

She got up to see if there was any Swiss almond ice cream in the freezer.

David Letterman and ice cream.

She had to get a life, she thought as she stood in the freezer light in the dark kitchen, eating from the carton by the spoonful.

The following evening found Max listening to the last speaker at a charity function before the Lions game. The function was held at the Missouri Athletic Club. The historic club was a throwback to the time when men were men . . . and women were at home where they belonged.

It now had a few women members, because the club had been forced to change with the times. Yet the place still retained its old boys' club atmosphere. There was dark paneling on the walls, and real paintings, and it was furnished with good, bulky furniture.

He looked down the dais. All the men looked properly important and at home. Chantal looked anything but. He could just imagine what she thought about this old boys' club.

Her opinion would no doubt be mirrored by Amy Jane's.

Finally the speaker finished and the function began to break up as everyone left to go to the game at the Dome. Max's plan for a quick getaway was scotched by a talkative CEO.

* * *

Now, for the first time...

You can find Janelle Taylor, Shannon Drake, Rosanne Bittner, Sylvie Sommerfield, Penelope Neri, Phoebe Conn, Bobbi Smith, and the rest of today's most popular, bestselling authors

...All in one brand-new club!

Introducing KENSINGTON CHOICE, the new Zebra/Pinnacle service that delivers the best new historical romances direct to your home, at a significant discount off the publisher's prices.

As your introduction, we invite you to accept 4 FREE BOOKS worth up to $23.96

details inside...

We've got your authors!

If you seek out the latest historical romances by today's bestselling authors, our new reader's service, KENSINGTON CHOICE, is the club for you.

KENSINGTON CHOICE is the only club where you can find authors like Janelle Taylor, Shannon Drake, Rosanne Bittner, Sylvie Sommerfield, Penelope Neri and Phoebe Conn all in one place…

…and the only service that will deliver their romances direct to your home as soon as they are published—even before they reach the bookstores.

KENSINGTON CHOICE is also the only service that will give you a substantial guaranteed discount off the publisher's prices on every one of those romances.

That's right: Every month, the Editors at Zebra and Pinnacle select four of the newest novels by our bestselling authors and rush them straight to you, even *before they reach the bookstores*. The publisher's prices for these romances range from $4.99 to $5.99—but they are always yours for the guaranteed low price of just *$3.95!*

That means you'll always save over $1.00…often as much as *$2.00*…off the publisher's prices on every new novel you get from KENSINGTON CHOICE!

All books are sent on a 10-day free examination basis, and there is no minimum number of books to buy. (A postage and handling charge of $1.50 is added to each shipment.)

As your introduction to the convenience and value of this new service, we invite you to accept

4 BOOKS FREE

The 4 books, worth up to $23.96, are our welcoming gift. You pay only $1 to help cover postage and handling.

To start your subscription to KENSINGTON CHOICE and receive your introductory package of 4 FREE romances, detach and mail the postpaid card at right *today*.

We have 4 FREE BOOKS for you as your introduction to KENSINGTON CHOICE

To get your FREE BOOKS, worth up to $23.96, mail card below.

FREE BOOK CERTIFICATE

As my introduction to your new KENSINGTON CHOICE reader's service, please send me 4 FREE historical romances (worth up to $23.96), billing me just $1 to help cover postage and handling. As a KENSINGTON CHOICE subscriber, I will then receive 4 brand-new romances to preview each month for 10 days FREE. I can return any books I decide not to keep and owe nothing. The publisher's prices for the KENSINGTON CHOICE romances range from $4.99 to $5.99, but as a subscriber I will be entitled to get them for just $3.95 per book. There is no minimum number of books to buy, and I can cancel my subscription at any time. A $1.50 postage and handling charge is added to each shipment.

Name _____

Address _____ Apt. # _____

City _____ State _____ Zip _____

Telephone (_____) _____

Signature _____

(If under 18, parent or guardian must sign)

Subscription subject to acceptance

KC 0994

We have
4
FREE
Historical
Romances
for you!

Details inside!

Amy Jane sat at the Dome watching the Lions play the Red Wings and wondering why Max wasn't in the broadcast booth.

She had made the trip up several times, but only Corey and Chantal were working.

Why would Max miss announcing an important game like the playoffs? She'd asked, but neither Corey nor Chantal knew where Max was. The last they'd seen of him had been at the Missouri Athletic Club where all three had been attending a charity function.

Was he with Miranda? Surely he wouldn't do something that foolish. No, this was too important a game.

Had something happened to him? Had his stalker moved from making threats to taking action—or hired someone to harm him . . .

"Did you see that?" Claire asked, jumping up.

"What?" Amy Jane asked, standing.

"Aren't you paying attention to the game? That bruiser on the Red Wings team blasted Bobby from behind, driving him headfirst into the boards. See, he just got a two-minute penalty against him."

Amy Jane tried to pay attention to the game as they sat back down, watching Bobby get set for a power-play goal. But she couldn't seem to keep her mind on the game or her eyes on the ice.

Where was Max?

Unable to sit still, she got up from her seat.

"Where are you going now?" Claire asked, dragging her eyes from the ice.

"I'm going to check the broadcast booth again to see if Max has shown up."

"Bring me a Coke on your way back," Claire requested, her gaze drawn back to center ice as a fight broke out.

The place was pretty much cleared out by the time Max had disentangled himself from the CEO, whose son played hockey.

As he stepped into the empty elevator, Max glanced at his watch. He barely had time to make it to the Dome and the broadcast booth before the game was scheduled to start. If he hit traffic, he would be in trouble.

He punched the button to go down from the main dining room to the entry level of the club and the elevator doors swished shut. The elevator began its whooshing descent, then suddenly clunked to an abrupt halt.

Damn.

He looked at the button panel and began jabbing the button for the floor he wanted, hoping the button was plain stuck. But the elevator car didn't move. It didn't even shudder. Nothing.

Max jabbed the red emergency button, but the alarm didn't ring. He jabbed it again. And again.

He picked up the emergency phone, but it

was dead. Great. He was going to be late for the game now for sure.

Though he tried every avenue available, the elevator refused to budge and no one came to his aid. He really hated things he couldn't control.

By the time the elevator started to move again hours later, he was annoyed, hot, and had missed announcing the playoff game.

When the car stopped at the lobby, he'd expected to see a maintenance man. But there was no one there. The elevator had evidently come unstuck by itself.

Max made his way to his car parked in the parking garage across the street from the club.

As he drove out of the parking space, he turned on the radio. It was already tuned to the station carrying the Lions game.

"McQuaid blasts one over the goalie's left shoulder and scores his second goal of the night making the score three to one here in the final minutes of the third period!"

"Looks like the Lions are going back to Joe Louis Stadium with a three-games-to-one winning advantage playing against the Red Wings. Richie Allen has played just an incredible game defending at goal while fighting off a bad case of the flu."

Max frowned as he listened to Corey Cohen and Chantal Perry announce the game like they'd been doing it together for years. If he'd needed a reminder of how expendable he was, he had it.

For the first time he wondered about the stuck elevator. Had it only been happenstance?

Or was it something much more sinister?

Twelve

"Where the hell were you tonight?" James Chadwick asked as Max and Amy Jane entered the sports bar with the rest of the hockey fans bent on celebrating the Lions victory.

"I got stuck in an elevator," Max explained.

"With Sweet?" he inquired on a wink.

"No, I was at the game," Amy Jane said, "with Claire."

"I'm hot and thirsty," Max complained. "I thought I was never going to get out of the elevator. I was beginning to see my life flash before me."

"Well, I can do something about the thirsty . . ." Uncle James said. "As to the hot—"

"Just send us over a pitcher of beer," Amy Jane said, shooting him a silencing look.

Uncle James just laughed at her attempt at being stern.

"Where is Claire?" Uncle James asked.

"She'll be here. She was waiting for Bobby to change."

"Yeah, the whole world's waiting for Bobby to change but I'm afraid he's gonna be a hothead anyway," Uncle James mumbled. "I can't believe she's still involved with him. He isn't her type at all."

"She says he is," Amy Jane countered. "Guess it's just bad luck he happened to ask her out."

Uncle James exchanged a look with Max that didn't go unnoticed by Amy Jane. She waited, however, to follow up on it until they'd slid into a booth in the back of the sports bar.

"What was that about?"

"What?" Max asked, trying to pretend he didn't know what she meant.

"The look."

"There was no look."

"You know I'm not going to give up until you tell me what you and Uncle James are hiding. What was that look the two of you exchanged about?"

"I can't imagine why your uncle calls you Sweet. You aren't at all, you know."

"Quit stalling—"

"I don't think I ought to tell you this . . ."

"Tell me anyway."

"Well if you must know, you were Bobby's first choice," Max said, laughing.

"That isn't funny."

"Says who . . . ?" Max asked, continuing to laugh until Amy Jane threatened to uncap the ketchup bottle in her hand and chuck the contents at him.

"Put it down, I'll tell you. I've had enough

trauma for one night. What happened was that your Uncle James mentioned he had two nieces one night. Bobby said he was sure he could get a date with one of you. We discouraged him from even trying to ask you out."

"Why?" Amy Jane interrupted—not that she'd have gone out with Bobby, but every girl likes to be asked.

"Because we told him it wouldn't be good for his health. That you were the princess of high sticking."

"Oh great, you make it sound like any man should be afraid of me."

"I'm afraid of you."

"Is that why you're here with me?"

"I'm here with you because I'm brave. I want us to begin publicly dating."

"We've already been over this. I told you before that I don't date clients."

"I know. I know," Max said, putting up his hands in defense. "I think you should make an exception in this case."

Miranda brought over a pitcher of beer. "Would you like a burger or something?" she asked Max.

"A burger sounds good. How about you, Amy Jane?"

"Okay, I want onions on mine."

"That's not an auspicious way to begin dating," Max said when Miranda left them. *"Onions—"*

"What? I like onions. Ask Uncle James if you don't believe me."

Max buried his head in his hands. Finally he looked back up at her. "Why are you so tough?"

She wasn't tough. She was a marshmallow. Okay, so maybe she was a slightly stale marshmallow on the tough side. "Maybe you just don't like dealing with a woman instead of a girl."

"Look, can't you at least pretend you like me? I've had about enough of my anonymous fan. It's making me lose my concentration. Besides giving me the creeps, I've been blowing calls at the home games, if you haven't noticed. And I'm getting paranoid. I don't even know if the stalled elevator was a fluke or something else. I figure if we dated openly, with you pretending you liked me a *lot* maybe we could flush out this fan."

"You could also be setting off something dangerous, you know," Amy Jane explained.

"I don't care. I just want it to be over. I want to know."

"You're sure about this?"

Max nodded.

"Okay, we're a couple. But it's just pretend, understand? I don't want anyone getting confused here about what's going on."

"I'm not confused."

Amy Jane was glad someone wasn't, 'cause she sure as hell was. Her feelings about Max ran the gamut, all the way from protective to predatory. Her feelings were all a jumble. She wasn't in control of any of her emotions; not the least of what she felt she knew was pure old-fashioned lust.

Like right now. He was a little pale and disheveled. She wanted to kiss him and make it better. He looked so appealing . . . Had she just moaned out loud?

"What?" he asked, watching her study him.

"Even if I didn't have a rule about not getting involved with a client, it wouldn't work between us, you know. You're all wrong for me."

"I'm all wrong for you—" he repeated.

"You're a Capricorn and I'm a Virgo," she stated as if that made perfect sense.

"You can't be serious. You don't really believe that stuff, do you?" he asked, as Miranda brought their burgers, then left when another table waved a five-dollar bill.

"Of course, I'm serious. You're a Capricorn and I'm a Virgo. We'd bore each other to death."

"Maybe. If I were a Capricorn. But I'm not."

"I thought you said your birthday was in ten months."

"I lied."

"You lied."

He nodded, picking up his burger and taking a man-sized bite. He let her digest that fact while he chewed and swallowed.

"So when is your birthday?"

"Next week."

"Then you're a—"

"Taurus."

He didn't have to look so smug. A goat, a bull. There wasn't much difference. One was stubborn, one was, ah, bull-headed.

"That's right, I'm bull-headed," he said, as if he were reading her mind.

"Domineering," she said, substituting a better word.

"So when's my party?" he asked, stealing one of her onions.

She slapped his hand. "What party?" she asked around a bite of her burger.

"You told everyone you were throwing me a surprise birthday party. I think you ought to do it. It would aid the charade that we're an item, don't you think?"

"I suppose. I'll talk to Claire about it. She's good at parties and stuff. It could be fun."

"And you thought our signs weren't right," he kidded. "This could be quite interesting. There's nothing more stubborn than a virgin and a bull."

"I didn't say I was—"

"Your sign . . ." Max explained.

"Oh." She felt herself blushing.

"Why don't you tell me a little bit about yourself?" Max asked.

"No, you," she countered, playing with the lettuce that had been on her hamburger. "How come a cute guy like you isn't married?"

"You think I'm cute?" he asked, brightening.

"You know what I mean." Here it came, the

answer; he lived with his mother, had an addiction to something or . . . liked to dress up in bustiers and . . .

"Yeah, you mean you think I have a problem making a commitment. Isn't that what you're saying?"

"Well, you're, what, thirty-fiveish?"

"I could ask you the same question."

"I'm not thirty-five."

"But you're around thirty." He grinned announcing his zinger. "That's like forty in men years, isn't it?"

"Oh, please, you don't buy into that 'men age more gracefully' nonsense, do you? That rumor was started by a male-dominated communications system."

"What, were you born a feminist? Did you come out asking why your doctor wasn't a woman?"

"No. But I'm told I was complaining," Amy Jane answered. "My father always said you could hear me screaming in three counties."

"I'll keep that in mind."

She kicked him under the table.

"Ouch!"

Amy Jane smiled innocently. "You still haven't answered my question," she prodded.

"You tell me. Why do you think I'm not married."

"No woman would have you?" she offered way too readily.

She saw the thought of kicking her under the

table flash across his eyes. His manners saved her.

"Okay, you want the truth; I haven't found a woman who satisfies all my needs."

Oh, great. They were already talking about . . . that. She gritted her teeth and plunged ahead anyway, ever impulsive and curious. "What needs?"

"You are nosy, aren't you?"

"I believe 'curious' is the better word."

"Right. Okay, my needs. I need someone with a sense of humor."

"Why, because you don't have one?"

"Of course not. I have a perfectly good one. I just think a sense of humor is a really important ingredient in a great relationship. You can get through a lot if you can laugh with someone."

"Yeah, yeah." It was really annoying that he had a priority that matched hers. "What else?"

"Well, I've been busy building my career."

"There's more to life than work." There had to be; so far she wasn't sure exactly what it was, though. Work was what had sustained her through her parents' death. It just wasn't sustaining her in the manner to which she'd like to become accustomed. Like paying for someone else at the bed and breakfast to dust and polish the silver so she wouldn't have to. Yech. It must have been a man who invented housework.

It was that old hunter/gatherer thing. We hunt it, you clean it. We build it, you clean it.

"You know what I think?" Amy Jane said. "I think men are spoiled. They don't want to lose their girlfriend, but they don't want to marry her either because if a better girl comes along, they can't date her. See, if marriage included dating privileges, men would marry like that." She snapped her fingers.

Max set down his mug of beer and smiled. "You've given this a lot of thought, haven't you?"

"No. It doesn't require any thought to realize men want variety. Hence the remote control. I rest my case," she said, triumphant.

"No, men want to be entertained. If they find something entertaining, they stop and stay with it."

She smiled and nodded, graciously conceding him his point, and maybe even victory. After all she wasn't unaware she had entertainment value.

"Hey, Armstrong, you're still alive. What happened, did you get stuck in traffic?" Bobby asked, when he and Claire had jostled their way through the crowd to their booth.

Max got up and slid in next to Amy Jane, offering Claire and Bobby the other side of the booth.

"I got hung up in an elevator," Max explained when they were all settled.

"I bet that was a bummer," Bobby said, not looking very sympathetic.

"So that's where you were," Claire said. "Amy Jane was looking for you all night. I don't think she saw much of the game. She kept popping up and down to the broadcast booth to check on you."

Max put his arm around Amy Jane and squeezed her to his side, taking full advantage. "It's good to know someone was concerned about me," he said, smiling at her.

"Want to come with me to the ladies' room, Claire?" Amy Jane asked, as Miranda came up to take their order.

"Do I? The line at the Dome was at least a mile long and hardly moving."

"We can only hope that one of these days a woman architect designs a sports facility so there will be more ladies' rooms," Amy Jane said, as the two women scooted out of the booth.

"Would you like something?" Miranda asked, as they stood.

"Why don't you order for me, Bobby," Claire suggested, then joined Amy Jane.

Miranda looked like she would have lingered to chat, but Chantal stopped by the booth to congratulate Bobby on his goals.

"Did you hear that?" Bobby said, looking from Chantal to Max. "She complimented my playing. Did you ever think of trying that?"

Max took a swallow of his beer, and set the mug down. "I say so, when you play well, as you apparently did tonight. I even say so, when you try and it doesn't work out. It's only when you're willing to settle for a tie over a win, or screw up showboating that I call you on it."

"Yeah, well, I think we're going all the way in the playoffs," Bobby boasted.

"I must say I agree with you, Bobby," Chantal said. "I think the team is psychologically and emotionally ready to win. Don't you, Max?"

"They're proving they can handle the pressure." He glanced at Bobby. "I think they'll do all right as long as they don't start reading the morning papers looking for glory."

"Corey said you were trapped in an elevator. What happened?" Chantal asked, steering the conversation away from hockey.

"Yeah, I guess it was just one of those fluky things, though I was in there so long, I was beginning to see my life flash before my eyes."

"You're lucky it didn't crash or anything," Bobby said, pouring another mug of beer from the pitcher he'd ordered.

"Yeah, guess so. By the way, Chantal, I caught the tail end of the game on my car radio on the way over. You did a great job."

"Yeah, I know. Corey made it easy for me."

"Really? That's never been my experience working with him," Max commented.

"Maybe if you had better legs," Bobby said, not realizing he'd insulted both of them.

Claire and Amy Jane stood in front of the mirror in the ladies' room. Claire was reapplying her makeup while Amy Jane looked on.

Claire applied a dab of perfume to her wrists. The scent of hyacinth teased Amy Jane's nose.

"You're wearing Mother's scent," she observed.

Claire smiled. "It makes me feel closer to her when I wear it, especially in the spring. Remember how she'd be almost giddy every fall planting hundreds of bulbs like some demented squirrel burying nuts for winter."

"I cried the first time the hyacinths came up after the accident, and then I cried with the daffodils, and the narcissus and the lilies."

"Stop, or you'll ruin my mascara," Claire sniffed, brushing the moisture from the corner of her eye. "Mother used say the bulbs were like ugly ducklings that flowered into great beauties."

"I used to always think I was the point of that story. I'm still waiting to flower."

"Oh stop, Amy Jane. You're beautiful."

"You're my sister. You have to say that."

"No, I don't. Besides, Max thinks you're beautiful, so there."

"Wherever did you get such an idea?"

"Bobby told me."

"Do you remember the year we helped plant the tulips, and we planted them upside down?" Amy Jane said, avoiding the subject of what Max thought of her.

Claire giggled. "Yes, Daddy banned us from the planting for a year."

"Yeah, but he gave us back the job the following year because he hated helping Mother put those smelly mothballs in the holes to keep the rodents away from the bulbs.

"Bobby really told you Max said that?" Amy Jane blurted.

"He really did."

"He probably just made it up to embarrass both of us," Amy Jane frowned, looking at her hair in the mirror. It was a dark cloud around her face. "Why won't my hair get the message that straight hair is in."

"The same reason mine wouldn't get the message curly hair was in when it was. We are what's in our genes."

"Heavens, what a thought. You know grease-paint is in our genes . . . that and ostrich feathers, and togas, and beards and wigs . . ."

"I don't think they ever got over our not wanting to follow in their footsteps. I think they thought there was a mixup at the hospital, sometimes," Claire said. "Not you so much, because you're just like Uncle James. I was really the odd one."

"You were the most like them. You always played pretend with your dolls."

"Remember the great parties they used to throw? They were grand."

"And why we're broke," Amy Jane said sardonically.

"I miss the parties. The after-theater parties that didn't start until after midnight and ran sometimes until dawn. I loved watching Mother get dressed. She'd wear these," Claire touched the pearls at her neck.

Amy Jane smiled. "I remember the noises and the smells from the kitchen," she said, closing her eyes to travel there for a brief moment.

"And flowers, there would always be the vases of fresh flowers."

Amy Jane's eyes popped open. "Let's have one," she said, excited.

"What?" Claire asked, putting her makeup back into her paisley makeup bag.

"A party. Let's have a party."

"What kind of party?"

"A birthday party. A surprise birthday party."

"For who?" Claire asked, trying to keep up.

"Max, of course."

Back at the Chadwick Bed and Breakfast after the sports bar had closed down, Max and Amy Jane sat on the porch swing on the veranda.

"I think I'm too old for this," Max said as the porch swing creaked back and forth.

"Too old for what?"

"Courting on a porch swing. I feel like your daddy is going to come out any moment and tell me it's time I went home."

Amy Jane laughed. "My father wasn't like that. He would have been out here regaling you with stories until you went home to escape. Speaking of which, if Bobby doesn't come out soon, I'm going to have to go in and clear my throat."

"Oh, a protective big sister, are we?"

"Claire's . . ."

"I know."

"What I don't know is what she sees in Bobby McQuaid," Amy Jane whispered.

"Opposites attract?" Max offered.

The sound of the front door opening silenced their discussion as Bobby came outside.

"Time to be going," he said, pausing on the veranda. "Tomorrow's a travel day. I have to rest up for the game. How about you Max, you coming?"

"Nah, I've got a later bedtime. I'll see you at the airport tomorrow. Good night."

Dismissed, Bobby left.

"Max, just a reminder . . . we're not courting."

"I know. It was only an expression. This place kind of reminds me of the place where I grew up. Not the estate; it's much more grand than the farm I grew up on. But the quiet night sounds and the clear starry skies are the same. My parents don't farm the land anymore, but they still live in the farmhouse."

"I bet they're proud of you."

Max sighed. "I guess. It was tough for a while when they found out I had no interest in farming. That I planned to move to the big city. Since I didn't have any brothers or sisters, I'm their one hope for grandchildren and I haven't given them much encouragement there, either."

"Do you see your parents often?"

"No. I go home for the holidays, of course. But other than that I keep in touch by phone."

"It must be lonely for them."

"Not really. They have each other. Theirs is a really good marriage. They loved me, but they didn't need me."

"Our parents were like that too, very self-contained. I think that's healthy."

"I do share one guilty little secret with mine, though," Max said, stretching.

"What's that?" Amy Jane asked, feeling around with her feet on the veranda for the shoes she'd slipped off when she'd made herself comfortable.

"I like staying home. Maybe it's because I travel so much for my job. But there's nothing better to me than an evening in. No plans."

"Me, too," Amy Jane said. "I love staying home. I'm sure Uncle James would disown me if he heard me say that. I don't think he's ever stayed home a night in his entire life."

"What do you do when you stay in?" Max asked. "Are you working or zoning out?"

"Zoning, what else? Well, I might do my nails or something. But generally I like to do nothing."

"I bet that goes over real big with Claire," Max said on a rich laugh.

"You got that right. She thinks I'm lazy. What do you do when you stay in?"

"I order in, for starters. Then I set my Jacuzzi for coma."

"Ummm . . . that sounds like heaven."

"It is."

"But I'm too lazy to order in, even. If Claire doesn't have something in the fridge, I'll even settle for stale donuts."

"I'm surprised Claire would have a stale donut on the premises, she's such a great cook."

"We get them day-old from the bakery to feed the raccoons and foxes."

"How lovely. Hypoglycemic wildlife," Max said, lending her a hand out of the porch swing after he got up.

Instead of releasing her hand, he pulled her into his arms.

"What are you doing?" she demanded, putting her hands on his chest to push him away.

"Hush," he whispered, nuzzling her ear. "Claire's at the door. I don't want her to get the wrong idea."

"Neither do I," Amy Jane muttered, trying to keep the quaver out of her voice as he continued to nuzzle along her neck.

Max's soft laugh was ragged. His hands moved to cup her face.

Amy Jane shivered at the gentleness in his touch, his caress of her as if she were fragile. She'd never thought of herself as fragile. Claire was the fragile, delicate one. She was strong.

He lowered his head, taking her breath away with his kiss.

She felt her body clench at the probe of his tongue against her lips. His tongue was hot, seductive and insistent.

She melted.

A moan escaped her lips as he increased the tempo, pressure of the kiss.

Her eyes were closed. His scent intensified, imprinting itself upon her memory. Electricity trailed off his fingertips as he moved his hand to caress her neck; to tilt her head back further for his exploring and passionate kiss.

They embraced in a sensual rhythm.

Amy Jane forgot that the kiss was for Claire's benefit. Forgot Claire was watching. She was lost in the intimacy of the kiss.

Claire opened the door and came out onto the veranda. "Excuse me, I just wanted to tell you I was going up to bed," she said, as the two of them broke apart.

"I'm coming up, too, in a minute," Amy Jane said, her voice sounding strange to her ears.

"Yeah, I've got to be leaving. Tomorrow is a travel day, so I need to get a good night's sleep. I never sleep as well on the road. And if the Lions win, I won't get much sleep at all, I'm sure," Max said, wordy, as though he was as disconcerted as she was after that kiss.

"We'll be watching the game on television, won't we?" Claire said, looking to Amy Jane.

Amy Jane nodded, and Claire went back inside.

"I guess I should be going," Max said, waiting.

"Right. Good night." Amy Jane turned and fled inside.

Thirteen

Up at the crack of 10:00 A.M., Amy Jane threw on an oversized T-shirt that read "I'm out of bed and dressed, what more do you want?" and snuck downstairs to the library for the morning newspaper.

She hadn't heard Claire about, she realized, as she headed back upstairs with the newspaper in hand. Maybe her sister had succumbed to sleeping in, for a change. No, on second thought, if the newspaper was in the house, then Claire had to be up somewhere. No doubt, quietly drawing up a list of chores for her. Amy Jane quickened her steps to her room, crept inside and closed the door softly.

The covers she crawled under were still warm. She made a quick survey of the sports page of the newspaper, to read about the Lions game, then turned to her horoscope and read:

> The sun and moon tryst
> in your fifth house
> governing romance. Expect
> to be surprised.

"Oh, sure, now you tell me," Amy Jane mumbled, tossing the paper on the floor beside her bed. She reached down for her purse, upending it on the bed. Searching through the dumped contents on the bed, she located the small daily calendar where she kept her daily appointments jotted down.

She wanted something to do, anything to do.

Her reason was twofold: one, she wanted with good conscience to escape Claire's chore list; and two, she wanted to keep her mind busy and off last night and Max's good-night kiss.

The kiss he'd staged for Claire's benefit.

She didn't want to wonder what she'd do if she were confronted with the real thing. Max was a good kisser. Truthfully, he was a great kisser . . . even when he didn't mean it.

She had quite liked being kissed by him. And that was the trouble—what worried her. So far, she hadn't been able to find anything wrong with Max.

It wasn't that there wasn't anything wrong. She was confident that something was wrong. She just hadn't found out what it was yet. It was necessary she keep reminding herself of that fact. It would be all too easy to let down her guard.

She flipped through the calendar pages to discover she hadn't any appointments, not one lousy one. She gathered the contents of her purse and replaced them while trying to think. There had to be something to get her out of the house. She reviewed the stuff she had pending on two insurance cases; nothing.

Max.

What about his case? Was there anything she could follow up on there? Not much.

The only new developments there, were a stuck elevator and a suspicious fan named Snoozy. It was hard to think of someone named Snoozy as threatening. She'd probably made Max too paranoid. But the stuck elevator had possibilities.

She'd go check on that.

A course of action decided, she threw back the covers and went to her chest of drawers for clean underwear before she headed for the shower.

The drawer was almost empty. She'd have to start picking up the piles of clothes scattered around the room and throw them down the laundry chute later.

When she selected her last clean bra, it revealed the gun lying beneath it. It was her gun from when she'd been a cop. The gun she'd learned to shoot with.

She picked it up. It was a silver, .38-caliber Charter Arms revolver. It didn't feel comfortable in her hand. She didn't like guns—didn't like living in a society that could only seem to find its self-esteem in a piece of cold steel.

She placed the snub-nosed gun back in her drawer, out of sight beneath her panties, then went to see if the coast was clear to take her shower.

A half hour later she was on her way to the

Missouri Athletic Club, having successfully cir-
cumvented Claire and her chore list. The traffic
on highway 44 was light, making her drive a
quick one. After parking next door to the club
in the parking garage, she crossed the street and
entered the club determined to bluff her way
into the elevator, while trying to look incon-
spicuous in the crowd of lunching males.

She'd found that if you looked like you knew
what you were doing and where you were going,
people seldom questioned you. Her plan worked
pretty well—she was only questioned once and
allowed past with her explanation of meeting
her uncle for lunch.

Finally reaching the elevator, she got on. What
she needed was a few minutes alone, but it took
several rides up and down until she became the
only passenger in the car. She acted quickly then
to stop the elevator between floors.

Opening her purse, she withdrew the screw-
driver she'd brought along to open the button
panel and check out the electrical guts of the
elevator. It would be easy enough to see if it
had been tampered with.

To see if Max had been trapped in the car
deliberately or if it was a fluke as Max wanted
to believe.

It didn't take her long to discover that Max
was wrong.

It hadn't been a fluke at all. Someone had
been at work on the panel's wiring, and they

hadn't yet come back to rewire away the evidence of their handiwork.

The emergency phone wire was disconnected, as was the alarm. She'd bet money the elevator's system had been rewired, to match a new code. The reason why was simple. Someone had coded it to match a remote-control device, using the remote to stop, then restart, the elevator.

Someone who'd wanted to scare Max, or at least give him pause.

She didn't think she'd tell Max what she'd found out. It was better for him to continue thinking it was a fluke. As it was, he'd said his concentration was suffering at the hockey games. He couldn't afford to be distracted any more than necessary during the playoffs.

She restarted the elevator once she had the panel back in place and rode it up to the fifth floor where the gym and swimming pool were.

Because she knew she wasn't supposed to.

The elevator doors whooshed open softly and she peeked out. It was disappointingly empty. There'd been no one to shock. Oh well, she thought, pushing the button to descend to the entry level, she'd gotten what she'd come for.

She'd validated her gut feeling that whoever was stalking Max was perfectly willing to act on her threats—had begun to, in fact.

It was important to Amy Jane to try to find the woman before she got any more daring.

Before Max got hurt.

* * *

Max finished studying his notes for the next game of the playoffs. He'd spoken to the coach and knew the bench. The team was healthy, with only one player on the injury list. Even though he had a great memory, Max always did his research, his homework. He was always ready when he stepped into the broadcast booth. He never tried to wing it. Probably because he'd lucked into his job after his career-ending injury.

It still bothered him that he'd blown those calls a few games back. Corey couldn't wait to jump on him when he made mistakes. It wasn't wise to feed Corey an opportunity to criticize him on-air. It didn't take a clairvoyant to know Corey would have Chantal in the booth with him in a heartbeat, if he could arrange it.

He couldn't feed Corey any more opportunities like that. He'd told himself his lack of concentration was due to the creepy feeling of constantly being watched. And that was true. Of course, Amy Jane was the only one who knew about it besides himself.

He put his notes away. It was time to shower off the plane flight and go out to get something to eat.

While showering, he finally allowed himself to admit the truth he'd been hiding from; there was more than the stalker distracting him from his work.

Amy Jane was doing her fair share.

She'd gotten under his skin to the point that he'd used deceit last night to kiss her. It hadn't been a wise move. It had made him even more distracted. If he'd thought the kiss would satisfy his curiosity, he'd been wrong. It had instead whetted his appetite.

She was intelligent, funny and adventurous. And she had dangerous curves; he'd felt them pressed against him last night. He'd almost been glad to see Claire. Otherwise he might have made a fool of himself.

Might have kissed Amy Jane for no reason.

Other than he just plain wanted to.

Had to.

He wondered if his parents were doing something back home in the barn with chicken bones to insure they had grandchildren, because for the first time he found himself thinking about what it would be like to be married.

Max turned off the shower, toweled dry, dressed and left his hotel room with Amy Jane still on his mind.

She was the reason he didn't see the hotel room door ahead of him open—why he didn't stop, and ended up sprawled on the floor with a woman and a bucket of ice.

"Why don't you look where you're going, you—"

Kerry Ashton's mouth dropped open when she saw who'd upended her. "It's you!" she accused, brushing the ice cubes off herself.

"What are you doing here? I believe we've already played this scene," Max said, not bothering to help her up as he righted himself.

"What's going on?" Richie Allen asked as he and Bobby McQuaid came out of their hotel room.

"He, he—" Kerry sputtered, pointing at Max.

"Was just leaving," Max finished for her and did just that.

Richie helped Kerry up as Bobby stared after Max, who got on the elevator.

"What happened, honey?" Richie asked, concerned, "Are you all right?"

"I'm fine," Kerry sniffed, brushing his arm away. "Give me a minute to change and I'll join you in the lobby."

Kerry went to change while Richie finished picking up the ice cubes and ice bucket. When he looked puzzled about what to do with it, Bobby took it from him and set it next to the door to their room. "Maybe room service will stick a free bottle of champagne in it."

Richie, preoccupied, didn't crack a smile. "What do you suppose that was all about?" he asked.

"Well," Bobby said, throwing his arm across Richie's shoulders as they headed for the elevator to wait in the lobby for Kerry, "if you ask me . . . Kerry hates Max more than she likes you."

Kerry stomped around the hotel room kicking off her shoes and peeling out of her wet dress.

Max had a nerve.

He hadn't even had the courtesy to say he was sorry for plowing into her and ruining her dress. Hadn't offered to help her up.

She looked at herself in the mirror and cringed. Her face looked awful. It was red and blotchy from flushed embarrassment. Her mascara was smeared on her left eye. And her stocking had a prominent run.

It was going to take more than a few minutes to repair the damage Max had done.

"What's taking her so long, I'm hungry," Bobby complained, looking at his watch again.

"Maybe I'll just go up and check on her," Richie suggested, nervously.

"Yeah, why don't you do that, man? If it gets much later, we're going to have to call it breakfast. Tell her to get her rear in gear and let's go already."

"Be right back," Richie said, heading for the elevator while Bobby struck up a conversation with a stewardess he recognized from their flight out.

Back up on their floor, Richie knocked softly on the hotel room door.

"Honey, are you almost ready? Bobby's starved."

"So am I," he heard her answer. "Come on in. I'm ready," Kerry called.

Richie opened the door.

"It's her," Max said, nudging Amy Jane, a look of surprise on his face. "I thought your name was Snoozy," Max said to the blonde.

"You two know each other?" Lance asked, not looking real pleased.

"No, he just signed my jacket like the rest of the guys," Victoria explained. Then turning back to Max, she said, "My name is Victoria. I had you sign my jacket to Snoozy because it's for my little sister. Her name is Snoozy. Well, her nickname is. She's crazy about hockey. The jacket is a present for her."

"How did you and Lance meet?" Amy Jane asked.

"We met when he signed the jacket," Victoria answered. "He was so sweet about it, and he gave me an eight-by-ten glossy of himself he autographed."

Lance blushed furiously and tugged her away, "Come on, let's go find the party."

"Well, that clears up that mystery," Max said, turning back to Amy Jane.

In the living room everyone was gathered around Tom Quinn as the coach expounded on the strengths and weaknesses of the Maple Leafs, the team the Lions would be playing next in the playoffs.

Finding a spot on the couch, Max sat down and pulled Amy Jane down onto his lap. "Have I told you how much I like your dress?" he whispered, his warm breath raising goose bumps along her arms.

"Okay, enough about hockey," Uncle James announced, interrupting. "This is a party."

"Does anyone want to play games?" Claire asked.

She was greeted with a chorus of *"No's."*

Uncle James switched on the stereo system. "Bobby, Lance, Richie . . . help move the furniture back against the walls so there's room to dance."

The strains of opera filled the room. It had been what Amy Jane had listened to late the night before when nerves over the party had kept her awake.

"We can't dance to that crap," Kerry complained. "Find something on the radio."

"What's this deal?" Bobby muttered to Richie as they moved the sofa back against the wall. "Chantal talks us into coming to Max's party, and then she has the nerve not to show up herself."

"Yeah, I'm going to give her some grief about it when I see her. She's the one who got Kerry all fired up about coming to the party."

"Look at Corey standing over by the window. He doesn't look any too pleased that Chantal hasn't shown, either. I know, let's go out to your car phone and try to reach her. If we have to be here for good public relations like she said, she has to be here, too."

Corey leaned against the wall, watching Max and resenting him. The guy didn't deserve his good fortune. He had a pretty girlfriend throwing a party for him, while Corey couldn't even get the girl he was interested in to show up for the party.

The radio disc jockey introduced a romantic ballad, and Corey made a snap decision to walk over and ask Max's girl to dance.

A look of surprise registered on Amy Jane's face when he asked her, but she allowed him to lead her out onto the makeshift dance floor.

Kerry, watching from the sidelines, was annoyed that Richie had disappeared somewhere with Bobby. Determined to gain attention, she walked over to Max.

"Looks like you lost your girl," she taunted.

"Go away."

"I think you should ask me to dance," she said, twirling around to show off her very short and sexy red dress.

"In your dreams," Max answered, turning away, dismissing her.

"You want me to make a scene?" she threatened, the tone of her voice telegraphing her intent to do just that if he didn't agree to dance with her.

"Let's dance," he said, deciding it was the wiser choice. He didn't want anyone ruining the party Claire had worked so hard to pull off.

Amy Jane felt an unreasonable flash of jealousy as she caught sight of Max dancing with Kerry. The smug smile Kerry flashed her didn't do anything to dispel her jealousy.

Corey was asking her something about the bed and breakfast when she saw Bobby and Richie enter the living room, and Richie make a beeline for Max and Kerry.

"Hey, leave her alone," Richie said, shoving Max.

"I'm dancing with Max," Kerry said. "You had something better to do," she sniffed at Richie. When Max would have released her, she snuggled closer.

"I said, leave her alone," Richie said, ignoring Kerry and spoiling for a fight.

"Go away, Richie. If you like Bobby so much, dance with him." Kerry was enjoying the male attention.

If Kerry meant to make Richie jealous, it worked.

Richie took a wild swing at Max.

Max stepped aside and the swing went wide. Just as Richie made to follow it with another swing, Tom Quinn and Uncle James stepped in to stop him.

"This is a party, not a street brawl. Be smart and save your energy for taking on the Maple Leafs," the coach said, holding Richie back.

"Didn't I hear something about birthday cake?" Uncle James said, nodding to Claire.

"Yes, you did. We're going to cut the cake in the dining room," Claire said, picking up on her cue to divert everyone's attention. "Let's light the candles so Max can make a wish for the Lions to destroy the Maple Leafs. Everyone, into the dining room." When no one moved, she coaxed, "The cake is chocolate, and we have homemade ice cream."

"I don't want any damn cake," Richie snarled, shrugging free of the coach's grip. He grabbed Kerry. "Come on. We're leaving."

Kerry didn't put up any argument. Richie led her out of the party.

The excitement over, everyone followed Claire into the dining room for cake and ice cream. When Claire had the candles lit, Max stood before the cake. "I'd like to thank all of you for helping me celebrate my birthday," he said, then proceeded to blow out all the candles. The wish he made had nothing to do with hockey.

Talk moved back to hockey as everyone sat around eating cake and ice cream. There was a lively argument about the woman goalie some of the pro teams were scouting. The conversation had just turned to the bruising defenseman the Maple Leafs had signed when Chantal arrived at the party looking anything but her usual well-put-together self. She looked like she'd been in a fight with a tiger, and lost.

"Chantal! Are you all right? What happened to you?" Claire cried, going to her.

"I'm okay. My car broke down a few miles from here. I tried to fix it but—"

"Here, come upstairs with me and I'll help you get cleaned up," Claire offered, grabbing Chantal's hand.

"Thanks," Chantal said with a weak smile,

shoving a limp strand of hair from her eyes and wiping at her dirt-smeared face.

"Amy Jane, why don't you put some music back on the stereo so everyone can dance," Claire instructed, as she led Chantal from the room.

Corey slipped unnoticed from the party to go try to find Chantal's car and see if he could repair it for her.

"Come on, I think it's time you danced with the birthday boy," Max said, taking Amy Jane's hand.

Amy Jane knew she was in deep trouble. It felt too comfortable in Max's arms. She had to bring reality back, and soon.

"Have you received any more notes, gifts or hang-up phone calls from your fan?" she asked, pulling her head from where she'd rested it so comfortably on Max's shoulder to look up at him.

"No, nothing. Maybe this party was all for nothing."

Amy Jane shook her head no. "Claire enjoyed putting it together. We haven't had any big parties in the house since our parents died. They used to have a lot of them. It's been good for us to do this. And anyway, with the mention in Berger's column about us being an item, we'll seal the impression that you aren't available for fantasies any longer."

Max winked at her. She'd swear he had.

"Oh, I don't know. I'm always available to some people—for some fantasies."

Chantal and Claire came back downstairs. Amy Jane broke away from Max to see if there was anything she could do to help.

"Where are you going?" he demanded, reluctant to let her go.

"I'm the hostess. I don't have time to enjoy myself. I have to help Claire make sure everyone has drinks and that they're enjoying the party."

Max's grin was full of conceit. "So you do admit, then, that you were enjoying yourself."

"I admit nothing," Amy Jane answered and flounced away.

"How about some cake and ice cream?" Amy Jane asked Chantal. "I don't know about you, but chocolate always makes me feel better."

"Sounds good," Chantal agreed. "Maybe while I'm eating it I can decide what to do about my car."

"I've already taken care of that," Corey said, coming inside on a draft of cool air.

"What are you talking about?" Chantal asked, as the three women turned to face him.

"Your starter has gone out. I called a tow truck to pick it up and tow it to a garage to have it fixed."

"They can fix a starter?" Amy Jane asked.

"No, they'll have to replace it."

"How much is a new starter?" Chantal asked, hesitantly.

"Don't worry. There'll be no charge. The garage owes me a favor," Corey assured her.

And now Chantal owed him one, Amy Jane

thought, as she handed Chantal a plate of cake and ice cream.

"I think the party went really well, don't you, Claire?" Amy Jane asked, as the last of the guests left. Only Uncle James, Bobby and Max were left for the clean-up crew.

Corey had given Chantal a ride home.

"Everyone seemed to have a good time," Claire agreed. "Except Bobby. I don't think he had any better time than Richie. We'd better get back out there before Bobby starts up with Max where Richie left off."

"Don't worry. Uncle James can handle them," Amy Jane assured her.

"I don't know. I don't think Bobby is any too thrilled I made him come to this party."

Amy Jane followed Claire back out to the living room carrying the cream and sugar for the coffee Claire had made.

"Who wants coffee?" Claire asked the silent room.

"I'll take some," Uncle James said while the two other men declined.

After pouring Uncle James a cup of coffee, Claire took a seat next to Bobby on the couch.

Uncle James sipped his coffee. "Good, as usual, Claire. I swear you're going to make some man a perfect wife."

"How come you never say that about me?" Amy Jane demanded to know.

"Because we all know you're going to drive some poor man crazy, unless he's as indulgent as I am."

"What happened to Miranda?" Claire asked, suddenly realizing she was no longer at the party.

"She had a headache and left with Corey and Chantal."

"Uncle James! She came with you, you should have driven her home."

"But I wasn't ready to leave yet. Besides, Corey offered, so I stayed."

"Well, I guess it goes without saying that you're never going to make someone a good husband," Bobby said, laughing.

"Well, you'd be lucky to get Claire. Though I have to admit I'm surprised I lost the bet," Uncle James said.

"What bet?" Claire asked, her eyes narrowing.

"Ah . . ."

"Uncle James—"

"Okay, I bet Bobby that he couldn't get you to go out with him."

"That's why you asked me out?" Claire said, turning to face Bobby.

His face gave away the truth.

"Get out!"

"Come on, Claire," Uncle James began, trying to make things better.

"And you can leave, too," Claire said, her eyes welling with tears, as she got up and raced upstairs to her room, slamming the door closed behind her.

"Well, I guess the party is over," Uncle James observed, looking guilty.

"I think it would be best if everyone left," Amy Jane agreed.

"Thanks for nothing," Bobby said to Uncle James as he followed him from the room.

"I didn't mean to—"

Uncle James's words were silenced by the kitchen door he closed behind him as he and Bobby left.

"This party certainly turned out to be a disaster," Amy Jane said, looking at Max.

"Don't be so hard on yourself. It's the best birthday party I've ever had."

"That would have to make it the only birthday party you've ever had," Amy Jane said glumly.

Max patted the sofa beside him. "Come here and sit down beside me. You've been so busy hostessing I haven't had a chance to spend any time with you all night."

"I'd better go up and check on Claire." She looked toward the staircase Claire had fled up when she'd found out Bobby had only gone out with her on a dare.

"Did you know about the dare?" she asked, turning back to him.

"I was there, yeah. You might say I saved you from a similar fate."

"I don't understand."

"Well, the original bet was that Bobby could

get either of you to go out with him. I told him not to even try with you."

"Why not."

" 'Cause I wanted you for myself. Now, come on over here. Claire will be fine. She didn't want to get mixed up with someone like Bobby McQuaid anyway. Uncle James did her a favor by letting her know. She's too good for Bobby by far."

Amy Jane gave in and went to sit beside him on the sofa.

"Have I told you how pretty you look in that dress?" Max said, putting his arm around her.

Amy Jane blushed, feeling herself grow hot under Max's close scrutiny.

"And your hair is different. You did something different with your hair, didn't you?"

"I put it up, that's all."

"I like it. It allows me to do this." He began kissing the side of her neck with tiny pecks that trailed up to the lobe of her ear. Her nerve endings went berserk. Her common sense was clearly about to take a long vacation, if she didn't do something about this immediately.

"I think I better clean up. Why don't you give me a hand," she said, jumping up from the sofa.

Max laughed. "Okay, we can clean up . . . first . . ."

He followed her into the dining room and helped her collect the dirty paper plates and plastic-ware. While she went out to the kitchen to get a plastic trash bag to stash the trash in, he used his finger to scoop off some chocolate icing from the cake. He was licking it off his finger when she returned.

"I caught you."

"Like you don't eat cake the same way," he countered, offering her a lick.

She surprised herself by spontaneously licking the chocolate from his finger.

"You missed a spot," Max said, wiping it on her neck and then slowly licking the speck of chocolate from her neck with his warm tongue.

"Don't do that," Amy Jane groaned, while her hormones clamored for more, more.

"Why not?" he asked, not stopping.

"Because you're a client. I told you I don't get involved with my clients. It isn't ethical."

"I'm not a client any longer. I'm firing you. I think my stalker has lost interest."

He scooped another finger of chocolate icing from the cake and offered it to her.

She gave in, licking it slowly, deliberately.

She looked up to find him grinning as he watched her.

"What?" she asked.

"I'm trying to figure out if it's me or the chocolate you like."

"I do like chocolate," she teased.

"Give me a try, plain," he suggested, pulling her close and lowering his lips to hers.

What started out friendly and teasing, soon turned hot and serious. The kiss escalated quickly and had her head spinning.

She pulled away. "What were you, captain of the debating team or something?" she asked, trying to regain her equilibrium. Trying to keep her emotions under control.

It would be so easy not to.

"What are you afraid of?" Max asked, as if he could read her mind.

"Myself," she answered truthfully. "I don't have a very good track record when it comes to picking out men who are good for me."

"I'd be good for you, real good. Trust me."

Amy Jane laughed. "Trust me? Does that line work for you often?"

"I don't use it often or ever. You're something very different in my life. I haven't ever met a woman like you before. You've got moxie."

"I've got what?"

"Moxie. You're a tough cookie, with a soft center. You don't cut me any slack, but you're up front with me. You tell me the truth. As a celebrity, that's a valuable quality to find in someone."

Her mouth was dry. How did she respond to what he was telling her? Did she give in to what they both wanted?

Did she believe him?

He didn't play fair. He kissed her again, and again, until she was weak, almost purring.

All she wanted to do was rub up against him. All she wanted was for him to stroke her.

"Trust me . . ." he whispered, coaxed again. His thumb caressed her pulse at her throat.

She arched against him, sliding her hands up his chest and clasping them around his neck. She lifted her lips, surrendering to desire.

"Amy Jane . . . have they all gone home?"

Claire's tearful voice sliced into the heated atmosphere between them, separating them.

Reason returned with her sister.

Sixteen

Max was dreaming about a wedding, as he slept late the following morning. He knew it was a wedding because the church bells kept ringing and ringing incessantly as he stood at the altar waiting for his bride, who had yet to show.

Annoyance at the church bells shoved him up several layers of deep sleep until he was tossing and fighting the sheets he'd become wrapped in.

He woke up with a start.

It wasn't church bells he'd heard, but the doorbell. Someone was on his front porch leaning on the damn bell, making it peal insistently.

"I'm coming, I'm coming," he mumbled, pulling on a pair of jeans and swearing when he stubbed his toe on the the doorjamb as he left the bedroom. He was entertaining thoughts of Amy Jane waiting for him with a changed mind, or at the very least her sister, Claire, sent with breakfast as a token that she still held him in some esteem, if not all that much.

He yanked open the door just as whoever was jabbing the doorbell stopped. The sudden silence was disconcerting, as was the person who stood on his porch.

It wasn't Amy Jane, or even Claire with her Little Red Riding Hood basket of goodies.

It was a deliveryman. Or rather a delivery kid. The kind you usually saw packing an aerosol spray can or heat. The kid had neither form of destruction in his hand, Max saw with some sense of relief. It was too beautiful a day to die.

"I was about to give up hope," the kid said, handing Max a clipboard with a paper attached that needed Max's signature.

"On a day like today?" Max said dryly. The wry remark sailed over the kid's head like a runaway balloon.

"You woke me . . ." Max tried again.

The kid nodded, bored and unconcerned.

Max studied the paper on the clipboard and then looked at the label on the package. "This doesn't say who the package is from. And I can't tell from the label because there isn't a return address."

The kid shrugged. "I don't know, dude. All I do is deliver. Maybe it's a surprise. If you don't want it, I can take it back."

Max knew he ought to have the kid do just that.

Packages without return addresses weren't a good sign.

If he accepted the package, Amy Jane would have his hide. She would be absolutely furious with him. What great incentive, he thought with a smile. He liked the way she looked when she got all heated up.

He signed for the package and gave the kid a nice tip. His manners wouldn't allow him to be as rude as the kid.

"Hey thanks, dude," the kid said, suddenly animated at the sight of the sizable tip. "You have a good day, hear?"

Max waved off the kid and carried the package back inside his condo.

After first listening to make sure the package wasn't ticking, he set it on the kitchen counter. Not certain whether to open it before he told Amy Jane about it, or to wait, he went to take his shower.

Amy Jane lay in bed thinking about the party. About what might have happened if Claire hadn't walked back downstairs to talk to her about what had happened between her and Bobby McQuaid.

Claire was bitter about Bobby's dating her on a bet. When Amy Jane had pointed out that Bobby was still dating her even after he'd technically won the bet, Claire had sniffed, and dismissed that as nothing more than Bobby going for a hat trick. Claire was a virgin and Bobby knew it. Since he hadn't slept with her, she was still a conquest for him to make.

It was the way athletes thought. You had to

rack up points, win the game. A draw or tie wasn't good for the same satisfaction.

Amy Jane was inclined to agree that Bobby was a rat. Agree with Max that Claire deserved far better.

She knew that what Claire was bemoaning had more to do with her sister's pride being in shreds than with her heart being broken.

Claire wanted to be married. Had wanted it since she'd seen her first bride doll. She pored over bridal magazines. Kept a file on wedding cakes and dresses. She romanticized what marriage would be.

To Claire it would be a soft cotton cocoon to buffer the world's hard knocks. A husband would support and cherish her. Claire's vision of marriage was as idealized as a diamond commercial.

Amy Jane, on the other hand, took a jaundiced view of marriage. She was a realist who didn't want to fit into a standardized ideal relationship. She wanted a relationship customized to fit her . . . or she didn't want one at all.

And last night she'd almost let herself be ruled by lust.

Lust had the worst judgment of all—the drunken sailor on shore leave of all the emotions.

But who could blame her when lust came courting dressed in Max's strong hands and supple lips. She wasn't the sort to wallow in guilt or recrimination. Instead she planned to celebrate escaping a close call. Because she was certain once she drew Max's fire into her depths, the blaze would be too hot to deny . . . too body-satisfyingly warm.

All her good intentions would be toast.

She needed to think as well as feel.

So the deal was, what did she think?

She thought she should tell Max that his stalker hadn't lost interest. That the elevator had been tampered with and it was just a matter of time until she decided to act.

He needed to remain on guard.

She needed to remain on guard for him.

And he would continue to be her client, and therefore he would be off limits to any personal relationship.

If either of them allowed themselves to be lulled into complacency, it would put Max in danger.

A warm breeze flipped the pages of a magazine she'd left lying on the floor. It stirred Amy Jane to leave her warm bed.

A soft clink sounded when she stepped out of bed naked. Amy Jane smiled down at the silver bangle bracelets she wore that had made the noise. Wearing nothing but the bracelets to bed was a guilty pleasure of hers; it made her feel wanton. She wondered what Max would make of that.

She slipped the bracelets off and laid them on the nightstand, then searched out a jersey tunic with a hood. She pulled it on before going to lean out the window. The secluded acreage of the Chadwick estate was bathed in brilliant sunshine. It had a grand country-house vista. The stonework and sweeping lawn setting off the Cotswold-style house could have come from a Katherine Hepburn movie.

It was the kind of glorious day made for driving around in a convertible. Something flashy with tail fins and a pastel paint job.

She'd have to settle for her dusty Jeep.

But before she could explore the day, she needed to check on Claire to see how she was faring after last night. Once she'd ascertained that Claire was all right, she'd go downstairs and try to satisfy her craving for a sugary donut. Later she'd connect up with Max. It was important she got things straight between them.

She left her room and padded barefoot down the hall to Claire's room. She respected her sister's privacy, even if Claire didn't often respect hers, so she knocked on Claire's bedroom door.

There was no answer.

Concerned, Amy Jane tried the door and found it unlocked.

"Claire, are you awake?" she called out, pushing open the door to peek inside. She glanced around the small wood-paneled bedroom swagged in peach linen and lace. It must be later than she thought. The room was empty. Claire's bed was made. Last night's party dress wasn't draped on the brocade chaise next to the window and the queen-sized lace-topped dressing table had every vintage perfume bottle in place.

Claire was not only awake, but already up and functioning. Bobby's deceit might have wounded her, but she'd survived. Claire was tougher than she appeared. She was the opposite of Amy Jane, who wasn't as tough as she liked to pretend.

Closing the door, Amy Jane headed downstairs in search of Claire, conversation, and a sugary donut.

She found Claire at the trestle table in the kitchen. The table's surface was covered with flower catalogues. Claire was coping. Her motto was, "When in doubt, plant."

"Do we have any donuts?" Amy Jane asked, opening the refrigerator, and taking out a carton of milk.

"No, but there's leftover birthday cake," Claire answered, not looking up from her order blank.

Amy Jane stuck the carton of milk back in the refrigerator and took out a Pepsi instead.

"How are you this morning?" Amy Jane asked. She walked over to the table and took a seat next to Claire. She wanted to see what her sister was ordering.

"I'm fine. Why?" Claire answered, looking up. Her eyes weren't red and swollen from crying. She, in fact, looked like she'd had a good night's sleep.

"I thought you might be bummed after what happened to you last night."

"You mean Bobby taking me out because of a bet and my finding out about it? Of course I was hurt at first. But his being a jerk really wasn't news to me, once I thought about it. All he had going for him was money."

"Yeah, about two million a year in salary alone," Amy Jane said, taking a long swallow of Pepsi to wake her up.

"But he doesn't have culture or manners like Max. I want the man I marry to be more Ivy League than Bobby McQuaid. With him I was settling for physical strength and money. It isn't enough. I know that I should continue to go for the kind of man I really want. How are you and Max doing?"

"It's not me and Max. Last night's party was just for business purposes," Amy Jane protested. "We are not a couple. I—"

"It looked to me like you were a couple. A very close couple, when I walked in on the two of you necking on the sofa after everyone was gone. How do you explain that, big sister?"

Amy Jane took a long swallow of her Pepsi. "I don't know. Bad judgment?" she offered. Lust, she thought.

Claire closed the flower catalogue she'd been perusing. A serious look crossed her face. "Do you sometimes think, Amy Jane, that we're too independent, too self-sufficient?" she asked.

"We are alike in that way, aren't we," Amy Jane conceded. "I suppose it's because our parents were such children." Amy Jane chuckled. "Do you remember how Mother and Father used to shake their heads and say we were nothing alike?"

Claire nodded. "We weren't. Do you remember the bikes we had growing up?"

Amy Jane stared out the window as if she could see them. "Yours was pink with a basket on the handlebars. The handlebars had pink and white ribbon streamers hanging from them."

"Yours was a black racer," Claire countered.

"Your friends were always girls."

Claire laughed. "And your friends were always boys."

They were both quiet for a long moment as they lingered in the past, lost in the pale ghostly images of their childhood. It was Claire who broke the silence. "Do you ever wonder what our children will be like?"

"Did you ever think we won't get married? That we'll be these two old maid sisters running the Chadwick Bed and Breakfast until we retire?"

"Perish the thought," Claire said, shaking off a shudder.

"I don't know," Amy Jane said. "It might be kinda nice. I didn't say we couldn't have beaux. We could be those scandalous old maid sisters who run that infamous bed and breakfast."

"You make it sound like a bordello!"

"Now there's a thought . . ."

"You might turn out just like Uncle James and be the female equivalent of a hound, but not me. I'm getting married."

"You sound pretty certain of that."

"I am. As a matter of fact I'm picking out white flowers to plant for my wedding bouquet. It's going to be beautiful."

"What about me? Do they have black flowers?"

"No!"

"Red, then. I choose red."

"If you're going to be in my wedding, you'll carry white roses."

"It sounds like you plan on getting married right here," Amy Jane teased.

"I do. I've planned that since I was a little girl. There's a lovely spot right by the fish pond."

"You aren't discussing where to bury my body, are you?" Max said, strolling in the kitchen door with two packages in his arms.

"Depends on what you've got there in your packages," Amy Jane teased.

"Well, this is for the both of you," Max said, handing over a big white box of turtle candies, which were a local legend. The sweets were made of whole pecans covered in caramel and coated with milk chocolate. "I wanted to show my appreciation for all your hard work on the party."

Claire took the box and Amy Jane urged her to hurry with the ribbon she was untying. When Claire lifted the lid, the rich aroma of fresh chocolate scented the air. The turtles were made fresh daily.

Amy Jane grabbed a turtle and bit into it, closed her eyes and savored the creamy, crunchy texture of the candy. Bliss, sheer bliss.

"We'll let you live," she said finally around a mouthful of candy.

"Yeah, for now," Claire agreed, licking her finger.

Amy Jane knew Claire was still sore about the bet Max had witnessed, so she changed the subject. "So what's in the other box?"

"Something personal," Max replied. "Do you think we could go up to your room to open it?"

"I don't know, Max. I'm not dressed." She turned to her sister. "Do you think it's proper for me to be entertaining a gentleman caller in my room when I'm not wearing underwear?" she asked Claire for shock value.

"Amy Jane!" Claire blushed and shook her head.

"Don't worry, Claire. She's not all that entertaining. I can vouch for that," Max countered, apparently shock proof.

Amy Jane knew his comment was a jab at her insistence that she didn't get involved with her clients, despite her momentary lapse in good judgment last night on the sofa. Thank goodness Claire had walked in when she had. For his part, Max Armstrong was entirely too entertaining.

"You know, Claire," Amy Jane began, studying her nails with feigned interest. "I'm beginning to think burying Max's body out by the fish pond isn't an idea entirely without merit. No one would ever suspect us."

Her eyes shone brightly with mischief. "Think of the great scandal when we die at ninety-plus and they find the body. And they *will* find the body, because we'll leave all our money to our seven cats and stipulate in the will that the money is buried by the fish pond. Why, we'll be legendary. We'll—"

"I think I've already seen this movie," Max said. "You don't scare me. All I have to do is remember not to drink the wine."

"Anyone ever tell you that you're entirely too cocky?" Amy Jane grumbled, getting up from her chair to lead him upstairs.

Max's sexy grin telegraphed the double entendre he could have pounced on, but wisely refrained from mentioning.

"Don't forget your package, wise guy," Amy Jane prompted from the hall. She went ahead of him, taking the stairs an unladylike two at a time until she remembered she really *didn't* have anything on beneath the jersey tunic.

Max was right behind her with the package in tow. He followed her into the bedroom and closed the door behind him.

"Is that necessary?" she asked, turning to face him.

"I'm not sure. Maybe. But I did warn you this was personal. I don't think you'd want Claire involved with it."

"So what's in the package that you don't want my sister to see?" she asked, arms crossed in front of her. "It can't be anything really good, because I've always heard good things come in small packages, and that's a fairly good-sized package."

"We'll have to open the package to find out, now won't we?"

"Aw, come on, Max. I hate surprises. Just tell me what you bought me, and I'll act surprised just like you did last night at your party. And while we're on the subject, you took advantage with that thank-you kiss you felt it necessary to bestow on me in front of the whole party."

"You liked it, huh?" he said, flashing a sexy wink.

She just looked at him. It was the look she usually reserved for salesladies who told her that's so flattering on you, dear.

"O-kay," he squirmed. "Maybe we should get to the package opening . . ."

"Good idea," she agreed. She picked up the package he'd set on her desk and carried it with her across to her bed.

Max followed her to the bed and sat down beside her, making himself comfortable.

Amy Jane cast him a sideways glance. That he took the liberty of sitting on her bed with her was perfectly innocent and really suspect all at once. But she didn't comment on it.

Instead she lifted the box and tested its weight. "It's pretty light. What is it, a hockey puck with your signature on it?"

"Cute, real cute."

She lifted the package to her ear. "It's not ticking . . ." she pronounced.

"I know. I already checked that."

"What do you mean you already checked it? Don't you know what's inside?"

"Nope."

"You mean you had someone else pick out something for me. Chantal or someone?" she tried, but didn't avoid sounding peeved. Maybe because her try was half-hearted.

"You don't understand. This package isn't for you. It's for me," Max hastened to explain.

"But I thought you said it was personal—" Amy Jane felt her stomach sinking. Had she really blundered into embarrassing territory, she wondered, knowing deep down that she had.

"It is personal. Personal business. The package was delivered to my condo this morning."

"Who sent it to you?" she asked, glancing down at the address label. "And why did you bring it here to open?"

"I don't know who sent it. That's why I brought it here. I figured you might want to have a look at it before I opened it."

"Oh." Amy Jane felt a cringe of total embarrassment. What an idiot she'd been. Here she'd been feeling giddy over a gift Max had brought her, when actually all that time he hadn't brought her a gift at all.

Worse, when she thought about it, was—he shouldn't have any reason for her to assume that he had.

She'd made a major leap in assumption. And she'd given away too much by doing so.

Not wanting Amy Jane to feel bad, Max tried to put her at ease. "You realize I'm going to feel pretty stupid if this is a corporate birthday gift from the Lions or something."

Amy Jane hoped that it was. It was easier to laugh at your embarrassment when you had company. But she had a feeling this was Max's stalker surfacing. Her gut instinct was kicking in, bigtime.

"Well, there's only one way to find out. Let's open it," she said, tearing the brown wrapping paper from the three-foot-by-three-foot package. The cardboard box beneath it gave away no clues. It was standard grocery store issue, the brand name of a major paper manufacturer printed on it. Someone had had a good time with sturdy clear packing tape. The cardboard box was thoroughly sealed with the stuff.

"Scissors—" Amy Jane said, holding out her hand like a surgeon for Max to fill it.

"Where?"

"My desk. The center drawer."

"Nope," Max said, after a thorough search of crammed papers and odds and ends like hard candy and old keys.

"Try the left-hand drawer, top," she suggested, closing one eye as she tried to recall when she'd last used them.

"Nope."

"Then your guess is as good as mine. They have to be in there somewhere."

After a search of all the desk drawers, Max

located the scissors under a stack of newspapers on the end of her desk.

"Scissors," he said, crossing to the bed and placing the scissors in her hand.

Amy Jane cut away the tape and pulled open the folded four-flap top to reveal crumpled newspaper. She tossed out the top layer of newspaper to reveal the contents of the box.

"Well, I don't think it's a corporate birthday gift, unless the Lions have a very odd corporate policy," she said, pulling the sawed-off hobbyhorse head from the box.

"What the hell is that?" Max demanded, grabbing it from her.

"I'd say it's a message. And I don't think the message is happy birthday."

"I'd say you're right," Max agreed, tossing the sawed-off hobbyhorse head back in the carton it had been packed in.

"I don't like this, Max. I don't like it at all. I think we should bring in the police. I can be discreet. I've got friends at the precinct who will keep it quiet, if I ask them to."

"No. No police."

"Max—"

"Come on, Amy Jane. A sawed-off hobbyhorse head . . . I'll look like a fool."

"Have you got any other ideas, like who might have sent you this?"

"Kerry Ashton comes to mind. She's got a weird sense of humor."

"This isn't funny."

"I know."

"Let's take this package apart piece by piece. There may be something here that will clue us in on who might have sent it to you. If something points to Kerry Ashton, then we can get a restraining order put out against her."

"Wait a minute. What's this?" Max asked, spotting a white card on the bed beside him. It had to have fallen there when he'd grabbed the hobbyhorse head from Amy Jane.

He picked it up and read it:

Dearest Max:

You belong to *me*.

I LOVE YOU

"This is really creepy," Max spat out, throwing the card into the box with the hobbyhorse head.

"Is there some reason other than Kerry's weird sense of humor that you think she might have sent it?"

"Pretty girls don't like being told no. Kerry isn't used to rejection."

Amy Jane wondered if anyone ever got used to rejection, pretty or not, as she started going through the newspaper crunched in the carton. But there was nothing to discover. Whoever had sent the package had been very careful.

They weren't dealing with anyone stupid.

They were dealing with someone who was sick.

Very sick.

She'd been reading up on stalkers.

They had obsessive thoughts like:

"I'm entitled to whatever I want. I am the only person who counts. I can destroy anyone I want."

And Max was right about one thing; they were unable to accept rejection. And jealousy was usually the trigger that pushed them over the edge.

Max's birthday party had worked.

So why didn't she feel good about that? She began stuffing the newspaper back in the carton.

"I still think we should go to the police, Max," she tried one last time.

"No. No police," he said, standing firm.

"Well, there isn't anything here to go on. The newspaper is the St. Louis *Post-Dispatch*. It would be unable to trace, same as the carton. Maybe the hobbyhorse. Let me get dressed and we'll see what we can do."

She set the box aside and got up and went to her closet.

"You want me to go back downstairs and wait for you?"

"No, just turn around," she said, pulling jeans and a crop top from her closet. She went to her lingerie drawer to get underwear, then remembered she didn't have a clean bra. Oh hell, she'd just go braless. That would keep Max's mind off the horse's head. He was looking kind of spooked.

She grabbed a pair of panties, then saw a rip

at the seam. She threw them back in the drawer and felt for another pair.

"Damn!" she cried and began throwing panties in the air.

Max turned and was hit in the face by a pair.

"What are you doing—not that I'm objecting . . ."

She began opening and closing the rest of the drawers in the piece of furniture, searching through them.

"What—"

Amy Jane closed the last drawer and turned to face him as he stood there with her panties in his hand.

"My gun is missing."

Seventeen

By Monday evening Amy Jane was thoroughly bummed.

She'd filed a police report, but her gun hadn't turned up. And she was no closer to finding out who Max's stalker was than she had been on day one.

As she sprawled on the couch in the library watching the first game of the second round of the playoffs, she was sure of two things: One, that someone who was at the party she'd thrown for Max had stolen her gun. And two, they meant to use it.

It wasn't going to be good for business to open the *Post-Dispatch* and see a headline, VICTIM SHOT WITH PRIVATE EYE'S GUN. And it didn't take a warning from her gut to tell her Max was the intended victim.

Even the hobbyhorse had been a dead end, so to speak. If only she could just get one decent clue she could crack this case before someone got hurt.

At the moment the Lions would have settled

for one decent goal. They were behind the Maple Leafs two to nothing.

"Aren't you going to watch the game at all?" Amy Jane asked Claire, who was curled up in the wing chair opposite her with a paperback novel.

"No."

"But the Lions are in the playoffs. It's your civic duty to cheer them on," Amy Jane cajoled. "It'll be your fault if they lose."

"I hope they do lose."

"Claire!"

"Well, I do."

Amy Jane knew Claire was listening to the game and just being stubborn. Claire hadn't turned the page in the book she was reading, for the past fifteen minutes. But she let Claire have her illusion.

Everyone was entitled to an illusion now and then. Claire's was that there was someone out there who was going to make her happy. Amy Jane knew better. You had to love yourself.

Finding someone to love you was a fluke at best. And it got harder as you got older; bars were for those under twenty-five, dinner parties were full of married couples, and women in the nineties were cursed with the freedom of choice that brought high expectations.

She'd lowered hers from "a man who met all her desires" to "a man who doesn't embarrass me in public or slobber when he kisses."

Max certainly fulfilled the latter. She wasn't

certain about the former. She had the feeling he got a kick out of embarrassing her in public.

"They don't want to get into a shootout with the talents the Leafs have." Max's rich voice came from the television. "Coach Tom Quinn has a lot to worry about with this team. Just shy of the three-minute mark in the opening period, no score. Uh-oh, folks, McQuaid draws a stick-in-the-face penalty again. McQuaid needs to get hold of his temper, or he's going to really hurt the Lions' chances in these playoffs. It'll be a two-minute high-stick penalty. At the break in the action . . ."

Max shook his head. "McQuaid's going to blow it for everyone," he said off-air to Chantal and Corey in the announcers' booth.

"Sure you're not just a little jealous?" Chantal asked softly, replaying Richie's accusation.

"Of what?" Max demanded.

"McQuaid is a damn fine player," Corey said.

"When he plays. Most of the time he's fighting, or starting a fight."

If Corey and Chantal were looking for an argument, he was ready to give them one. He wanted to strike out at someone, since he couldn't fight what was happening to him. It made him angry that one person could ruin another's life because they took a mind to. Much like the victim of a drive-by shooting, he railed that he hadn't done anything to deserve it.

The game was starting up again, the noise of the crowd swelling. The organist was whipping them up.

Chantal passed him an envelope.

"What's this?" he asked, with a raised eyebrow.

Chantal shrugged. "I don't know. A kid handed it to me on my way back from the ladies' room, asked me to give it to you."

"What did the kid look like?"

"I don't know, a kid."

"And the puck is loose in the neutral zone," Corey began announcing. "Number five is offside on the near right wing, just ten minutes into play."

Max ripped the envelope open with dread. He took out the note and read:

> Dearest Max:
>
> Either you announce you
> plan on becoming engaged
> on-air during tonight's
> game—or else.
>
> I LOVE YOU

Max put the note back in the envelope and slipped the envelope into his blazer jacket while picking up the game in progress.

"This is where the Lions have to take advantage. They've got to work over the Maple Leafs' defensemen," he said into the microphone. He announced the rest of the hockey game by rote, his mind on the note in his jacket pocket.

It didn't help any that it was a terrible game for the Lions, including a bench-clearing brawl near the end of the third period. The Lions ended the night by losing to the Maple Leafs without scoring even one goal.

The mood in the broadcast booth was glum.

The mood in the locker room for the post-game rehash was worse. Bobby and Richie avoided Max. Even the normally talkative coach didn't want to talk about the game. Max finally got an interview with the defenseman, Lance Thomure.

His night got worse when he made his way out to the parking lot of the Dome.

The tires on his car were slashed.

All four of them.

He walked around his car a second time in utter disbelief.

What the hell was going on?

Max stood leaning against his car waiting for Amy Jane to arrive. He'd figured he might as well call her to come fetch him, as he'd planned on going to see her after the game. He'd turned down several offers of help, and withstood some curious stares without explanation.

Finally he saw her Jeep, and pushed himself

away from his car as she pulled up in the empty parking lot beside him.

"You've got car trouble, huh?" she said, getting out of the Jeep and walking toward him.

Max nodded.

She shook her head when she got a look at the slashed tires. "Somebody doesn't like you, Max."

"Why you must be Amy Jane Chadwick, the famous detective," he muttered, as she took a slow walk around the car, stopping to kneel and study the slashed tires as she went.

"I'd be nice to me, if I were you. I'm the one with the tires that roll. What do you want to do about this?"

"Leave it. I'll have it taken care of tomorrow. If you'll give me a ride home . . ."

"Let's go."

"Why don't I drive," Max suggested, holding out his hand for the keys.

Amy Jane frowned. "Don't tell me you're one of those guys who always has to drive because he doesn't feel macho sitting in the passenger seat when a woman is doing the driving?"

"I want to drive because I've got something I want you to look at while I'm driving," he explained.

"What?" she asked, tossing him the keys and going around to the passenger door.

Max followed her, opening the door for her.

When she was settled, he withdrew the envelope from his jacket pocket and handed it to her, then went back around to the driver's side and got in. As he drove off the parking lot, Amy Jane put on the overhead light and withdrew the latest note.

She turned off the light when she finished reading the note.

"Unless I missed it, you didn't announce your engagement during the game tonight," she said, putting the note back inside the envelope. "I did doze off."

"You're right, I didn't," Max agreed, swinging the Jeep onto the entrance ramp to the highway.

"And you think your slashed tires are the 'or else'?" Amy Jane asked.

"Don't you?"

"There's something I should have told you," Amy Jane said.

"What?" Max accelerated and switched lanes as he neared Chesterfield mall.

"Remember getting stuck in the elevator at the Missouri Athletic Club?"

"Yeah . . . that's not something I'm likely to forget."

"It wasn't a fluke."

"What do you mean—"

"The control panel had been tampered with. Someone deliberately trapped you in that elevator."

"Why?"

"To scare you, same as the tires were meant to scare you tonight."

"But it doesn't make any sense. Why are the notes all signed, I LOVE YOU?"

"From what I've been reading up on, it's because whoever it is wants to be in control and isn't. Wants to intimidate and threaten you because you aren't returning the love they feel for you. When love is denied, it becomes necessary for a stalker to demonstrate how powerful they are at all costs. That's what causes them to perform acts of criminal behavior."

"There isn't any way out of this, is there?"

"Only one. We have to discover who the person is that has a desperate obsession with you."

"Any luck finding your gun?" he asked, exiting the highway.

"None."

"Damn," he swore, beating his hand against the steering wheel in frustration.

She was struck by his vulnerability. He was a strong man made weak by an enemy he couldn't vanquish.

And she was a woman in too deep.

"Look, if you want to hire someone else—"

"No, I want you."

They'd stopped in front of his condo.

"But I don't have experience in this kind of . . ."

"I want you."

His hand stroked her shoulder.

She panicked, pushing open the door of the Jeep and getting out. She came around to his side of the Jeep and waited expectantly. "Call me if you want a ride in the morning."

"Aren't you coming inside?" he asked, his disappointment plain, as he got out of the Jeep.

"No. And you're going to be very careful about accepting packages and answering the door. I'll hate you forever if something happens—"

"Hush," he said, placing his finger on her lips. "Nothing is going to happen." And then he shifted his weight and pulled her into his arms.

"Ah, Amy Jane," he sighed, then pressed a kiss on the top of her head. "When this is all over—"

"When it's over," she agreed, pushing him away.

Amy Jane sat in her room berating herself.

She should have seen this coming. When the hang-up phone calls had stopped coming to Max, she should have known his stalker was planning to act.

Time was running out. She had to find out who Max's stalker was before the stakes were upped any higher.

Something about the hang-up call she'd listened to on Max's phone bothered her. If only she could put her finger on what it was. But the harder she tried, the more elusive whatever it was became.

She went to the closet and pulled down a yellow-pages telephone book and began flipping through it until she came to the toy-store section. Pulling a pad and pencil from her desk, she began making a list.

In the morning she would call every one of them and try to locate which one carried the hobbyhorse that had been in Max's package.

She would justify Max's trust in her. She had to.

"With 4:01 gone in a scoreless third period, this is St. Louis Lions hockey," Max said, leading into a beer commercial the following night.

His eyes were gritty because he hadn't gotten a wink of sleep. The game wasn't helping him stay awake, even if it was a playoff game. It was the dullest game he'd witnessed the whole season; as dull as rooting for the American League in baseball's All-Star Game.

The commercial over, Max tried to concentrate on the hockey game before him instead of his stalker. He was rewarded, calling, "a dazzling save by the Lions goal tender, Richie Allen. Big save by Allen with 11:45 left to go in the third period, Lions trailing four to nothing."

He caught himself yawning a few minutes later.

A minute after that there was blood on the ice.

Bobby McQuaid had smashed a Maple Leafs' player against the perimeter wall and then cuffed him. It was the final play of the game and had nothing to do with scoring goals and everything to do with scoring points.

The Maple Leafs' player was carried out on a stretcher as the Lions went down in scoreless defeat, leaving the Maple Leafs out ahead two to nothing in the second round of the playoffs.

An unrepentant McQuaid raised his fist, gladiator-style, before the crowd.

Max saw red. McQuaid's right hook helped fuel hockey's reputation as the fastest most violent professional sport. When he was playing, Max had played clean. He loved the sport and hated when thugs and goons used it as a bullying ground.

After the game, when the players were showered and dressed to leave, Max called Bobby on his responsibility for losing the game.

"You don't want to skate. You don't want to score. You don't want to win. All you want to do is be a fighting machine."

"Shut up, Armstrong. You don't know what you're talking about. All you are is a washed-up ex-hockey player who couldn't take it. A cry baby. Why don't you put your fists up and back up your words like a man."

"A man doesn't have to use his fists to be heard," Max answered, avoiding Bobby's shove with a quick side step. His hand, however, snagged Bobby's jacket and something fell out of Bobby's pocket.

Bobby quickly retrieved it, pocketed it and walked away.

But not before Max saw what it was.

A rolled up fifty-dollar bill.

That explained a lot.

Bobby wasn't just a goon, he was a loser.

On the drive home from the game Max's thoughts were on Bobby. His efforts to get Bobby to clean up his game and play to his great ability weren't working. He knew it wasn't his job. It was the coach's job, but he had a hard time standing by while someone as talented as Bobby pissed away a career Max would have given anything to have had.

Maybe he needed to talk to Richie Allen alone. Richie was Bobby's best friend. Someone needed to tell Bobby that cocaine wasn't the answer to his problems.

It was about that time that Max sensed someone riding his bumper. He glanced in the rearview mirror and saw Bobby's black Land Rover practically on top of him. He sped up and Bobby sped up, continuing to crowd him.

Max slowed down. Bobby stayed with him, moving into the passing lane and bumping Max's car. The guy had to be high to try something this stupid.

Max suddenly realized he was in a very dangerous situation. Bobby McQuaid was a time bomb just waiting for someone to set him off. He had to lose him before someone got killed.

Max's mind raced through the possible ways

to avoid having Bobby's rage culminate in disaster on the highway. Bobby was crazy enough to take out a lot of innocent people to exact his revenge on Max.

A highway exit up ahead gave Max an idea.

Max sped up. He waited until Bobby fell in behind him. As he approached the exit ramp, Max delayed until the last possible second, then swerved onto it. He felt his car actually go airborne for a brief time. It settled down and skidded sideways as he applied the brakes.

Bobby hadn't made it. He'd had to continue on the highway. Even he wasn't crazy enough to turn around and face oncoming highway traffic to try to follow Max off the exit ramp.

Max took a deep sigh of relief.

He'd lost Bobby. He'd managed not to flip his car or his lunch.

He waited for his heart to stop pounding as he sat at the red light. That had been too close for comfort. Clearly Bobby couldn't be reasoned with. Not by him, anyway.

Now his dilemma was whether to tell Tom Quinn about his player's flirtation with cocaine.

Amy Jane was frustrated.

She'd called every toy store in town. Not one of them carried the hobbyhorse Max had been sent. Nor had they carried it in the past.

In all likelihood, the hobbyhorse had been handmade.

The telephone beside her on her desk rang. She picked it up distractedly, certain it would be impossible to track down something that had been handmade, yet trying to come up with a way.

"Well, I made it through the night without any more mash notes from my fan," Max said. "Looks like things are beginning to pick up. How's it going on your front? Are you having any luck figuring out who wants to love me to death?"

"No, it's going slow. About as slow as the Lions game was tonight," Amy Jane compared. "It's been a pretty boring evening all around. I'm glad you talked me out of coming to the game, though. I wouldn't have wanted to witness live what Bobby did to that Leafs' player. Did you see all the blood? I hope the player is all right."

"Yeah, he is. The player's nose is broken. When you think about it, I guess I got off easy. Bobby just tried to run me off the road," Max said casually.

"Bobby did what?"

"I called him on his grandstanding after the game. I shouldn't have done it in front of the team, but he deserved to be embarrassed. He blew a lot of chances to score tonight when he was playing because he was too busy playing tough guy. Anyway, he followed me home, tailgated me and tried to run me off the road."

"Are you all right? What happened?" Amy Jane asked, concern etching her voice.

"I'm fine. I managed to lose him finally by ducking off an exit ramp when he wasn't expecting it. I guess he went on home."

"You can't be sure he won't show up at your place. Make sure you keep your doors locked and don't hesitate to call the police if he does show up. And call me."

"Sure you don't want to just come over here and protect me?" Max coaxed, his tone warm and suggestive.

"What is it with all you men that violence makes you horny?"

"I never said—"

"Good night, Max."

Bobby pounded on the front door loud enough to wake the dead.

"I know you're in there."

No response.

"Come on. Let me in," he said, pounding on the door again.

When that didn't work, Bobby went to his car at the curb and began blowing his car horn.

The car horn had the desired effect.

The front door of the apartment flew open and Richie Allen tore out onto the porch in his underwear. "What the hell are you doing, man?" he demanded, jerking Bobby's hand away from the car horn. "You're going to wake all my neighbors and get us lynched."

"I don't care about your damned neighbors."

"Well, I do. Come on inside and tell me what you're doing here," Richie said, heading back inside his apartment.

Bobby followed him, swearing all the way.

"What's all the racket?" Kerry Ashton asked, coming out of the bedroom in Richie's shirt.

"Nothing. Go back to bed. I'll be in in a minute. Bobby's got something he wants to talk about."

Kerry sat down on the sofa instead of going back to bed. She ignored Richie's look to leave them to talk in private.

"I want you to come with me," Bobby insisted.

"Come where?"

"To Armstrong's apartment. I want to kick his ass. The sonovabitch won't get off my case."

"Cool down. You don't even know where he lives," Richie said, a cooler head prevailing.

"I do," Kerry piped up. "I could show you where he lives."

"You shut up," Richie admonished.

"Well, someone needs to teach Max a lesson," she pouted.

"Maybe, but not tonight," Richie said.

"Why not?" Bobby asked, belligerent. He paced nervously around the room.

"I'm busy . . ." Richie said, nodding to Kerry so Bobby would get a clue.

"Oh. Right. Sorry, man."

"It's all right. Listen, maybe you ought to sleep it off on the couch," Richie suggested.

"No. I'm going home. See ya."

James Chadwick was in a good mood as he closed up the sports bar.

He was making headway with Miranda.

They had a date planned for their night off. He'd promised her a motorcycle ride.

There was a knock on the door to the sports bar. He smiled. Miranda must have forgotten her keys. She was always forgetting something. Yet she was great at remembering complicated drink orders.

He went to let her back in.

"Oh, it's not you."

"No, I think it's me," Amy Jane said, grinning.

"I meant, I thought you were Miranda coming back for her keys."

"Sorry to disappoint you."

"I'm never disappointed to see you, Sweet," Uncle James said, following her back into the sports bar.

"Does that mean I get a free drink? I could sure use one."

"One Pepsi coming up," Uncle James promised. "Things going that bad for you?"

"Things aren't going at all. I'm stalled out on Max's case."

"You worried he's going to fire you?"

"No, just worried," Amy Jane admitted, taking a sip of the fizzy drink Uncle James sat before her.

"Oh, it's a good thing you stopped by. Miranda said to give you this."

"What is it?"

"I don't know. She said someone left it on a table with a tip."

"She doesn't remember who?"

"No, it wasn't someone she waited on. She just found it on a table with a tip as she was cleaning up."

Amy Jane opened the sealed envelope with her name on it and read the note inside:

> STOP TRYING TO STEAL MAX
> OR YOU MIGHT BE THE KNIFE'S
> NEXT TARGET.

"What's it say?" Uncle James asked, his eyes curious.

"Someone's idea of a joke," Amy Jane said, not wanting to worry him. She slipped the note back inside the envelope, studied her name typed on the front in all caps, then tucked the envelope in her jeans pocket.

"Listen, someone slashed Max's tires the other night. He had to buy four new ones. You ever see anyone in here with a knife?"

"You mean they did it outside the sports bar?"

"No, it was on the parking lot of the Dome."

Uncle James thought a moment and shook his head. "The only knife I've ever seen anyone use is a big pocket knife Bobby McQuaid uses to clean his nails sometimes."

"Oh, gross—"

"Well, you asked," Uncle James said with a shrug.

Amy Jane took the last swallow of her Pepsi as she thought. Reaching a decision, she pushed the empty glass toward Uncle James.

"How would you like to join me on a caper, Uncle James?"

"Would I!" His eyes lit up with relish.

"Come on then, close up this popsicle stand and let's go," Amy Jane instructed.

Eighteen

Amy Jane finessed her way past the guard at the Dome.

She'd used her relationship with Max, pretend though it was, and Uncle James's bogus impersonation of a responsible citizen to gain entry. The guard believed her story about retrieving something for Max he'd left behind. He'd dismissed a girlfriend and an older man as harmless, allowing them entry while he went back to his paperback thriller.

"What are we doing?" Uncle James asked when they were out of the guard's earshot.

"I told you. We're detecting. You're an official associate detective of the A. J. Chadwick Detective Agency."

"Yeah, yeah. But what exactly are we detecting? You deliberately neglected to tell me that little detail, Sweet. I need to know, so I know what to lie about when we get arrested."

"We are not going to get arrested."

"Right." He put a spin of disbelief on his affirmative reply.

"Come on, I want to you stand guard outside

the dressing room. I told the guard we were going up to the broadcast booth."

"What are you going to do, go through the lockers?" Uncle James asked, standing where she'd posted him.

"There are no lockers in the dressing room, just cubicles. I'm going to have a look around. See what I can find," she said, going in.

She was in the dressing room only a few minutes, when she heard a knock on the door. After a quick glance around discovered nothing untoward, she heeded the warning knock.

"What?" she asked, peeking her head out the door and looking at Uncle James.

"I thought I heard a noise," Uncle James whispered.

They both listened and heard the sound of approaching footsteps.

"Come on, let's get out of here," Amy Jane said, motioning for Uncle James to follow her.

When they passed the guard's post, he wasn't there. Only his paperback book laid face down guarded the door they let themselves out.

"Did you find what you were looking for?" Uncle James asked as she drove him back to his car at the sports bar.

"No. The place was clean. There were no clues left behind. I'm still trying to fight my way out of a cotton ball, or at least that's how it feels," Amy Jane said, disgusted.

"Don't worry, I have every faith you'll figure it out," Uncle James assured her with a hug before he got out of the car at the sports bar. "Oh, and Sweet," he said, sticking his head back in the car, "just let me know if you need my help again. I had fun playing detective tonight."

"You would."

Amy Jane went straight from the sports bar to Max's condo. While she hadn't found Bobby's knife as she'd hoped she might, she was sure Bobby was dangerous.

He might not have been the one to slash Max's tires, but he was out of control. A sane person didn't attempt mayhem on the highway.

She needed to warn Max that things were getting more complicated.

She didn't like knowing the team was going on the road to Toronto for the next game.

The night air was chilly as she left her Jeep at the curb. She could see her breath as she stood waiting for Max to answer the door after she rang his bell.

Max came to the door with a glass of wine in his hand and a surprised look on his face when he saw her waiting on his doorstep.

"I was just getting ready for bed," he said, explaining his wearing apparel—jeans and nothing else.

"I thought I told you to be careful about opening your door," she grumbled, taking the glass of wine from him. "It could have been someone dangerous."

"What do you mean, 'could have been.' You are someone dangerous at this time of night," Max said, following her to where she sank down on the sofa.

"I'm not dangerous. I'm tired," she said, taking a sip of wine.

"Then that isn't going to help." Max nodded to the wine she was sipping.

"It's not going to hurt." She drained the wine and handed him the empty glass. "It's been a bitch of a day."

"Why? What happened?" he asked, concerned, leaning toward her protectively.

Amy Jane reached into her jeans pocket and withdrew the envelope Uncle James had given her, handing the envelope to Max.

"It seems your stalker has taken a dislike to my poaching her territory."

Amy Jane leaned forward, her chin in her hands, as she watched Max slip the note from the envelope and read it.

He just stared at her when he was done.

She drew in a deep shaky breath.

"Okay, that's it. We go to the police."

"The police? What are you talking about? I thought you said you didn't want to go to the police. As I remember you were adamant about not wanting the publicity."

"I've changed my mind."

"Why?"

"Because while it's one thing for me to be in danger, it's quite another for me to put you in danger, I won't be a party to that. We go to the police," he vowed, a note of finality in his voice.

"But what about the publicity?"

"Hang the publicity—this has gone too far."

"No, it hasn't gone far enough. The legal system isn't set up to give anyone protection under the law until the stalker actually *acts* on a threat."

"I'm not prepared to wait for someone to harm you. There's no way."

"We don't have any choice. There isn't an anti-stalking law in the state of Missouri. The anti-stalking laws are only just now starting to get on the books in some states. There's a law pending in Missouri, but that doesn't do you any more good than the practically useless order of protection currently on the books and in use."

Max shot her a stubborn look.

"Promise me you won't do anything foolish, Max."

He didn't promise her.

"I need you to cooperate with me, and let me do my job. All contacting the police will do is generate publicity, if you go to them." Amy Jane could see that she wasn't getting through to Max. He was no longer concerned about his career in the face of any possible danger to her.

She tried another angle.

"The publicity would wreak havoc on the Lions' ability to concentrate during the playoff games. Now you don't want that, do you?"

She could see that argument weakened his resolve, but only slightly. His concerns were still very real. And she was touched by them.

"Trust me," she coaxed.

He smiled, and she knew he remembered trying that very line on her.

"I'll sleep on it. That's all I can promise you," he said, yawning.

Amy Jane wondered if she should voice her suspicions. Would Max take them seriously? Hell, she had trouble taking them seriously herself. But her gut instinct told her there was something to them.

She took a deep breath and plunged headlong anyway.

"Max . . ."

"Ummm . . ."

"Before you nod off, there's something I'd like to run by you."

"Sure, shoot."

Amy Jane tried not to notice as he rubbed his bare chest absently, then stretched, displaying the unconscious catlike grace of an athlete. He might no longer play hockey, but he certainly did something to keep himself in excellent shape. She shook her head, trying to clear it of the distraction of Max's appeal.

"Now I want you to keep an open mind about this, to listen to what I have to say, before you form an opinion about it . . ."

"Okay, I'm listening," he agreed, dropping down on the sofa beside her and setting his empty wineglass on the coffee table.

She cleared her throat.

"You know how your tires were slashed the other night on the parking lot of the Dome . . . ?"

He nodded. "I'm not likely to forget. It cost me a bundle to have a garage go out and replace all four of them."

"I went by the sports bar tonight on my way over here, and talked to Uncle James."

"I bet that was a real lively place tonight after the second Lions defeat in a row," Max said dryly.

"I don't know. I got there after everyone was gone. Uncle James was locking up. But I'm sure you're right. The town is pretty bummed."

"It wouldn't be this way, if McQuaid—"

Amy Jane stopped him. "That's who I wanted to talk to you about. I think he's the one who slashed your tires."

"But what about—"

"I think he's your stalker, too."

Max hooted. "That's a good one. Bobby McQuaid is my stalker."

"I'm serious."

"Oh, come on, Amy Jane. Sure, Bobby McQuaid isn't my biggest fan, but—"

"Uncle James told me Bobby carries a big pocket knife with him," she offered, crossing her arms in front of her. "I think he used it to slash your tires."

"So, okay, maybe he did. But all that proves is that Bobby is a hothead."

Amy Jane was quiet. Finally she spoke. "You said you'd hear me out . . ."

"I know, but I thought we'd agreed it was a woman who was stalking me. I mean, after all, the letters were, well, they were sexy."

Amy Jane remained quiet.

"Okay, okay. I'll listen," Max conceded.

"There are several reasons that point to Bobby McQuaid being your stalker, when you stop and think about it objectively. First, you've been criticizing both Bobby and Richie on the air for being lazy, hotshot stars."

"Well, they are. Richie's improved since he started dating Kerry, which I can't figure at all. But Bobby's out of control. I think he's doing cocaine."

"An even better reason to suspect Bobby. Maybe he and Richie cooked up the female angle to the mash notes as a prank to get back at you. A prank that Bobby took over the edge once he started dating my sister. He'd heard Claire and I openly discuss your hunk appeal and that would only fuel his obsession with you."

"My hunk appeal . . ." Max picked up on the admission. He preened like a peacock, his smile full of amused self-satisfaction.

Amy Jane punched his arm. "Don't take it to heart. The hunk-appeal list Claire and I run is lengthy and can change on a whim."

Max rubbed his arm thoughtfully. "You're serious, though, about thinking Bobby McQuaid is behind all of this—"

"Yes. I think it's reasonable to assume Bobby could be out for revenge because he's embarrassed and jealous. And Bobby could be gay."

"I don't know, Amy Jane. It's a lot to—"

"You know, Max, now that I think about it, I don't see rewiring an elevator as a thing a woman would tend to do. I'm not saying she couldn't but . . ."

"You know what, I've got a headache. Let's sleep on this, okay?"

Amy Jane nodded. Now that she'd voiced her suspicions she wasn't sure if they sounded more ridiculous or less. She only knew that Bobby McQuaid was her best suspect, and that it was nice to finally have one instead of a thousand.

"I'm going to bunk on the couch," she said, planning to stay the night.

"That isn't necessary," Max said, getting up. "I don't think there's going to be any more trouble tonight. It's late."

"I'm staying," she insisted.

"Okay, but not on the couch. You can sleep in my bed."

"I don't think so. The couch is fine," Amy Jane declared, using good judgment instead of impulsive want for a change. If she slept in Max's bed, she wouldn't sleep at all. And sleep was what both of them needed.

Sleep wasn't what both of them got.

Despite her original protest, Max wound up winning his bid to have her take his bed and let him sleep on the couch. Now she lay awake listening to the sounds of the house, familiarizing herself with the refrigerator kicking on, the furnace blower and the ticking clock on Max's bedside table.

She was keyed up, restless and strangely happy.

Max's scent was on his pillow and she was as giddy as a high-school freshman in a gym decorated with miles of crepe paper for prom night.

Expectant. She was waiting and ready for something. And being patently foolish.

She was in the middle of a possibly dangerous case and her client was in the next room probably sleeping soundly.

What would he think, and would he be sleeping as soundly if he knew she was sleeping in the nude in his bed?

Max lay on the couch staring at the ceiling.

He wondered if Amy Jane always slept in the nude, as she had that morning he'd barged into her room at the bed and breakfast.

He closed his eyes. He had to get some sleep. Tomorrow he'd be traveling with the team to Toronto for the third game of the playoffs.

His mind replayed how inviting Amy Jane had looked with nothing more than her sheet and her anger wrapped around her.

In his mind she dropped the sheet . . .

Oooooh, baby!

* * *

Claire's eyes flickered open when the weight of the magazine in her hand caused her wrist to bend. She'd been dozing on and off while waiting for Amy Jane to return home.

Her bath water was tepid, the foamy bubbles having gone from lush to sparse. The candles still burned, and their scent permeated the small bathroom.

Reaching for the tap, Claire turned on the hot water to elevate the water temperature. She wiped the water droplets from the page of her new bridal magazine and studied the lush photograph of a bride with white garden roses wreathed in her hair.

The model was blond so it was easy for Claire to picture herself as the bride.

Why, she wondered was it so hard for anyone else to picture her as a bride?

A salty tear trickled down her cheek and onto the page. She sniffled and threw the thick glossy magazine across the room with a sob.

Kerry Ashton stood in front of the mirror in her bedroom in her parents' home.

Richie couldn't believe he'd let her talk him into sneaking in while her parents were asleep in the master suite down the hall.

Kerry had a way of getting her way.

Yet he had to admit, being in Kerry's room

like this gave him a sexual thrill. Her bedroom was that of a girlie girl. The wallpaper was a pink and white cabana stripe, and the bed linens were pastel with lots of ribbon and ruffles. He stretched out his arm against the pale pink sheet and admired how the olive of his skin looked so masculine against it.

On the wall were hooks with ballet slippers dangling from them by their shiny ribbons. He wasn't surprised Kerry had been a dancer. She was very limber and had a supple body.

His eyes settled on her. She was posing in just a pair of panties that had ruffles reminiscent of a ballerina's tutu as she admired herself in the mirror. Yeah, he was real glad he'd let her talk him into leaving the apartment and coming here.

This was really sexy.

"Come here, and bring a pair of your ballet slippers with you," Richie said from where he reclined against the painted four-poster head-board against a pile of frilly pillows.

"What for? They don't fit me."

"They don't have to . . ."

Kerry shrugged and lifted a pair and brought them to the bed with her. "Do you think I'm pretty?" she asked crawling over him.

"Yeah, real pretty," Richie said, rolling over and positioning her beneath him.

"Prettier than Amy Jane—what are you do-ing?"

"Making sure I get what I want for a change," Richie said, tying her wrist to the bedpost with one of the ballerina slippers, looping the ribbon in a slip knot.

"Maybe I don't want—" she started to object.

"I wore my goalie mask for you . . ." Richie countered, continuing to fasten her other wrist to the bedpost with the remaining pink slipper, the pale ribbons trailing down in a flutter.

He leaned down and licked her armpits.

"That tickles," she squealed, squirming, the movement of her arms pulling the ribbons tighter.

"Be quiet, I don't want your parents in here, for heaven's sake," Richie said.

He moved his mouth to cover one breast, the movement of his tongue lazy, signaling he meant to take his own sweet time.

"Richie . . ."

He looked up at her while continuing to lathe her nipple, pearling it.

"I think Bobby is right. You should help him teach Max a lesson. Max doesn't give the two of you the respect you deserve. He doesn't pick on the other players the way he picks on the two of you."

"I don't want to talk about it right now," Richie said, his hand sliding into her panties to distract her.

She began to moan and arch against his hand.

Her moans grew louder until Richie covered her mouth with his, stealing her cries of pleasure as he replaced his hand with his rock-hard penis.

* * *

Chantal Perry couldn't sleep.

Giving up the ghost, she got up and pulled on a robe and turned on the light at the desk in her bedroom.

She pulled open the center drawer and took out the file of unpaid bills. It was thick with second and third past-due notices.

Her excuses were wearing thin with her creditors. She didn't think she could bear the embarrassment of her employer finding out.

It wasn't fair. It just wasn't fair.

She tried—she really had given everything she had and more to make a life for herself. To do it on her own.

She knew Corey would loan her the money she needed. It would be so easy to take it.

But it wouldn't be easy to repay.

Loans made you vulnerable.

She didn't like being vulnerable, not one damn little bit.

Taking out her calculator, she began adding up her balance, checking it. And then she made a surprising discovery; she had more money than she'd thought because she'd forgotten to record a deposit.

The discovery made her high with determination to take control.

Not only wasn't she going to owe anyone anything, but she was going to collect on what was owed her. Either she got more money from the

Lions or she'd find another way to get what she'd worked so hard for.

No man was ever going to stand in her way— or buy her.

The price would be much too high.

"Hello . . ."

"Miranda, were you asleep?"

She rubbed her eyes and looked at the clock on her bedside table. "It's one o'clock in the morning, everyone is asleep."

"Not those of us who have places to go and things to see."

"James, you aren't making any sense. Have you been drinking?" Miranda asked sitting up in bed, cradling the phone by her neck and stretching.

"No, I haven't been drinking. I've been thinking."

"Just as dangerous," Miranda said laughing as she snuggled back down in her bed, warm and comfy in her Lions jersey.

"What have you been thinking?" she finally asked, giving in to curiosity.

"I've been thinking that we ought to go to Toronto and cheer on the Lions."

"You have, have you? And have you been thinking about just how we might get tickets to a sold-out playoff game?"

"Is that a yes, if I can manage the tickets to the game?" James asked.

"Maybe if you'll give me the night off—with tips," she countered.

"Miranda—"

"Ummm. . . ."

"Start packing."

"You're kidding," she squealed, sitting straight up in bed.

"Nope."

"But how—"

"Max came up with—"

"Of course. Of course he would. Your niece is his current squeeze."

"So your answer is yes, then?" James prodded.

"Yes, yes, yes! When do we leave? Are we flying with Max and—"

"No. I have to book a later flight. Their flight is already full."

"James . . ."

"What?"

"This is so cool. It's excellent."

"Okay, go back to sleep and I'll take care of all the arrangements."

"Sleep. No way."

James chuckled. "Well, I'm getting some. Good night, Miranda."

The telephone rang.

And rang.

And rang.

"Come on, man. Pick up."

But the phone kept ringing.

Bobby slammed down the phone in disgust. Where the hell was Richie? Was he at home and not picking up? That thought made him even angrier.

He took another drink of his can of beer, setting it back down next to the line of empty cans in front of him.

He was almost out of beer. And he was completely out of money.

And he was all out of patience with Max Armstrong.

It was time to make the announcer eat his words. Time to make Max admit that he, Bobby, was the better player. He was going to enjoy hearing those words from Max Armstrong's lips, a welcome change from Max's constant criticism.

The Lions were going to win in Toronto and then they were going to come back home and finish off the Maple Leafs in St. Louis.

The city would go wild.

The Lions would proceed to go all the way to win the coveted Stanley Cup, bringing honor and prestige on the city.

Bobby McQuaid was going to be the most celebrated hockey player St. Louis had ever seen.

And Max Armstrong was going to be forced to sing his praises.

"Yes, yes, yes!"

Corey watched Chantal's eyes sparkle with delighted excitement; the sparkle in her eyes eclipsing the sparkle of the five-carat diamond solitaire engagement ring he was slipping on her finger.

"May I kiss my intended?" he asked when he'd finished the task, watching her turn her hand to catch the light.

"Of course, darling." Chantal threw her arms around him and he captured her lips with a pent-up groan of sexual longing.

Now he would be able to sleep.

And then he woke up.

Clutching nothing more than his pillow and his dreams.

Nineteen

Amy Jane woke up slowly and found herself disoriented by the strange surroundings at first.

Her mouth was dry and her eyes were sandy. She blinked, taking in Max's bedroom. It was a warm and comfortable cocoon.

In other words, a trap.

Never get too comfortable. That was a good motto for a private eye to live by. Unfortunately, comfort was high on her list of priorities.

She threw back the covers and got up, pausing a moment to listen for sounds of life in the condo. Hearing nothing, she decided that Max was still asleep.

Good, it would give her time to take a shower, brush her teeth with her fingers, and get dressed. She found herself at a distinct disadvantage when she was naked when she talked to Max. She'd been almost tongue-tied when he'd marched into her bedroom at the bed and breakfast.

She decided turnabout was fair play, feeling brave since Max was asleep.

Wrapping her sheet around her, she traipsed

into the hall, then crept into the living room where Max was asleep on the couch.

She knew with one glance what Max had looked like as a boy and what he looked like as a man.

His dark paintbrush-straight eyelashes shadowed his cheeks and an innocent half smile played at his lips. His breathing was shallow, his mouth closed. His hands were tucked under his head and folded prayerlike, suggesting the innocence of an altar boy.

His bare chest rose and fell as he slept. Her gaze lingered to travel the path of dark hair down his concave belly to where a riot of it escaped the V-shaped opening of his unsnapped jeans.

Amy Jane caught a quick intake of breath at the guilty sexual thrill she felt.

Her horoscope had said he was the man she shouldn't have, but for the life of her she couldn't think of one single good reason why not. Not that she was trying to, at the moment. At the moment her thoughts were illegal in several states.

Tearing her eyes away from the visual feast he provided, she made herself leave the room. She didn't want him to wake up and find her lusting for his bod.

It would give him too much satisfaction.

In his bathroom, she turned on the shower, thinking maybe she ought to make it ice cold.

When she'd showered, she stood before the sink brushing her teeth with her fingers. She'd stopped evading thinking about Bobby McQuaid. He had to be dealt with, but she needed some sort of evidence that he was the one behind the threats to Max.

She needed his knife.

And the timing couldn't be more perfect. While the team was away, she could get into Bobby's apartment and search for it and anything else that might incriminate him.

Amy Jane smiled at herself in the mirror, her mouth foamy with toothpaste. This necessitated another call to her associate, Uncle James.

She slapped her palm on her forehead, remembering that everyone, including Uncle James and herself, was going to Toronto for the game.

Rinsing her mouth, it came to her . . . the solution. Uncle James was taking a later flight with Miranda, if Miranda had agreed to go. She would have to make some excuse to Max to take that later flight as well. That would give her and Uncle James just enough time to check out Bobby's place.

And maybe Richie's. Richie could possibly be in on it as well. Especially with Kerry Ashton to encourage him.

Going back into Max's bedroom, she listened for any sign that he'd awakened and gotten up, but it was still quiet. She went to the sliding glass doors and pulled back the curtain, looking out at the pale colors of early dawn. While her eyes drank in the beauty of morning, her stom-

ach told her she'd yet to feed it that sugary donut she'd been craving every morning for days.
Letting the curtain drop, she went to dress, pulling on what she'd worn the day before; jeans, a
white T-shirt and a vanilla weskit sweater vest.

She slipped her feet into her black leather
slides and was off in search of a donut shop.

Fixing breakfast for Max, had never entered
her mind.

It didn't take long to find a Dunkin' Donuts
and make her purchase. She bought two sugary
twists for herself and made a guess at what Max
would like, selecting two glacé rounds and two
fudgy chocolate cakes. She'd forgotten to check
the refrigerator before she left, so she added two
cartons of milk as an afterthought.

On the way back to Max's condo with her
booty, she stopped at a convenience store for the
newspaper. It was high time she consulted her
horoscope.

If Max was the wrong man for her, she needed
to know why.

Opening the newspaper to her horoscope
while she waited at a stoplight, she read:

> Whatever happens and
> whoever you meet, is
> serious.

Amy Jane frowned.
What the hell did that mean?
It sounded both promising and ominous at

the same time. Was the horoscope talking about Max? Or Bobby? Or both? Or something else entirely.

The light changed and she laid the newspaper down on the seat. An uneasy feeling in the pit of her stomach made her press her foot down harder on the accelerator.

Max awoke with a yawn and a stiff neck.

Why was he sleeping on the couch? he wondered, looking around. If he'd fallen asleep watching television, the set would still be on, and it wasn't.

He rubbed his eyes, and then remembered.

Amy Jane.

She'd slept over. She was asleep in his bedroom—in his bed. He looked at the clock on his VCR. It was early.

But he was hungry. And there wasn't any food in the refrigerator.

He'd let Amy Jane sleep in while he went out to get breakfast for them. With any luck, he might be able to scare up some fresh flowers for the table to surprise her. It wouldn't be one of Claire's gourmet feasts, but then nothing could compare to those anyway.

Things between him and Amy Jane had gotten complicated. Things she wouldn't talk about as long as he was her client. He was almost more eager to solve the case because he wanted to settle things between them. This dance they were doing was maddening.

Though he couldn't argue with her reluctance to give in to what had flared up between them. It might well be only the danger that created the chemistry. He'd heard of such things. It might be, but he didn't think so.

This was more than just chemistry.

It was his parents wanting grandchildren. It was what had made him start thinking maybe that wasn't such a bad idea. It was this rightness he felt, a comfort along with the excitement. He'd felt it every time he'd gone to the Chadwick Bed and Breakfast. So much so that the first time, that rainy night, it had scared the hell out of him.

Domesticity wasn't his bag.

Or so he'd thought.

He rubbed his jaw and drew back his hand at the razor-sharp stubble. Maybe he could sneak in and shave and shower without waking Amy Jane.

He went down the hall into the bedroom, tiptoeing so as not to wake Amy Jane. But he was not so gentlemanly that he didn't sneak a quick peek at the bed, the memory that she slept in the buff indelibly imprinted on his mind.

He stopped short upon seeing the bed was empty, the impression of her still on his pillow. He walked over to the bed and placed his hand on the pillow. It was still slightly warm, or so he imagined.

He glanced to the bathroom, but it was easy to see that she wasn't there either. Then he thought of the deck just off his bedroom. Maybe she'd gone out to sit on it to watch the sunrise.

But all that greeted him when he moved aside the curtains to look out was an empty deck and the pale fluid wash of a melting sherbet-colored dawn sky.

Well, she had to be somewhere, Max thought, dropping the curtain back in place. Perhaps she'd decided to make him breakfast. It could happen. And then he thought of Amy Jane and decided that no, it couldn't.

He went to the kitchen anyway, wondering why Amy Jane had gotten up so early, when she was the type who liked to linger in bed until noon. It occurred to him then that she might not have slept at all, awake and worried about Bobby McQuaid . . . or him.

The kitchen, however, was also empty.

He almost missed seeing the sign that she'd been there only just catching it out of the corner of his eye as he turned to leave the kitchen.

It was a note stuck on the refrigerator with some sort of Lions promotional giveaway magnet.

Going to the refrigerator he read the note she'd left for him:

Dearest Max,

Stay put. I went for donuts.

I LIKE YOU.

Max laughed out loud.

The note had certainly given him a start at first. Amy Jane had a very wicked sense of humor. He definitely owed her one when this was all over.

Still determined to do his part, he pulled on a shirt and slipped on some loafers to go out into his back yard where he pinched some flowers from his neighbor's cutting garden. He'd remember to get them a game pass or something later.

After putting the cheery flowers in a tall glass in the center of the table, he went to take his shower and clear the stubble from his chin.

When he was done he smelled like sandalwood. He hoped it wasn't a scent Amy Jane hated.

He searched his closet for something comfortable to wear and pulled out a pair of baggy pants and a collarless shirt. Then he added a relaxed-fit linen jacket and worn-out suede buck shoes.

When he was dressed, he went out to the kitchen to make some coffee. After grinding some coffee beans, one of the few things he kept stocked in his refrigerator, he put the coffee in the automatic coffeemaker and looked for a couple of clean cups.

Not finding any, he pulled two from his dishwasher and washed them by hand. He set the cups on the table along with some paper towels he pulled off the roll to serve as napkins. A couple of spoons, some sugar and cream and he was all set for Amy Jane's return with the fresh donuts.

There was just one fly in the ointment. He was out of milk. It didn't matter to him because he drank his coffee black, but what if Amy Jane took cream in her coffee. He supposed that he could go next door and wake his neighbors to borrow some milk. Looking at his watch, he decided that wasn't such a great idea. It was too early to impose on a neighbor.

He'd have to make a quick trip to the convenience store. If he hurried, he might beat Amy Jane back. So, ignoring the instructions in her note to stay put, he picked up his wallet and headed outside.

He went jogging down the walk because he wanted to avoid having Amy Jane return before he did and read him the riot act about being careless. While he respected her opinion, he wasn't convinced Bobby McQuaid was anything more than a hothead. A spoiled, though talented, showoff who hated being called on his lazy attitude and lack of drive.

Sure Bobby might have sliced his tires on his

car in a fit of anger, but he wasn't dangerous. Bobby was all mouth.

Just as he was about to step off the curb and cross the street to his car, Amy Jane appeared in her Jeep. She pulled up to the curb and parked.

He waved to her and started to cross the street, but just as he stepped into the street, a black car suddenly seemed to come out of no-where, speeding full throttle toward him.

Seeing only the goalie mask on the driver, Max froze in confusion for a second. What was Richie doing? Why was he—

Everything seemed to happen as if it were in slow motion. Amy Jane floored the gas pedal on the Jeep. The Jeep surged away from the curb as she purposely crashed into the speeding car to stop it, to save Max from being hit and surely killed.

"Noooo!" Max cried out. He ran for the Jeep and Amy Jane.

"Amy Jane . . . Amy Jane!" he called out. He pried the door of the Jeep open to get to her.

Her body was slumped over the steering wheel and wedged against the dash.

"Say something, Amy Jane," Max begged, pulling her into his arms and cradling her.

Her eyes slowly fluttered open.

"You're an idiot," she grumbled.

Max laughed out loud with delight and relief. "That wasn't what I had in mind, but I'll take it."

"I told you to stay put," Amy Jane said, stirring and rubbing her shoulder. "You could have been killed."

"I was just going for cream for your coffee," he tried to explain.

"I don't drink cream in my coffee."

"Yeah, you're a tough guy. Right—you drink it black."

"Let me up," Amy Jane pushed at his chest. "What's happened to Richie?"

Max had forgotten all about him in his concern for Amy Jane. He wasn't sure he'd ever forget the screech of grinding metal the impact had made. He'd never been more frightened in his life—even when the car had been heading straight for him.

"Are you sure you're all right?" Max asked, following her to the black car that was welded to her Jeep.

"Yeah, my shoulder hurts where I was thrown up against the dash, but I'm only battered and bruised. That's all. I'll no doubt feel a lot worse tomorrow, but I was very lucky today."

Max held her back. "Wait."

He moved in front of her as a crowd gathered in response to the crash.

"Someone call an ambulance," he called out to the crowd, as Amy Jane pushed her way in front of him. The door to the car had flown open. The driver, not wearing a seat belt, was lying half out of the car with his neck twisted in a peculiar position.

"I think it's too late," Amy Jane said, leaning

forward and checking for a pulse. Finding none, she stood up. She shook her head, signaling the lack of a pulse to Max.

"Let me get his mask off before the police arrive," Max said at the sound of approaching sirens. He bent forward and tugged, freeing the goalie's mask.

When he did, Amy Jane gasped.

"It's not Richie, it's Bobby!"

"You were right about him all along," Max said, completely stunned.

The siren's wail sounded closer and Amy Jane knelt down beside Bobby's body. She placed her hand in his pocket and came up with what she'd expected to find there; a large pocket knife. The one Uncle James had told her about. She handled it gingerly, concerned about fingerprints.

She showed it to Max, opening the blade. There was an incriminating black rubber residue on the blade and an oily feel.

Max nodded. "Okay, so he did slash my tires with his knife. But why did he try to kill me? What set him off?"

Amy Jane reached across Bobby's body to replace the knife in his pocket. Her eye was caught by the newspaper on the front seat. It was the morning newspaper and it was opened to the front page of the sports section.

"I think this is your answer right here," she said, picking up the newspaper and handing it to Max.

The banner headline on the front page of

the sports section read: BOBBY MCQUAID TRADED!

Max looked from the headline to Amy Jane. "I didn't know anything about this."

"I'm sure Bobby thought you did. He, no doubt, blamed you for the trade instead of his own immature and hotheaded behavior."

The ambulance and police sirens wound down as they pulled up to the scene of the crash.

"Okay, what've we got here?" the senior police officer said, walking up to the tangled automobiles.

Max looked at Amy Jane.

"What we have here, officer, is a hero."

"Are you sure you're going to be okay?" Max asked, his voice tender as he sat beside Amy Jane's bed, rubbing her hand.

"Yes, I'm going to be fine. Now will you please go and catch your plane before you miss it? You, too, Uncle James. The Lions need all the cheering section they can get. Especially now that—"

"I still can't believe that Bobby tried to run you down and kill you, Max," Claire said, plumping Amy Jane's pillow.

"Neither can I. I'm just lucky your sister was looking out for me." He squeezed Amy Jane's hand. "She saved my life, you know." He turned to Uncle James. "You were right after all, you old reprobate. A. J. Chadwick is the best private eye in town."

"You may change your mind when you get your bill," Amy Jane said chuckling, then wincing because it hurt to laugh.

"Hey, I'll gladly pay any bill you send me," Max assured her.

"Hmmmm . . ." Amy Jane made a show of touching her thumb to her fingertips in turn, as though she were adding up something.

"What are you doing?" Max asked.

"I'm trying to figure out how I'm going to list a new car on my expense report."

"You know what, I think you're feeling better already," Max said, standing. "I think it's called full of . . . ah, something and vinegar."

"Well, it's certainly not sugar and spice and everything nice," Claire declared.

"I can vouch for that," Uncle James agreed.

Max lifted Amy Jane's hand to his lips and kissed it gallantly. "I'd better be going if I'm going to catch my plane. I need to work so I can pay off my detective bill."

"Oh, that reminds me. I've got to turn in my expense report to you," Uncle James said to Amy Jane.

"What expenses?" Amy Jane demanded.

Uncle James just grinned. "I'm sure if I think hard enough there's something."

"You're working for Amy Jane," Claire cried. "Oh, no, that's all we need. The two of you together only means double trouble."

"Excuse me, you-all will have to have this family discussion in a minute. I'm leaving and I want to make sure Amy Jane doesn't need anything before I go."

"Go," Claire shooed. "Don't worry, I'll be taking good care of her."

"Okay, okay, I'm going. I'll call you from Toronto," Max promised Amy Jane, bending to buzz a quick kiss to her forehead as he left the room.

"I'm glad to see you two are speaking again," Amy Jane said to Uncle James and Claire after Max had left. "Even if I did have to get myself half killed for it to happen."

"Aw, that wasn't necessary, Sweet. Claire would have come around. She's just stubborn. But she knows in her heart of hearts that I would never do anything to hurt her. The bet was stupid, I agree, but it wasn't meant to hurt Claire. I never dreamed in a million years that she would go out with Bobby McQuaid."

"I wouldn't, normally. You can thank Amy Jane for that lapse in judgment. She's the one who always goes on about how I need more excitement in my life. I accepted that date with Bobby because of her."

"Wait a minute, I'm the patient here. You're supposed to be nice to me. You know, feed me chocolate and plump my pillows."

Uncle James just looked at her. "Like you're going to actually stay in that bed long enough for anyone to plump your pillows."

"She'd better not. I've got a full house at the bed and breakfast booked. There's beds to be made, silver to be polished, floors to be waxed . . ." Claire teased.

"I've got to get another case quick—" Amy Jane said, sitting up and pushing her hair out of her face. "Are there any messages on my answering machine? Did anyone call for my services? Someone bring me my machine."

"Oh, no, you don't. You promised you'd stick to only insurance cases."

"I had a bump on my head. I didn't know what I was saying . . ."

"Amy Jane . . ."

"But Claire, I need excitement. I'd drive you nuts if I was under foot all the time."

"Come on, Uncle James, I've a few chores you can help me with," Claire said, dragging him from the room. "Let Amy Jane get some rest."

"But—" Uncle James objected, looking to Amy Jane to save him from whatever Claire had planned. "Sweet . . ." he pleaded.

Amy Jane just waved him off. "Good idea, Uncle James can help you. I'll get some rest." She waved off a glowering Uncle James with her remote control.

Amy Jane hated being right.

She did feel a lot worse the next day. Every move she made reminded her that she'd been in a car accident. Pushing off the covers had revealed a nasty bruise on her hip where it had hit the door handle of the Jeep when she'd been thrown against it.

A movement at the door caught her attention and she looked over to see a young girl watching her.

"Hi, what's your name?" Amy Jane asked.

"Tessa . . ." A pair of big blue eyes watched while one finger twisted in blond ringlets. Amy Jane guessed her age to be about four.

"Are you visiting St. Louis with your mom and dad?" Amy Jane asked, surmising she was one of the guests she'd heard arrive last night.

Tessa nodded.

"My mommy said you were sick and not to bother you," Tessa reported, continuing to hang out in the doorway to Amy Jane's room.

"It's okay, I just got some boo-boos," Amy Jane explained. "I'm not contagious. You can come on into my room if you want to."

Tessa hesitated, clearly wanting to, but also not wanting to get into trouble. "Whatcha watching?" she asked, her attention caught by the television's flicker.

"Beauty and the Beast," Amy Jane explained. Claire had brought her the tape, insisting she watch it. It was animated and one of Claire's favorite tapes. "You want to watch it with me?" Amy Jane offered.

"Uh-huh," the little girl nodded, skipping over to Amy Jane's bed and climbing up on top to sit at the foot of the bed close to the television, her wide eyes captured by the animated characters on the screen.

"Tessa, do you think I could have a bite of that?" Amy Jane asked, nodding to the sugary donut Tessa clutched in the hand that wasn't twisting her hair.

Tessa nodded and Amy Jane reached for the donut the child offered.

"Amy Jane!"

Amy Jane took a bite of the donut, nonrepentant, as Claire stood in the doorway with her hands on her hips and an exasperated look on her face.

"Well, I was hungry and I was just going to take a bite," she explained, handing the donut back to Tessa.

"There are plenty of donuts downstairs. I can't believe you. Stealing sweets from a child."

"I used to do it to you all the time, don't you remember?" Amy Jane said.

Tessa was involved in the cartoon, oblivious to the two sisters.

Claire smiled sweetly. "Yes, I do. That's why you got pimples and I didn't."

Twenty

"Hello," Amy Jane said groggily.

"Did you watch the game?" Max asked.

"Yes," she lied. She'd fallen asleep right after the game had started.

"You don't sound very excited about the Lions having won tonight."

"They did? I mean, they did. It's great."

"Are you taking pain medication?" Max asked.

"I don't know. Claire gave me some kind of pill with my soup and insisted I take it."

"And you actually took it . . . you didn't try to hide it under your pillow?" Max said on a laugh.

"She stood there watching until I swallowed it," Amy Jane said dryly. "Claire's being a real tyrant. I've taken to calling her Nurse Ratched."

"So you aren't up cleaning and waxing?"

"Are you kidding? Ooowie . . . ohhh . . . doesn't that sound like I'm too hurt to work?"

"Amy Jane, you should be ashamed of yourself."

"Yeah, well, I'm not. Claire thinks dust is her enemy. But I've never met a dust ball I don't like. Hell, I've given names to the ones under my bed. They're my pets. You don't have to feed them or let them out. It's a great relationship. Besides, I help Claire when she truly needs it."

"How are you really feeling, seriously? Are you sure you're all right?" Max asked with concern.

"I'm fine. A little sore and achy, but fine. How is the team? I guess it was pretty hard on them to have to play."

"Everyone is pretty much in shock. Especially Richie. But he played his heart out tonight. He made some amazing saves. Look, someone else wants to use the phone, so I've got to go. Are you going to watch the next game?"

"Of course. I'll be watching," she promised.

"Good, then I'll say hi to you on the air. Don't forget."

"I won't."

Of course, she forgot.

Well, not actually. It was Claire and her damn pain pill.

"Hello . . ." she said into the phone and reaching for her remote to turn the sound down.

"It's me," Max said expectantly.

"I know."

"Well?" he asked, waiting with that same expectant tone in his voice.

"Well what?" Amy Jane asked, rubbing her eyes and yawning silently.

Max's sigh on the other end of the phone was audible.

"What's the matter?" Amy Jane demanded to know.

"Nothing."

"Max? What is it?"

"I just wondered if you heard me say hi, is all."

"Sure I heard you. Thanks. It was sweet of you to do that on the air." She felt crummy for having missed it.

"Sweet?"

"Uh-huh."

"Anything you want to tell me about?" Max asked.

"No. Everything here is pretty quiet. I've talked to the police, of course. But there is no problem. They wrapped everything up with Bobby. I'm so glad that's over."

"Yeah, me, too. Well, get some rest and take care of yourself. I'm going out to celebrate with the team."

"Oh, you mean for winning," Amy Jane quickly surmised.

"Yeah, for winning."

"Okay, I'll see you when you get back. Good night, Max."

Amy Jane hung up the phone feeling like she'd missed part of the conversation. There was something definitely strange about Max tonight.

Maybe it was just the shock of finding out Bobby was planning to kill him finally sinking in.

She lay back down against her pillow and fell back asleep.

Amy Jane got up the following morning feeling great. Her bruises were fading and she could move without saying "ouch!" all the time. A nice hot shower only perked her up more. She was her old self again, ready to take on the world.

When she walked into the kitchen, there was a definite happy bounce in her step.

"Well, I guess I don't have to ask what your answer was?" Claire said, sitting at the trestle table with a cup of coffee and the morning newspaper before her.

Amy Jane stopped humming the Motown hit on her lips and looked at Claire with puzzlement.

"What are you talking about?" she asked, her head in the refrigerator so that her question was muffled.

She closed the refrigerator after scoring a cold can of Pepsi. Popping the tab, she waited for the hiss of fizz to stop then slaked her morning thirst. "Do we have any of those sugar donuts left from the other morning? I'd settle for even a stale one right now. I've had this craving for sugar donuts for a week."

"You're not pregnant, are you?"

"What an idea! Why would you suggest such a thing to me?" Amy Jane continued her search for a sweet.

Claire shrugged. "I thought that maybe that was why Max asked you to marry him."

"What?" Amy Jane stopped what she was doing and stared at Claire. "What did you just say?" she repeated, her mouth open.

"I said, I thought maybe you were marrying Max because you were pregnant."

"Where did you ever get such a harebrained idea. I'm not marrying Max or anybody. And I'm not pregnant. Not unless you can get it from kissing. You can't get it from kissing can you?" she teased Claire, completely befuddled by Claire's turn of conversation.

"Does Max know?" Claire asked, frowning.

"That I'm not pregnant? I don't know. It's not something I announce once a month to every man within earshot. And I doubt that Max would be all that curious about it, anyway."

"No, I mean that you aren't going to marry him," Claire clarified.

"Well, we've never talked about it. There was no reason to."

"You mean he didn't call you?" Claire asked, her eyes wide with surprise.

"Yeah, last night after the game. He just asked how I was doing and if I'd seen the game. We didn't have a discussion about marriage. Sorry to disappoint you. You've really got to get marriage and weddings off your brain," Amy Jane teased.

"But didn't you watch the game last night?" Claire persisted.

"No. But I heard the Lions won, so they're still in the playoffs. I guess it was pretty exciting at the sports bar last night with Uncle James. It was great of you to fill in for Miranda when she broke her ankle, sky diving with Uncle James."

"Amy Jane, Max asked you to marry him," Claire said, losing patience.

"No, he didn't. I would remember something like that, I promise you. We talked about how I felt and the Lions winning. That's all. The subject of marriage never came up."

"Yes, it did," Claire insisted.

"You weren't even home when he called. You were helping Uncle James at the sports bar. Why do you keep—"

"Max asked you on-air during the wrap-up of the post-game interview."

"He did what!" Amy Jane cried, coming to the trestle table and sinking into a chair.

"He asked you to marry him, on TV."

"You're kidding me, right?" Amy Jane coaxed.

Claire took a sip of her coffee and shook her head no.

"So that's why he acted so strange on the phone. He thought I'd heard his proposal and that I was avoiding responding to it. Oh drat, Claire. I'm such a jerk."

"What are you going to do?" Claire asked, giving her no argument on her character flaw.

"I don't know."

"Do you hate me?" Amy Jane asked.

"I don't make it a habit of asking women I hate to marry me," Max answered, standing before her with a bouquet of white roses.

"I didn't know, Max. I can't believe I missed seeing you ask me to marry you on television. I can't believe you did it."

"It was an impulse . . ."

"A very romantic one." Amy Jane smiled.

"You haven't said yes," Max observed.

"I haven't said no, either," she countered.

He handed her the bouquet of roses.

"Are you trying to bribe me?" she asked, bringing the roses to her nose and inhaling their heavenly sweet perfume.

"Will it work?"

"It might," she answered, still noncommittal. "I'd better put these in a vase of water."

Max followed her out into the kitchen.

"Where's Claire tonight?"

"She's upstairs in her bath with a good book. She was tired from the full booking and from waiting on me. We won't see her for the rest of the night. Claire loves to soak in her bath for hours. There," she said, pleased with the arrangement of roses in the vase. She set the vase in the center of the table and turned back to face Max. "So, have you bought the ring and everything, Mr. Impulsive?"

"Uh-uh. I'm not telling until I get a yes."

"That could take a while." Amy Jane grinned with mischief.

"I'll take my chances."

"I'd have to break the hearts of all my other beaux, you understand . . ."

"There is that to consider," he played along.

"Max . . ." she said, coming to put her arms around his neck.

"Ummm . . ." he murmured, nuzzling her ear as he embraced her.

"Let's go for a swim."

"Now?"

"Of course, now."

"But it's cool outside. You'll catch—"

"The pool is heated. Come on, be impulsive."

"I already tried that, and it didn't work out so well. It appears all I did was make a fool out of myself in front of millions of people."

"Sorry to disappoint you, Max, but no one is going to be watching tonight."

"Good, because I don't have any trunks with me. Swimming wasn't uppermost on my mind tonight."

"Really? What was?"

Max escalated the intimacy of his embrace. "I thought I'd work on my bribing."

Amy Jane slipped from his embrace, dancing away. "Hold that thought while I go up and change into my swimsuit," she instructed, then raced upstairs.

Lucky she hadn't gotten her fill of sugar do-nuts, she thought, stripping off her slacks and sweater. This was a night for her black bikini if there ever was one. She wasn't sure she wanted to marry Max; she wasn't sure she wanted to marry anyone. But she liked the idea of Max wanting to marry her. A lot.

Her legs were freshly shaved. Her nails were freshly painted. Even her eyebrows were tweezed. She'd been really bored while recuperating.

She studied her naked reflection in the mirror.

Oh, well, it would be dark soon.

Pulling on her black bikini bottom, she gazed at herself in the mirror. Now this was a look she liked. Maybe she'd shock Max by going down-stairs like this.

She liked the bounce of her breasts when they were unconfined. It was sort of a fun, happy, free thing. A sort of rebellion against men, who must have invented bras—had to be, because they never had to wear them.

Feeling a bit rebellious and sexy, she decided to improvise and pulled a color-drenched pareo scarf from a drawer. Wrapping it towel-like around her torso, she tied it in front and then looped it around her neck and tied it. Stepping back, she studied the effect.

Perfect. It hid a lot and suggested more as the length of it fluttered around her knees. When she walked it revealed a flash of leg and clung to the bounce of her soft breasts.

"Hell, I'd ask you to marry me, too," she laughed at her reflection and hurried downstairs to Max.

"It took you long enough—never mind, it was worth it," he said, turning at the sound of her footsteps.

"You're still a bit overdressed," she said, noting his jeans and jacket.

"Give me time, I'm shy." His grin was anything but.

"Yeah, in your dreams." Amy Jane grabbed his hand and led him outside. "It's really not that cool out. Kinda balmy actually."

"Just balmy enough." Max was staring at her chest and Amy Jane looked down to see her nipples had peaked into hard buttons beneath the gauzy scarf.

"Come here." He reeled her into his body, put his arm at her back and flicked back her hair. Sliding his hand to the nape of her neck he tipped back her head and gave her a killer kiss.

"You aren't supposed to bring out the heavy artillery right away," Amy Jane moaned, feeling her knees go weak on her.

"Says who?"

"I don't know. I think I read that in *Teen* magazine or something. It said to beware of guys who took your breath away with the first kiss."

"But you're a big girl now. Kiss me back."

Max's lips coaxed hers and he drew her closer, painting his body with hers.

The kiss she gave him back signed the contract to be intimate, dotting all the *i*'s and crossing all the *t*'s.

It was Max's turn to be rocked back on his heels and she stopped regretting every bad boy she'd ever dated who helped her stock her arsenal.

Max cleared his throat. "Maybe we should head down to the pool now."

"Okay," Amy Jane agreed brightly, pleased at her kiss's effect on Max.

He wrapped his arm across her shoulder and they strolled down the path to the pool. The night sky was full of twinkly bright starry dots set off by the inky backdrop. The moon had come out soon after the abrupt sunset and it shone on the dark water of the fish pond.

"What do I have to do to get another kiss?" Max asked when they stopped beside the water.

"A full gainer with a half twist . . ."

"How about a back flip from the side of the pool."

"You can do that?"

"Piece of cake," he promised with a swagger in his voice. "And Amy Jane . . ." He looked back over his shoulder at her as he pulled off his jeans.

"What?"

"Watch when I tell you to."

Like she could look away. Still, he was letting

her know he was never going to let her live down not watching his marriage proposal.

"Okay, now." Max was down to nothing more than a pair of silk boxers as he pulled off the back flip from the side of the pool, with panache.

He bobbed up in the water and grinned at her wildly enthusiastic applause.

"Nice touch, but I still get that kiss." He sliced the water with ease, swimming to her where she waited at the side of the pool. "The water feels great. Just warm enough to take the chill off."

Amy Jane knelt down beside the pool and cradled his head in her hands while beginning a tender kiss that got away from her, taking a hairpin turn at full-out throttle.

"I think I'd better get out of the pool before the water starts to boil," Max said, pulling himself up on the side of the pool with ease when their kiss ended.

Her heart made a slight leap when he grinned down at her, a grin that shone from his eyes as well. It was a grin of acknowledgment and appreciation.

This was a man with an appetite. A man who knew a feast when he saw one. He was seductively confident and at ease. Confident enough to give her space. To wait.

She reached out her hand tentatively, running it through the short strands of his dark hair, slicking it back against his beautifully shaped head.

His hand captured her wrist.

"So are you going to test the waters, Amy Jane? You aren't afraid of getting wet with me, are you?"

His eyes danced.

The sexual message in them was unmistakable.

He was strutting out his libido for her to take a look at.

"I'm looking forward to it," she said, deciding out loud. With that she undid the pareo from around her neck, untied it at her breasts and slid it in front of her like a shield. In a blink she'd slipped into the water, quickly balling the filmy scarf into a ball and tossing it to him like a gauntlet.

Her pale breasts were buoyed to centerfold perfection in the water. It was a fact that tickled her more than anything else. It was her turn to smile up at Max. Her turn to beckon.

He pushed himself to his feet. The wet silk of his boxers molded his appreciation, announcing it. He strutted to the end of the pool. He was dripping wet.

And so was she as she savored his broad shoulders and lean legs; the perfect body for the perfect lover.

He dove into the water, cut it cleanly and disappeared until she felt his head between her legs. He'd come up behind her and raised her from the water astride his shoulders. It felt incredibly sexy. He held onto her, his long fingers gripping the insides of her thighs.

"Put me down," she squealed, feeling very naked, so high above the water.

When he didn't respond to her wishes at once, she began to squirm, thrashing about and squealing louder.

They both started laughing and collapsed in the water with a splash. He reached for her, pulling her up and against him where she clung while they both caught their breath.

"Did you know there are four types of orgasms?" she asked.

"Four, really?"

"Yes, four. Do you want to know what they are?"

"Sure, why not."

"Well, the first is the okay orgasm. It's . . . oh . . . oh . . . oh! The second is the positive orgasm. It's, yes . . . yes . . . yes! The third is the religious orgasm. It's, oh God . . . oh God . . . oh God! The fourth is the fake orgasm. It's, oh Max . . . oh Max . . . oh Max!" Amy Jane broke into a hoot of laughter at the astonished look on Max's face.

"Well, I guess I know when I've been challenged."

"No, I just think sex with laughter is the best thing. Don't you?"

"I guess then I won't worry so much about finding your G-spot as finding your funny bone."

"Go ahead, I dare you." Amy Jane raised her arms above her head in surrender.

The invitation was r.s.v.p.'d immediately. Max bent his head and closed his mouth over her breast. He suckled gently.

She swallowed air in a gulp when he brought his hand to the breast he suckled, kneading it softly.

"Max . . ."

He looked up at her, but continued what he was doing, essentially making her weak-kneed and shallow-breathed.

"We're going to have to get out of the pool."

At his look of puzzlement, she explained. "I may drown."

"Well, we can't have that." Max scooped her up into his arms and walked up the steps with her at the shallow end of the pool, all the while engaging her with tiny foraging kisses.

He placed her on the grass and lay down beside her and placed his cheek against her hair. It was a moment of still intimacy with the quiet night wrapped around them. A rush of tenderness washed over her.

She didn't hesitate to pull him over her, wanting to feel his weight. His kiss claimed her, while his hands slid beneath her buttocks. Their bodies ground against each other until he swore an oath and lifted himself, urgently shoving his wet boxers from him.

Her hand closed over him and she heard his sharp intake of breath, followed by a groan low in the back of his throat. He shuddered against her.

Her hands moved then to roll down her bikini bottom. He tugged it free and tossed it to join his boxers in an intimate pile.

When he returned to her, he entered her with a deep possessive thrust.

Amy Jane moaned with delight, meeting his thrusts, welcoming them. And then pleasure flooded her, suddenly. So quickly she cried out a startled "ahhhh . . ." It was all the encouragement Max needed for his own release.

His hand stroked the trembling length of her body, while he whispered endearments that scattered her senses.

She was limp and excited.

"Again?" he coaxed, minutes later when their breathing had returned to normal.

"Again," she pleaded.

This time he was no gentleman and she was no lady. This time they both took freely, like jewel thiefs who'd stumbled on an open safe of untold riches.

He pushed every button from the ground floor to the penthouse suite and then the fall back down was exhilarating, a roller coaster rush.

"Ohhhh, baby!" he cried.

And she smiled.

Max flung himself on his back on the grass beside her. "I see stars, do you see stars?" he asked.

"Yes," she said, her eyes open to a brilliant night sky.

She glanced over at Max to see that his eyes were closed.

"Are you all right?" she asked.

"You tell me," he chuckled.

"Ohhhh, baby," she replied.

Their chorused laughter sealed the moment forever in their memories.

"Are you sure you're not just telling me that so I'll do it again? Because if you are, I feel I should warn you—I can't." He took her hand and pressed a warm kiss against her palm.

She smiled, happy in her soul.

"Shhh . . . we don't want to wake Claire," Amy Jane said when Max banged a pan down on the stove.

"Sure we do. If we wake her, maybe she'll come down and cook for us. That way we'll have something edible to restore our strength."

"While that's true, I don't think Claire would be thrilled with the prospect. Come on, we can do this. What's that old saying, Two heads are better than one?" Amy Jane suggested.

"There's another old saying, Too many cooks spoil the stew."

Amy Jane giggled. "Well, we're safe there. There are no cooks in this room. But surely we can manage an omelet; we don't even have to keep the yolks whole for it."

"Okay, you're on. Let's see what possible ingredients you have on hand," Max said, standing over the empty omelet pan. He looked incredibly sexy in nothing more than his jeans. She felt a little naked in just the filmy pareo scarf wrapped around her body.

But he'd told her more than once, he really, really liked it.

Max began calling out the ingredients while Amy Jane rummaged in the refrigerator.

"Butter," he started.

"Butter," she repeated, handing over a stick of butter.

He cut off a chunk and it sizzled in the hot pan.

"Onions . . ."

"Onions!"

"Okay, maybe not onions. Ah, bacon, ham . . ."

"Bacon . . ."

The smell of frying bacon filled the kitchen in just minutes, making Amy Jane's mouth water.

Max continued with his list when the bacon was ready.

"Eggs."

"Eggs."

"Milk."

"Milk."

"Cheese."

"Cheese."

"Marriage."

"Yes."

"Yes?"
"Yes."
"Ohhh, baby!"

Twenty-one

"I can't believe I'm looking at this bridal magazine instead of you," Amy Jane said to Claire, as they sat in the library talking about Amy Jane's engagement the next afternoon.

"Neither can I."

"You are going to be my maid of honor, aren't you?"

"Of course. And I'm going to plan everything. You can be married in the garden, just like I planned to."

"I don't know, Claire. Maybe we'll just run off to Las Vegas one weekend."

"You will not!"

"Why not?"

"Uncle James will be crushed. He'll want to give the bride away."

"Uncle James would rather go to Las Vegas," Amy Jane suggested.

"Never mind. The wedding is going to be here and you are all going to be proper for a change. Do you know what kind of dress you want to wear?"

"No, I've never really thought about it."

"How can that be?"

"Well, for one thing, I never thought I'd get married. I'm still a little shaken over how quickly this has all happened."

"Amy Jane, are you thinking of changing your mind about getting married?" Claire's eyes were wide with surprise.

"If I am, I have to do it today."

"Why?"

"Because Max plans to announce our engagement tonight on-air. I kind of left him hanging out there for a while, you know. I couldn't do that to him again."

"But you're not certain . . ."

"I suppose I am. I'm just really nervous for some reason."

And she continued to be nervous for the rest of the day. Something was stuck in the back of her mind bothering her, but she couldn't retrieve what it was.

She spent the day trying to dispel her nervous energy and the sense of doom that haunted her.

Up in her room she worked on her desk, doing paperwork until the surface was clear. When that was done she found herself straightening the files in the desk drawers.

Claire came upstairs when it was time for them to get dressed to go to the Dome for the game. She peeked her head into Amy Jane's room.

"What happened in here?" Claire asked, coming in and surveying Amy Jane's handiwork. The room was free of clutter. Amy Jane had gotten out the baskets and hat boxes Claire had given her and used them.

"I don't know. I can't seem to stop straightening things."

"Well, you'd better stop now and get ready, or we are going to be late for the game. It's going to seem strange watching the team without Bobby playing."

"How are you about that?" Amy Jane asked, feeling guilty for her own happiness. While Claire hadn't fallen in love with Bobby, she had dated him.

"Oh, I'm fine. I threw him out, remember?"

"How could I forget. You threw Uncle James out, too."

"I doubt it's the first time Uncle James has been thrown out of a place," Claire said, smiling.

"But it was the first time he'd been thrown out by us. He was crushed."

Claire left to get dressed.

With a deep sigh, Amy Jane got up from her desk to do the same. This pervasive feeling of unease was getting to her. Was she that panicked about getting married? If so, she really should think about calling it off. She should be feeling happy.

If Claire were in the same situation . . .

Claire would be over the moon.

But then Claire had a dress picked out, flowers planted, a cake recipe and no doubt had hand-designed her own invitations. Claire had everything she needed for the perfect wedding— but the groom.

Maybe that was what was bothering her. She felt bad that she was getting what Claire had always wanted.

It wasn't fair.

But then life wasn't. It sucked that way.

She tried talking herself out of her funk, as she went through her closet looking for something to wear. Just because she was getting married, didn't mean Claire wasn't. Claire could meet someone at any time. Could even beat her to the altar. Probably would, as, at the moment, she could feel her own feet dragging.

Claire would have babies quickly to fill the Chadwick estate with the patter of little feet. There would be no more bed and breakfast. Claire would have her own family to take care of.

For some reason that thought saddened her. For all she groused about the bed and breakfast, she'd come to really like the idea of it.

Perhaps the bed and breakfast kept her parents in mind. They would have loved the idea of the bed and breakfast. It kept the house filled with interesting people the way it had been when they were still alive. Then there had always been some theater friend needing a place to stay, always the parties.

Maybe that was why she was sad.

Marriage brought closure to things as well as new beginnings.

She shook off the feeling and pulled a suit from her closet, supposing she ought to dress up for Max. It occurred to her that Max hadn't ever seen her in a suit.

The one she'd selected was as casual as a suit could be and still be a suit. The relaxed four-button jacket was made of parchment wool crepe and had a bias-cut short skirt. She wore the jacket unbuttoned with a bone silk charmeuse tank beneath it.

And beneath that—nothing.

Rebellion never went out of her makeup.

She had washed her hair after Max left at noon, wanting to rinse out the chlorine that had gotten on it when she was swimming in the pool. Now it was a cloud of waves framing her face.

Max liked her hair. He played with it like it was a toy. Maybe it was because his own hair was cut so short.

She liked the feel of his hair, too. It was sexy to touch.

Max.

That was it!

That was what was wrong, her gut instinct told her.

Max was still in danger. Something was still very wrong.

"Are you ready to go?" Claire asked, coming into her room.

"Yes, but I'll drive."

"Oh, no you won't," Claire vowed, pulling her hand with the keys to her car out of reach. "You already crashed one car. I plan to keep my car in one piece."

"Okay, but let's go. And hurry."

"Why? We aren't that late."

Amy Jane didn't want to alarm Claire, so she made up an excuse. "I want to get to the Dome a little early so I can get my nerves under control."

At the entrance, they handed their tickets to the ticket taker at the turnstile and then Claire pushed the turnstile to go on through. The turnstile let out a loud squeak when Claire went through it.

"That's it!" Amy Jane cried out.

"That's what?" Claire asked, looking back over her shoulder at Amy Jane.

"Nothing," Amy Jane answered, her mind racing. "I just thought of the answer to a crossword puzzle clue I was trying to get today."

"Oh." Claire looked at her strangely but accepted the lie. There was no reason for Claire to suspect she was hiding something.

Amy Jane had recognized the squeak of the turnstile as the noise in the background on the hang-up call she'd listened to on Max's phone.

A piece of the puzzle fit. But it didn't help much.

Bobby could have easily called from the Dome

to unnerve Max. She glanced to the bank of pay phones next to the turnstiles. Anyone could have.

The Dome was packed, she saw, as they made their way to the great seats Max had gotten them. They were close enough to the ice to feel the spray from the hockey players' skates.

"I'm going up to tell Max I'm here," Amy Jane said, when they had secured their seats. "Do you want to come along with me?"

"No. I'll get us something to drink."

"Okay, I'll be right back," Amy Jane promised.

She went up the aisle and then on upstairs to the broadcast booth.

Corey and Chantal were there with Max.

Max reached out and drew her to him in a body hug, not missing a beat on his commentary.

"Another power-play goal! Ohhh, baby! Number six came in low on the ice and slid the puck in beneath the goalie. That's a big goal for the Lions."

The crowded Dome went crazy cheering. Amy Jane stood in the broadcast booth listening to Max announce the playoff game as it continued, wanting to talk to him.

To warn him.

But of what?

Chantal whispered to Corey that she was going to the restroom and Amy Jane dropped down into Chantal's chair.

Max picked up a pencil to scribble a note to Amy Jane. As he was writing, the pencil broke.

He signaled for her to find him another, while he continued announcing the game along with Corey.

Not seeing any pencil, Amy Jane lifted the lid of Chantal's briefcase and searched inside for one. She located one beneath the pile of papers and was withdrawing it when her eye was snagged by a slip of paper hidden in the stack. The typed message was familiar in style.

Amy Jane quickly scanned the note, her stomach dropping in a free fall.

> Dearest Max:
>
> If I can't have you,
> no one can. You will
> die while she and
> everyone else watches.

"What do you think you're doing, letting *her* sit in my chair? Did you think I'd let you take my place that easily?" Chantal looked from Amy Jane to Max, stepping in front of Amy Jane to confront Max, showing her disdain for Amy Jane by presenting her back to her.

Amy Jane dropped the briefcase lid abruptly, but not before she'd seen the edge of a pair of silk boxer shorts peeking out from the elastic pocket in the lid.

Everyone's eyes in the broadcast booth were riveted one place . . . to the gun Chantal held in her hand pointed at Max's head.

"You don't want to do this," Corey said. "Please, Chantal."

"Shut up."

"What do you want from me?" Max asked, as the cameraman scrambled to keep the tape rolling.

"It's too late to ask. But I'll tell you anyway I want your job. No, *my* job. It was supposed to be my job, until you stole it. I worked damn hard for it; I deserved it. Not you. It isn't fair that you were handed it on a silver platter because you were a celebrity and a man. You didn't have to work for it like I did. To make the sacrifices I had to make. It was my job," she sobbed, hysterically.

"Now I have to kill you. Bobby botched the job. I sent a man to do a woman's job," she announced, with a note of irony.

"What are you talking about? You sent Bobby?" Max repeated, obviously trying to keep her talking playing for time.

"It was so easy. Bobby hated you, did you know that? He was jealous of you. I pushed him, deliberately fueling his anger until he went over the edge and after you."

"Why?" Max asked, his voice deadly calm, his eyes searching for Amy Jane.

"Because you wouldn't answer my notes. I wrote you sexy letters. I planned to get you to incriminate yourself sexually so I could file suit against you. So I could ruin you. So I could have your job, the one I'd worked so hard to get."

Amy Jane's eyes locked with Max's. Her eyes told him to keep playing Chantal along. Not to do anything. Just to trust her.

"I didn't know," Max said. "I'm so sorry, Chantal . . ."

Amy Jane nodded her head. He was doing good. Then she stepped a little to the right to get a better position. She needed a clear view of the gun in Chantal's hand.

Her gun.

The one she'd reported missing from the drawer in her room.

She remembered Chantal arriving at Max's birthday party late with grease on her hands and an explanation of her car breaking down. Chantal had gone upstairs with Claire to wash up.

And to steal her gun, it seemed.

Amy Jane breathed a sigh of relief. The gun Chantal held at Max's head wasn't cocked. It was a double-action weapon—you had to pull the trigger to fire.

Amy Jane took a deep calming breath. Then she made the only move she could, to try to save Max's life. She lunged forward to grab the gun in Chantal's hand—by the cylinder with a death grip. With the cylinder of the gun immobilized, the gun couldn't be fired.

She wrenched the gun away from Chantal. Max grabbed Chantal. He pinned her against the wall.

Corey fainted.

Security took Chantal away.

Max turned to Amy Jane, who laid the gun down on the briefcase, her hand now shaking badly.

Max pulled her into his arms.

"Ohhh, baby," he said with a shudder. Amy Jane began to cry tears of relief.

Twenty-two

Amy Jane looked out the airplane window at the blanket of white puffy clouds that obscured the ground below. The "fasten your seat belts" sign came on, signaling that the plane was about to land in Las Vegas.

Max squeezed her hand.

She turned from the window to look at him.

"You know we're both going to be in a lot of trouble, don't you?"

Amy Jane nodded. "Since you're an only child, will your parents forgive you for eloping in Las Vegas instead of having a traditional wedding?"

Max grinned. "My parents will be ecstatic if they hear my name and the word wedding in the same sentence."

"Good. That just leaves Uncle James and Claire to worry about."

"I think we're in trouble," Max said. "Claire told me Uncle James was looking forward to giving you away at the wedding."

Amy Jane chuckled. "When Uncle James

manages a wedding for himself, then he can give me grief. Before that, I'm not listening."

"That leaves Claire," Max said as the plane taxied down the runway after a clean landing.

"Claire's going to be the problem," Amy Jane agreed. "She's got this dream in her head of a big fairy-tale wedding in the garden. You know, the kind with the big white canvas tents and white linen-covered tables with bouquets of fresh flowers on the table. She even had a recipe for an apricot wedding cake with white-chocolate ribbon icing picked out that she planned to make."

"Sounds lovely," Max admitted.

"But it sounds like Claire, not me. It's the kind of wedding Claire should have. She should have the six bridesmaids in strapless blush-pink gowns. She should have the precious flower girl and ring bearer. The traditions suit her."

"And they don't suit you, right?"

"Right."

"Well, let's get our luggage and find a place to stay so we can honeymoon after we do the deed."

"We have to wait till after . . ." Amy Jane whispered as she pulled down her overhead bag.

"I'm open to negotiation on that point," Max assured her.

* * *

"So what do you want to do first?" Max asked, sitting on the edge of the flowered plush pink and green bedspread in their room at the Golden Nugget. Leafing through the brochure, he read off a list of possibilities; "we could luxuriate in the spa, play golf, the outdoor pool is heated," he said with a wink, "have pizza at the California Pizza Kitchen, find a wedding chapel or go downstairs to the casino and try our luck."

"The casino," they chorused.

Leaving their suitcases still packed, they left the room arm in arm like two teenagers playing hooky from school.

The casino had an air of European elegance. It was decorated with Grecian marble and glittering crystal chandeliers. Amy Jane elected to get her feet wet with the slot machines. Within twenty minutes she had more than her feet wet, she was soaked—down one hundred dollars.

"Let's try one of those classy table games," she suggested, growing bored.

"Roulette?"

Amy Jane nodded, and Max led the way, looking very handsome in his linen double-breasted suit and white band-collar shirt.

She wore black silk, an elegant long sarong skirt with coordinating tank top. She had her silver bangle bracelets on for good luck.

They stood at the table watching the spin of black and red as the small ball came to rest in one of the compartments. Black seventeen.

Amy Jane leaned into Max, whispering in his ear.

"Do me a favor . . ."

"What?" he asked.

"If Robert Redford comes along and offers you a half million bucks—don't quibble about the money."

Max laughed. "I wouldn't have."

She punched him.

"Are you going to play or fight?"

"I'm out of money," she said.

"A hundred dollars and you're out of money?"

Amy Jane nodded. "Private eyeing doesn't pay like hockey—yet."

"I suppose I could float you a loan," Max said.

"And the interest, if I lose your money?"

Max leaned in and whispered something in her ear that made her blush becomingly.

"Then I can't lose . . ." she said.

Max bought her some chips.

She bet them all on one spin of the wheel.

And lost them.

Max looked entirely too happy about it.

"Double or nothing," she said on impulse.

"Sure," Max agreed, being way too accommodating.

Amy Jane bet the chips all on one spin of the wheel again, holding her breath until the ball dropped into the compartment with the number she'd picked. Perversely, it was the same number she'd picked the first time.

"Max, I won!" she squealed, throwing her arms around his neck and jumping up and down in excitement. "Do you freaking believe it? I won!"

She let go of him to gather up her chips. "Let's go cash these in. I know enough to quit while I'm ahead. I think I won enough to pay for the wedding."

"Then let's go, by all means."

"Do you think we did the right thing?" Amy Jane asked, her head on Max's shoulder.

"I think we did."

"I feel sort of stupid."

"Don't."

"But—"

"We did the right thing," Max reassured her.

"You aren't angry with me?"

"I love you."

"But we didn't get married. We came all the way to Las Vegas and then I got cold feet."

Max kissed her nose indulgently. "But you didn't get cold feet about marrying me. You got cold feet about getting married in Las Vegas, when you realized it wasn't right for you." He smiled at her, his green eyes twinkling as the "fasten your seat belt" sign flashed on while they prepared to land back in St. Louis. "Think of it this way. Getting married at the Elvis Presley Wedding Chapel in Las Vegas was too traditional for you. It's been done."

"I love you, Max."

"You should."

"Max!" She punched his arm, and smiled secretly.

"When did you think up this idea, that's what I want to know?" Claire complained.

"Two months ago on the plane from Vegas. I wanted a wedding the four of us could all have a part in."

"Okay, so what have we got here?" Uncle James asked, ready to get the show on the road, and observe the seen-it-all-before look being permanently erased from the minister's face.

"Remember, we need 'something old, something new, something borrowed and something blue,'" Amy Jane prompted.

"Only my bride would come up with a scavenger hunt wedding. I suppose it's what I get for marrying a detective."

"And what is that?" Amy Jane demanded to know, ignoring his crack about her great wedding idea, while pointing to the very annoyed-looking gray striped cat in Max's arms.

"Something borrowed, of course." With that the cat bolted from Max's arms and crept down to the fish pond to gaze at the koi that were bigger than he was.

"And who's this?" Amy Jane asked Uncle

James about the disgruntled retiree in his jammies.

"Something old," Uncle James said, proudly.

"Can I have a piece of cake now?" the retiree demanded.

"In a minute," Uncle James promised. "I might even spike the punch."

"What about you?" Amy Jane asked, turning to Claire.

Claire laid down a video tape she produced from behind her back.

"What's that?" Amy Jane asked

Claire sighed. "Something blue. The title is "Beauty and the Beast"—but it's not the title I meant to buy at the video store. It got mixed in with—"

"An X-rated tape, Claire! What a great wedding present," Amy Jane cried.

Now all cycs had moved to Amy Jane.

"Okay, this was your great idea. What have you brought to the wedding?" Max asked for the three of them.

Amy Jane spread her arms wide and gave the equivalent of a drum roll . . . "Ta da!"

"You didn't bring anything," they all chorused, ready to throttle her.

"Sure I did," she insisted.

"What?" they insisted on knowing.

"Something *new.*"

"Where?" Max asked.

"I'm pregnant," Amy Jane answered, smug as hell.

Max couldn't stop smiling.

Uncle James couldn't stop laughing.

Claire couldn't stop crying.

And the minister pronounced them nuts and married, the former under his breath.

Dear Reader:

I grew up with a love of fairy tales and things fanciful. Like a storybook heroine, I am good at getting into trouble. However, I have no patience with waiting around to be rescued. It seemed to me Prince Charming had all the fun. So I thought, why not write about 90's women rescuing men? Why not do Men In Jeopardy?

SWEET AMY JANE, so named because she isn't, insists on having fun—insisted on being the private eye in the story. She knows that life isn't fair, and just sometimes she'd like to help even the score.

We share a love of happy endings that leave the reader feeling better about life and themselves.

I love hearing from my readers. Please address your correspondence to:

ANNA EBERHARDT
1515 North Warson Rd.
Suite 106
St. Louis, Missouri 63132

Anna Eberhardt